LOPER

T. L. BLANKENBURG

*I wish to express my sincere gratitude to Tracy Obey
for her ideas and editing the initial two drafts of this book.*

*Special thanks to Donna Blankenburg
for her love and support during the writing process.*

*Most of all, thanks to my parents and the community
of New Lothrop for all you have given me.*

CONTENTS

PROLOGUE

"Beauty is no quality in things themselves. It exists merely in the mind which contemplates them." —David Hume

I f one stands in the Upper Great Lakes Plain, in the State of Michigan at forty-three degrees seven minutes and two seconds north and eighty-three degrees fifty-eight minutes and eight seconds west and faces east, one will see a grove of trees with a water tower sprouting from the north side. In the midst of this copse is the distinguished village of New Lothrop. New Lothrop is a typical small central Michigan hamlet in structure, architecture, and personality. What one cannot see is exactly what has made this village so notable: its people.

New Lothrop is flat, with the exception of the area carved out by the Misteguay Creek along what is now the division between the east and west sides of town. Like many small towns in Michigan, New Lothrop emerged as the center of the local farming community. Its location along the creek spurred a grist and saw mill, which led to a cheese factory, which led to the store fronts, school, businesses, and homes that now grace its streets.

During the years following the "War To End All Wars," prosperity took hold in Michigan and New Lothrop gradually became inhabited with blue and white collar workers from the nearby city of Flint who did not like the metallic life of the city and sought refuge from the factories and crowds. They built small, but attractive and comfortable homes: most of which had porches for sitting and conversing with friends and neighbors during the long summer evenings.

New Lothrop was a safe place to live, and its residents were hardworking, industrious, and intelligent. Although there was a small minority who would be considered rubes, most of them were scattered about the vast rural areas that surrounded the small town. To the north of New Lothrop, was the farming township of Maple Grove. Both communities shared the same schools and distinguished themselves as "Lopers" or "Grovers": Grovers being primarily farmers while Lopers were represented by middle class occupations such as engineers, assembly-line workers, teachers, accountants, house wives, and the local business owners.

The village grew to a population of about six hundred at the end of the 20th century and covered sixteen village blocks. It was rare at this time for a person to be recognized as a stranger. All were welcome as long as they did not disturb the beauty and serenity that had been created by the residents. Despite the growth, the community took great effort to maintain its quiet, small-town status and a bit of disengagement from the rest of the world.

The greed and ignorance that corrupted the world in the late twentieth and early twenty-first centuries led to a deep economic crisis, the Millennial Depression. This was a dark time in the world and America. The cities were hit hardest with unemployment at its highest level on record which led to a plague of violence and hunger. The small towns were hit a bit less hard, but hard enough. New Lothrop managed to survive as the government managed to keep the farmers going to produce much needed food.

The Old Republic died. As America began to recover from the depression, a New Republic emerged and a new enlightenment occurred: the 2nd American Enlightenment. The depression had initiated a time of reflection as failure usually does, and a new way of thinking began to rise from the ashes of the human mind. Much like the first, the 2nd American Enlightenment was characterized by advances in liberty, democracy, and technology.

Since the end of the Old Republic, New Lothrop had grown to twenty-five hundred residents and transformed into a community that exemplified the characteristics of the Enlightenment and the New Republic: wisdom, intellectual accomplishment, physical wellbeing, tolerance, and a strong sense of obligation to the human race. The town, throughout the years, had still maintained its solitude and simple elegance.

This is the town, and the world, in which we find Will Warren.

LOPER

1

"If I have seen further, it is by standing on the shoulders of giants."
—Sir Isaac Newton

Will was running along Orchard Street, through the heavy gray air, on his way to his Uncle Jaxon's estate at the north end of town, "Riverside." Beads of moisture collected on his forehead as he wished for a slight breeze to come along and swirl through his long, sandy-brown hair. His mane was certainly a bit longer than his Aunt Abby liked, but she promised he could wear it long only if he kept his grades up. And with a 3.95 GPA going into his senior year, she had no basis to force a haircut.

Will glanced at his rocky, distorted image in the blue-textured glass of the Bradley Shane Library or "The Brad" as Lopers called it. He was a bit thinner than he would like, but his lean frame and excited metabolism would only offer him well-nigh 150 lbs.

The library was a flutter of activity, which was the usual for a Saturday morn. Mostly mothers with children were exiting, their tablets filled with books to consume during the long summer days. A few of Will's peers were certain to be inside using the vast resources to prepare for the upcoming school year. The Brad was the social center of New Lothrop as it contained much more than just the normal books, databases, and newspapers that one would expect of a library. Thanks to Uncle Jax's generosity, as he had endowed it with funds that would be the envy of most universities, it also included a café, ice cream parlor, and tavern.

Once through the Orchard/Easton traffic circle, he passed the large, red-brick building which housed Gracie's Restaurant, making a note to stop on the way back home and get some lunch. He continued his trek and passed the homes that lined Orchard Street as he covered the final three blocks. Some were old, some new, all quaint. As he passed, faces were looking out kitchen windows and screened doors, none of which would be locked. Each of these faces were certain to recognize him, and not because he was the nephew of Jaxon Warren. Rather, it was just the way rural Michigan towns operated. One cannot hide in a small town as even the slightest aberration from the daily routine would be noticed. The sight of Will running along Orchard Street was a normal part of his Saturday summer schedule. In fact, its absence would be the anomaly and raise the curiosity of those glancing faces.

This and the adjacent streets that formed the village of New Lothrop contained the timeline of Will's past. He worked, played, made friends, and walked to school all within the confines of these streets. However, his future was completely unknown to him, and this was the source of Will's agitation. With apparent ease, his classmates had narrowed their choices of universities and determined their majors: Will had not. He felt like a sculler who had spent the last seventeen years training for the race of his life and, as the race begins, rows with futility as he falls further behind, watching the other rowers pull slowly away.

Now on the outer corner, where Orchard Street bent to the west, Will stopped and gazed at the house before him. Riverside was an estate like no other. A production that only very few had the means to create; large but not gaudy, just unique. Uncle Jax liked things round. The house was round with a circular driveway. The swimming pool was round, and the library on the 4th floor was round. Rumor had it that the old man was also responsible for the four traffic circles in town. Uncle Jax and Aunt Jeanna had the estate built about twenty years ago and placed it on forty acres near the north end of the old residential area. There was no gate, nor fence, as Aunt Jeanna would not hear of it. She felt it would clutter the front lawn and that those passing by could not see the beautiful lilies and bleeding hearts that she tended to so gently.

The house appeared to have grown right out of the earth with tall vertical sheets of white and oak-colored fiber cement arranged in a pattern to resemble an Elizabethan Theater. However, the soaring windows and charmingly decorated grounds reminded an uninformed passerby that it was a home. But in truth, no one, with the exception of a young child coming to the earliest stages of knowledge, would be ignorant to the fact that this was the home of Jaxon Warren.

Jaxon Lester Warren was born some time ago in the nearby city of Flint and raised in New Lothrop. His parents were hard-working blue-collar workers, and they raised Jaxon and his sister, Abigail, in the traditional rural Michigan manner: chores, church, and class work. Neither of Jaxon's parents had a college education, but they were determined that their children would have instilled in them a deep sense of value in regards to developing the mind and a strong character.

After graduating from New Lothrop High School and obtaining his university degrees, Jaxon Warren went on to become a decorated war veteran, businessman, and founder and CEO of the largest company in America. Uncle Jax was considered, by many, to have greatly influenced the 2nd Enlightenment. Throughout this long list of accomplishments, he managed to acquire more wealth than any man in history, and, in fact, most countries.

The house itself had twenty rooms, six of which were bedrooms. It was simply furnished as the host and hostess were partial to comfort rather than elegance, although the interior architecture was rather distinctive. The most lavish rooms in the house were the library and the "College Room." The library was on the 4th floor, which topped the house. It had a surrounding circular, glass wall that acted as an impediment to nature's elements with the exception of the rays of sunshine that penetrated the grand room. The floor was engineered, red oak hardwood, and the ceiling was made of sun glass, which could be shaded by a release of an inert gas between the panes, thus allowing the room's occupant to reduce the harsh effects of the summertime sun or allow the full strength of the sun to enter on the infrequent occasion that an appearance was made during the ruthless, Michigan winter. There were two automated doors in the glass wall that one could use to gain access to the roof garden that surrounded the library. Several wrought iron chairs were located around the garden for reading or simply enjoying the surroundings. Two oversized couches, two love seats, and two rocking chairs were located inside for all who had the opportunity to enjoy the room which was primarily designed for comfort while reading. The interior temperature of the room was always set at sixty-two degrees Fahrenheit as Jaxon had decided that this was the optimal thinking temperature for a human being. This caused the room to feel a bit cool for some, which explained the blankets and quilts neatly strewn about the room.

The library collection consisted of 500 hardcover books located in the center of the room as well as several electronic tablets for reading in the more conventional style. Uncle Jax and Aunt Jeanna had built a digital library of more than 20,000 volumes in a central storage unit which was available from any tablet in the house. The central storage unit was also connected to an online service that allowed access to any periodical published in the world. In short, there was no better place in the world to read than this library.

The "College Room" was on the ground level. The room was octagonal and had no side windows, but rather, was illuminated by nine skylights, which ported light through a series of tubes and mirrors that ran in unique arrangements from the base of the rooftop garden. During darker hours, the room could be lit by recessed lighting in the ceiling. The floor was covered in Victorian tile which showed leaves, vines, and flowers combined into geometric forms. The botanical elements were adorned with the school colors of each institution from which Uncle Jax and Aunt Jeanna had graduated. The walls were painted maroon with gold trim, and the room held all types of paraphernalia from these same institutions. Uncle Jax had three diplomas on the wall, a Bachelor's of Science in Mathematics and General Science from Indiana University, an MBA from Oakland University, and a PhD in Philosophy from Oakland University. Aunt Jeanna contributed to the decorations with two diplomas, a Bachelor's of Science and a Master's of Science in Education from Central Michigan University.

Despite its unique exterior, the most unusual characteristic of this estate was its name. The nearest river was over six miles east, and the Misteguay Creek would certainly not qualify. Those who inquired of its origin were met with a wry smile from Uncle Jax, followed by a coy reply— "It was the most beautiful name I could think of." This response left little doubt that Uncle Jax preferred that it remain a mystery to all but him, and presumably, Aunt Jeanna.

The house was currently unoccupied. Each August 2nd, Uncle Jax and Aunt Jeanna would retreat to the northern lower peninsula of Michigan and the town of Horton Creek. Here, years back, they had discovered a "piece of heaven," the Horton Creek Inn Bed and Breakfast, which was nestled into the woods just north of town. Uncle Jax rented all six rooms for the entire month, inviting various guests to join them either for pleasure or business.

Will had been there once, about seven years ago, for Christmas. He and Aunt Abby braved the Michigan winter for the five hour ride to join Uncle Jax and Aunt Jeanna for a family Christmas gathering. Will remembered being excited, as it was a rare opportunity to gain an appearance with Uncle Jax. Aunt Abby was often aggravated by Uncle Jax's reclusive behavior and more than once commented that he was less approachable than most Kings or Queens of England, unless of course, you transacted business with him.

It was just the four of them as Aunt Abby was Uncle Jax's only sibling. Will stayed in the "Moose Room" while Aunt Abby was close by in the "North Woods Room." They were separated by a common room with a fireplace and various pieces of furniture that formed a half circle around a spruce that was well decorated by Will, Aunt Abby, and Aunt Jeanna. Uncle Jax and Aunt Jeanna occupied the "Tree Top Suite," where Uncle Jax, apparently, spent most of his time. Although he did make an appearance on Christmas morning, and after exchanging gifts, Uncle Jax engaged Will in a conversation regarding his education. Will was polite but less than eager to talk about school during Christmas break. The conversation continued during the grand dinner which was served to them by the host and hostess in the sun room, overlooking the white-coated gardens.

Those few hours were the longest Will had ever spent with his uncle. Aunt Jeanna was much more approachable and altogether fun to be around. But Jaxon Warren was Jaxon Warren, and one could not help but be intrigued by a man of such grand accomplishments. Many thought Uncle Jax to be a bit eccentric, which he was; others considered him to be a genius, which was also true. No matter what people thought, Uncle Jax had accomplished pretty much everything that a human being could in one life time.

Will passed along the side entrance to Riverside and headed to the four-car garage to begin his duties. Each week, from April to October, Will arrived on Saturday morning to cut the lawn. He was certain a professional could have done a much better job, but he was grateful for the $5 each week that he pocketed for the chore. Altogether, it was a fairly easy job. Over half the grounds were gardens, and then you also had the house, garage, swimming pool, tennis courts, and hobby shop, leaving only a small amount of grass to cut with a large John Deere, thirty horsepower, riding mower.

September would mark the beginning of Will's senior year in high school. He was looking forward to this with one exception, the dreaded USCEE, the United States College Entrance

Examination, or as most called it, the "Uskey". The exam served a twofold purpose: to prove a student deserved to receive their high school diploma and, secondly, as achievement criteria for entrance into a tertiary educational institution. The test consists of a written examination and three essays. The written examination tests basic command of the English language, critical thinking skills (divided into two portions, math and science), and reading comprehension. The essay topics this year were to be modern history, global business environment, and philosophy. Students sit for the exam on a Saturday in October and have from November through March to write the essays. The written portion of the test is weighted as 70% of the score, whereas 30% is credited for the essays. Due to the educational reforms that took place during the early years of the Enlightenment, very few students failed to graduate high school. As a result, most people now earned some type of degree, be it from a trade school, college, or university.

The exam results are tiered numerically, identifying those who have the greatest potential for achievement by placing the students score on a scale. Where one was located on this scale directly impacted their next level of education, be it a research university, college, trade school, or the dreaded LPA rating, Low Probability of Achievement, which gave the student a choice of another two years of secondary school or to simply dropout. Fortunately, this was a very rare occurrence.

Will was confident that he would do well with all but the history essay. New Lothrop was a public school system. All schools had greatly improved during the Enlightenment, but history had taken a back seat to the math and science curriculum that made up the core of all public schools. The private schools were able to expand their curriculum to offer additional math and science as well as the essential history classes by extending their school day and adding additional time on to the end of the school year. The public schools had failed in their endeavor to do the same. They adapted an extensive and disciplined math and science curriculum but sacrificed history and art classes in order to reach agreement with the government bureaucracies that held a strong influence over the public schools. As a result, many graduating students had outstanding critical thinking skills but lacked an equal understanding of society and culture.

The Uskey was a difficult exam, and its creators did not care if you went to a private or public school. The student still had to take the exam, and if they scored poorly, they could kiss goodbye the acceptance letter from a top notch school.

Will put his index finger on the scanner, and the large, wooden garage door slowly retracted. He grabbed the safety glasses hanging on the wall and saddled up on the large John Deere. Will moved about with the gracefulness of an accomplished athlete. He was a three-year letterman in wrestling and track, having won the state championship in the long jump just a few months ago. He pressed the round panel mount push-button to engage the contactors that transfer power to the electric motor which created a slight hum as the electrons began to flow. The touch screen display came to life showing a 75% zinc capacity, enough to last another month. Will chose the "Riverside" cutting pattern from the list of displayed programs, and the mower began to move, freeing Will to now sit back and read his Uskey study guide for the next hour and a half as the mower followed the instructions of the on-board computer. He was just along in case of a malfunction.

As the John Deere maneuvered its way around the intricacies of the estate grounds, Will efficiently paced through the Taylor polynomials and Taylor series exercises in his study guide. Will enjoyed doing mathematics, and it was a good thing as he and his classmates spent three hours each day of the school year studying the discipline. Many of his friends despised the cryptic formulas and calculations, but not Will. He found a sense of order and discipline to the problems that liberated him for a short time from the disarray and confusion of a typical teenager's world.

The morning haze was beginning to lift, leaving behind a dull, gray scene, and Will could feel his skin warming as he progressed with his task. The program was almost complete, and he decided to take a dip in the pool to cool off before heading back home.

The mower pulled into the garage, parked itself, and turned off. Will then exited the garage, shut the door, and headed to the pool. He strolled slowly across the freshly cut Fescue/Bluegrass combination, enjoying the thick scent released by the lawn he had just tended. He reached out and laid his index finger on the scanner, and the enclosed gate that allowed entrance to the large swimming pool opened and immediately closed as he passed through.

The pool was large, at least two-thousand square feet and six feet deep all around. Not suited for diving, rather, it was built for swimming. Aunt Jeanna had at one time been an amateur triathlete and still enjoyed swimming laps across the diameter of the pool.

Will took off his t-shirt and threw it on the tri-fold lounge chair. He ignored the depth of the pool and jumped in, pressing his hands into the bottom of the pool and diverting his body to the surface. The cool water hit his warm body like a mild shock of electricity, briefly scrambling his brain as it quickly analyzed what was happening. His mind relaxed as he adjusted to the water, and he turned to float on his back and relax for a few moments.

As he lay there, he once again smelled the flavor of the day: the fresh cut grass mixed with the fresh hay and cow manure blowing in from the farms south of town. It didn't bother him. In fact, as with most people living in rural areas, he found a sense of comfort in the smell. It was the smell of home. New Lothrop was Will's home. The community and the people were his family. They had all shaped him into who he was today, and who Will was on this day, would be the foundation of who he would be tomorrow.

"Thank you," Will whispered to no one in particular, but at the same time, to all of New Lothrop.

"You're welcome," said a man standing on the side of the pool.

Will was startled and turned over, splashing erratically. He gained his composure, wiped the water from his eyes, and raised his hand to block the sun, which radiated around the shadowy speaker who had interrupted his reward. As the figure moved toward the house, clad in black khaki's, a beige long sleeve cargo shirt, and brown wool felt hat, he turned his head toward Will. It was Jaxon Warren. Will was too terrified to speak.

"Come in the house when you're done flailing around in my swimming pool." Jaxon ordered, gruffly, continuing toward the house and entering through the French doors.

Will was stunned. "He wasn't supposed to be here," he said to no one but himself. *Crap, what kind of trouble am I in? All I did was use the pool. Aunt Jeanna told me it was ok!*

As Will pondered his offense, he swam over to the side of the pool and pressed his hands down on the warm stamped concrete to raise himself from the water. He turned and sat for a moment, procrastinating as he enjoyed that last bit of cool water on his legs, and then stood up, retrieved his t-shirt, and walked over to the bathhouse to dry off under the air dryer. Aunt Jeanna would have a fit if he was the slightest bit damp upon entering the house.

Will walked around to the front of the house, hearing the Westminster chimes announce his presence as soon as he stepped up on the landing after climbing the ten wooden stairs that formed a half circle. He could have used the back door, but he was always nervous and unsure how formal to shape his mannerisms around the estate when Uncle Jax and Aunt Jeanna were home. The large burgundy fiberglass door opened a moment later to reveal Aunt Jeanna, greeting him with the usual expansive toothy smile and wide festive eyes that revealed so much of Aunt Jeanna's character.

"Hello, Will. Come on in," she welcomed. Will stepped in and gave his Aunt a strong hug.

Aunt Jeanna shut the door behind him as he took in the beauty of the vestibule with its bisque, arched, cathedral ceiling with stone ribs and sconces holding white, unlit candles. At the far end of the vestibule, the grand hallway maintained the theme as it lined the middle interior of Riverside. Will was often in the house with Aunt Abby, checking on things during Uncle Jax and Aunt Jeanna's long absences. When he was younger, he liked to wander the great halls and explore the rooms, fascinated by its unique architecture and dreaming of living in such style.

"Sorry to bother you, Aunt Jeanna. I'm sure you were busy," Will politely asserted. Despite her enormous wealth, Aunt Jeanna had worked as a 4th grade school teacher for most of her life, and Will was not foolish enough to use bad manners while in her presence.

"If busy is watching the back of your eyelids while holding a book, then I was swamped," Aunt Jeanna joked and put her hand on Will's shoulder. "We're never too busy for you, Will."

"I was swimming out back after I finished the lawn. Uncle Jax came back and asked me to come in the house. He didn't look all too pleased. I thought it was ok to use the pool?" Will said apologetically, hoping for her support.

"Oh it's absolutely fine, Will. He's been wishing to speak with you."

"Why aren't you in Horton Creek?" Will asked.

At this, Aunt Jeanna's smile remained, but her eyes turned somber. "Oh, some things came up, and we had to come home." Will thought this was dismissive but didn't pry. "Go on down the hall. Jaxon is in his study. Probably coming up with some great idea," she laughed half sarcastically, waving her hand in the air as she walked away. Jaxon was always working on a great idea, which is probably why he had so many great accomplishments.

Will walked down the long, curved hallway. The walls were garnished with several decades of pictures housed in various frames. Most of them typical household photographs: vacations, wedding photos, et cetera. But the subjects were certainly atypical. Will was not eager to confront Uncle Jax and took his time gazing at the pictures.

As he neared his uncle's study, Will felt a twinge in his stomach, and his lips grew dry. He was surprised how warm Aunt

Jeanna kept the house and was hoping she might follow, in her usual style, with a nice large glass of lemonade.

Will turned left into the study and there was Uncle Jax sitting behind his oak desk. Uncle Jax looked up with his long slender face, a face that was hard and intense, reflecting a long life of harsh experience. Despite the high level of fitness he maintained, Jaxon's face looked every bit his sixty-eight years, as did most who had lived through the depression. He had hazel eyes with distinctive trails of green leading out to the edge that looked through rectangular Armani glasses. He held a pained look as if he was sitting on broken glass. Will had not seen Uncle Jax for several years, but was certain that this was not normal. For a moment, Jaxon looked like he had forgotten that he told Will to come into the house. But his face quickly revealed that the memory had come to light.

Jaxon's office was plain, but the few decorations were elegant, as was the small desk, which contained only his tablet, his brown hat, and a half-empty bottle of brandy. Two chairs of differing style stood facing each other in front of the desk, separated by a square oak coffee table. On the wall opposite the desk was a large forty-two inch television. There were no books in the room as none were needed. Jaxon could access his library from his tablet. A large window lit the room. Sunbeams cut across the chairs. Standing in the office gave one the feeling of being in the northern Michigan deep woods. The walls were covered in oak wainscoting and wallpaper decorated with pine trees. The only real color in the room was a lamp in the corner with a burgundy shade.

"Hello, Will," Jaxon said in his typical low, gravelly voice. He slowly raised his slender body from the chair, showing strain on his face. He reached out with his hand and shook Will's with a grip that caused a bite in the nerves throughout the younger man's palm. "Thanks for coming in."

This was not the Uncle Jax that Will had last seen years ago. Uncle Jax's eyes were still eager and energetic, but his movements were terribly awkward, as if someone had tightened his spine with a crank.

"Hey, Uncle Jax," Will replied nervously. He had always greeted his uncle with an abbreviation of his given name. Uncle Jax never had any objections.

"We haven't spoken in some time."

We have barely spoken in all our time, thought Will.

"I've followed your grades. Aunt Abby keeps me filled in." Jaxon placed a high value on a good education and appreciated the high grades that normally reflected a serious student's regard for education. "You've done quite well. I'm glad to see that."

Uncle Jax always looked like he was searching for something in Will's face: a reaction, a sign of understanding. Mostly Will found that it raised a feeling of awkwardness at the least, and certainly intimidation. It kept Will engaged.

"I like what you did with that contract scandal over the new track and field facility at the high school, especially since I had donated the money for it," Jaxon continued in his slower style of speaking with a slight smirk on his face. "Posting a letter to the congressman's web site took guts. Nobody else was willing to do it. When the congressman had the nerve to pay me a personal visit and lodge a complaint, I told him to... Well, never mind what I told him." Jaxon had actually told the congressman to pull his head out of his redneck ass and proceeded to remove the man from Riverside's front porch. Sometimes people, to their own chagrin, forgot that Uncle Jax was a Marine. Not a former Marine, as some would mistakenly say. There was no such thing as a former Marine.

The previous fall, a new track and field facility was built by a construction company owned by the local congressman and his brother. After just a few uses during the spring track season, the 400 meter track began to crack and deteriorate, leaving it in an unsafe condition and forcing the cancellation of all home meets. The team and coaches complained to the school authorities to remedy the situation, but their efforts were to no avail. After several weeks, Will became frustrated and took matters into his own hands. He analyzed a chunk of the track in the schools physics lab and, with the help of his physics teacher, determined the Butyl Rubber used in its construction was of such poor quality that its facilitated degradation was inevitable. Will took his findings, hacked into the congressman's web site, and posted them for all to see. Will attached his name to the posting and stated that he had no choice but to take this route in order to reveal the corruption in the ranks of those representing the district. Within two months, the school had a new track and field facility that was fully functional. Elections were coming up in November, and the common theme around the county was that the congressional seat was likely to turn over.

Will smiled, wily. He knew how to take a compliment and was happy with his uncle's approval. But he was still troubled as to why he was summoned into the house and even more curious as to why Uncle Jax and Aunt Jeanna were here at Riverside. Aunt Abby obviously did not know, she most certainly would have brought it up that morning before he left the house.

Jaxon motioned to one of the sitting chairs in the study. "Have a seat, Will."

"How about some iced tea, gentlemen?" Aunt Jeanna asked as she walked in carrying a tray on which sat two tall glasses filled with ice and some very tasty looking tea. *That will do,* thought Will, grateful for the interruption and the cool liquid. He took a drink. The tea immediately relieved his parched throat.

"Thanks, Jeanna," Uncle Jax said.

Will took a seat on the soft, beige leather chair, holding on to his glass of tea. Jaxon sat opposite in his "Captain's Chair." Will speculated that nobody other than Uncle Jax had probably ever sat in that chair. He was certain nobody dared. Being in the presence of Uncle Jax was no less intimidating than being in the presence of other great figures in history. One certainly felt the tension of being inadequate and small.

Jaxon paused, glancing toward the door as if he was waiting for Aunt Jeanna to move out of ear shot. "I know over the years I have not been around all that much, Will."

"You're a busy man, Uncle Jax," Will noted, wondering where this was going.

"Yes, I certainly have been busy. But, one should never be too busy for family," Jaxon said firmly. "I know Aunt Abby has done an excellent job raising you. She's an excellent role model, the best. I should have been around more. I'm not travelling for the next several weeks, Will. And I'd like to take that time for us to get to know each other a little better if you like. Maybe stop by during the week if you have the time."

If I have the time? Will thought, relieved that he was not in any trouble with the old man.

"You're in the final year of high school. Have you thought about what you will do after graduation?" Jaxon asked.

This was a subject Will often tried to avoid, at least with Aunt Abby. "Thought, yes. Decided, no," Will said dejectedly. "I'm working hard on studying for the Uskey. But I just don't know what to do with my life after high school. I know I want to go to college, but I have no clue what to study." Will surprised himself at how casually he blurted this out to Uncle Jax. "I'm sure I'll do well on the Uskey, but the history essay will be a challenge for me."

"Well that's no surprise," Jaxon smirked with derision. "They hardly teach it anymore. Even with the improvements made over the last several years, politics still plays a strong role in setting secondary educational programs. As we were crawling out of the Millennial Depression, people finally opened their eyes and realized we had to crank up the curriculum in our schools. Globally we just were not keeping up with the rest of the world. Private, mostly parochial, schools led the way. They did it right, they extended the school year, cut out the weaker recreational classes, and filled the time with math and science while maintaining history classes. The public schools were hindered by inefficient bureaucracies that were unable to make the same adjustments. People are better now. I think they have finally wised up and made the connection between learning and achievement. The result? I could go on about that, but the fact is you have fewer history classes but still need the knowledge to do well on your Uskey."

Will continued, "I want to be prepared for whatever I end up doing after graduation. I could get a tutor, but they will just have me memorizing a bunch of facts." Aunt Abby had pushed him to sign up for an online course over the summer, but Will danced around the topic and had come up with a variety of excuses.

"Good thinking," Uncle Jax said. "Maybe I can help you there." Jaxon looked away, obviously churning over an idea. "Tell you what, we'll spend some time talking about history during your visits. Hell, I've lived 21st century history. How about this: as I said, I'm not traveling for the next several weeks, so I'll make some time to spend with you. Be here every Sunday at 0800, and we'll work through 21st century history. I'll tell you what I know and what I've experienced, but remember, it will all be from my point of view. You'll have to do some reading, check the facts, and do some thinking for yourself. Always question and ask yourself if something makes sense."

Will smiled. "I can do that."

"I have high expectations for people, Will, and if we are going to work together on this, I'll expect a lot out of you. Many people I have known and worked with have been uncomfortable with that, but it is my way of showing respect." Jaxon leaned forward and peered deeply into Will's eyes, scanning for evidence of his thoughts. "I have a lot of faith in you, Will; I know intelligence when I see it. Stop by the library on your way home. Pick up Daton's 'American History At Its Core.' I know they have a copy because I donated it. It's not like a typical history book filled with dry timelines and superficial rhetoric. It goes deeper into the development of American society. It will be a good start in understanding how we got to our current situation."

Will nodded his head, affirming to concede to Uncle Jax's wish.

"Do you like to read books, Will?" Jaxon asked.

"I guess," Will answered in the usual short format of a teenager.

"If you want to succeed in life, you better. You'll run into many people who don't and just as many who should. They'll tell you that common sense is more important. If you look deeply enough, you'll see that they're making excuses for their mental laziness. Common sense is important, but my common sense always told me that I better be able to read a book and understand it."

Jaxon stood up and Will followed, taking the hint that this was his dismissal.

"Thanks, Uncle Jax. I won't disappoint you." Will attempted to sound confident but knew his lack of mettle could be perceived by Uncle Jax.

"I don't think you will. See you next Sunday," Jaxon said as he turned and walked toward the large window.

Will walked out of the room and through the hallway. He glanced into the sitting room as he walked by and spotted Aunt Jeanna seated in a reading chair with her eyes closed and her book fallen into her lap. He smiled and let himself out.

As Will shut the door behind him and stepped off the porch, the sun, which had decided to show itself, warmed his face. The sky had cleared and was turning into a promising day. Will decided to walk to the library and, on the way, recollect the conversation with Uncle Jax. He had hung on every word the old man said. An uncommon event in anybody's lifetime, but this was certainly the first time Will had the experience of having a serious conversation with Uncle Jax.

***

Jaxon unfolded his tablet and scrolled through the headlines of several major newspapers in order to satisfy his daily news requirement. He was a bit of a news junky and had been since he was old enough to remember. An article caught his attention and he tapped on the video icon. An attractive blond filled the screen and reported in a stressed tone that Southern Calidum, west of the White Nile, was facing a humanitarian crisis as Northern

Calidum had invaded and launched simultaneous attacks on the cities of Aveel and Bentu. After these cities quickly fell, the military moved south in an attempt to cut off the western half of South Calidum from the more populated eastern half. This apparently was an attempt to isolate the valuable zinc mines west of Umbec. *Sure, take it at the point of a gun,* thought Jaxon with a deep-seated animosity: One he had developed over the years towards those who chose to acquire by force that which they mistakenly believed they were entitled to rather than earn through hard work and ingenuity.

North Calidum was one of the few countries that had shown little progress since the Enlightenment. When the price of oil tanked and terrorism faded, those who still clung to the religion of terror and violence were imprisoned, exiled, or killed. Those who escaped found a new home in the barren region of North Calidum and quickly turned the northern territory into a hotbed of violence and war, turning once again against their brothers in the south.

South Calidum had chosen an altogether different path. They had utilized foreign investment to develop their zinc mines in the west which proved to be a considerable resource after the development and application of zinc-air batteries that were now widely used for various applications including automobiles. South Calidum had become prosperous despite the disadvantages of a landlocked position and febrile temperatures.

The western countries intervened and defeated the North Calidumese, establishing peace only after an agreement between the countries was enacted that secured the original borders set during the initial split in 2011. Since the end of major hostilities, there had been much saber rattling over the years by the North Calidumese who claimed that Southern Calidum had diverted large quantities of water from the White Nile for its industrial growth and caused economic turmoil in the north.

Jaxon folded the tablet and placed it in the breast pocket of his cargo shirt. He then poured himself a brandy and stared out the window, looking for the view of the gardens to re-establish a sense of peace in his own mind. After a few long breaths, he recalled a phrase he often used, *"you can either be part of the solution or be part of the problem."* He drank the brandy.

Jeanna walked into the room.

"A little early for that, don't you think?" Jeanna asked.

"I've earned it," Jaxon replied too harshly, then reached out for her hand in a sign of repentance.

I suppose you have, she thought, taking his hand. "I think you scared Will a little bit, Jaxon," Jeanna scolded.

"He's a smart kid, no doubt about that. But he's a teenager. He's been accepted into this community, and he's going to have to overcome that level of comfort and take the required risks if he wants to succeed. He definitely has the potential, though. We're going to meet for a few weeks. I'll reserve my judgment for now. If he's not the right fit, so be it, but I don't know where to look next."

"I think you can do it," Jeanna encouraged and kissed Jaxon on the forehead. "But don't forget that not everybody agrees with your ideas of success."

"They should," Jaxon grunted.

Jeanna walked out of the room, thinking to herself... *They probably should Jaxon, and I certainly hope Will does.*

LOPER

2

"Being ignorant is not so much a shame as being unwilling to learn."
—Benjamin Franklin

Will lumbered slowly down the stairs. His body and mind filled with dullness like the heavy mist that filled the air on a humid day. He had spent the last few hours reading the Daton book in the small library he and Aunt Abby maintained on the second level. Procrastinating as long as possible, he was in no hurry to move this night forward, other than to expedite its conclusion. The elation that Will had felt earlier in the day after his encounter with Uncle Jax had now faded into a heavy, escalating sense of foreboding. The family of his girlfriend Ronni was hosting their customary bonfire, and he was obligated to attend the dire event due to their relationship. The union was certainly not binding in any manner, and in itself did not require his attendance; rather, it was the local social norm that people attend family parties of those with whom they were romantically involved. At least that was the law in the greater New Lothrop/Maple Grove community. *Most anybody would be delighted to be going to a party,* thought Will. *But most people have never attended a Sperling party either.* His night was going to be filled with small talk, sots, and most certainly, a dreaded talk with Ronni's father. Will paused at the penultimate stair; he closed his eyes and tilted his head back slightly, searching his mind for a reason not to go. *Maybe I can claim I'm sick. Fat chance*, he told himself. *August isn't a legitimate sick month.*

Will continued down the hallway and stepped into the kitchen to grab a snack. He pulled open the refrigerator door and found the contents well stocked. *Way to go Aunt Abby*, Will thought, as a smile emerged on his face. He grabbed a handful of his favorite snack, quinoa bites, and tossed a couple in his mouth. The puffy, rice-like seeds had been mixed with a heavy dose of chopped green onions and carrots, just the way he liked it.

Will had lived in this house with Aunt Abby since before he could remember. Shortly before his fourth birthday, Will had asked Aunt Abby why all the other kids had moms and dads while he had an aunt. Aunt Abby gently explained to him that his parents had died, and so he came to live with her. As Will grew older, he learned that his mother and father had been research scientists at Uncle Jax's company, the Michigan Energy Corporation. They had worked in the development laboratory where they ran experiments and tested various combinations of enzymes used in hydrolyzing the cellulose used in biofuel. Apparently, there had been an enormous explosion that killed both of them. Uncle Jax, knowing that the couple were raising a baby boy, took action. He and Aunt Jeanna had no children of their own, and determined their busy lifestyle and frequent travel were not practical for raising a child. So Uncle Jax arranged an adoption for his sister, Aunt Abby. Although Abby had been everything a mother should be to Will, she insisted that he address her as Aunt Abby. She told him that he only had one mother and that he should always remember that.

Will thought about his parents frequently, but knew little of them. Uncle Jax and crazy Abner were the only two, as far as he was aware, that knew his parents.

Will continued out the kitchen and into the garage. He walked over to the battery storage cabinet and pulled out a fresh zinc-air pack and slapped it into the power unit of his Trig motor bike. Will had saved his money for three summers, working any job he could get, to purchase his Trig Model 613. Jet black,

20kW of power provided by a zinc-air battery pack, hydraulic shocks, front and rear disc brakes, automatic fingerprint start: all wrapped up into a package that weighed less than 175 lbs. Will mounted his Trig and put his thumb on the power start. The green "Ready" LED oscillated several times and then remained steady indicating the on-board processor had completed the "Start" sequence. He moved slowly down the driveway and sped silently onto Orchard Street. Dusk was beginning to fall as he drove west. Two hundred yards later, he turned north on Northwood Street and then two blocks up he hit the traffic circle at Easton. Will glanced quickly to his left, no cars in sight. *No surprise there*, Will thought. As he leaned around the traffic circle, he accelerated out of the turn and headed straight west on Easton Rd.

In less than a mile, Will turned north on Durand Road, and one mile later he entered Maple Grove Township. Nothing but flat farm land as far as an eye could see, broken up only by the occasional dull-green cow pasture, tree cluster, or wind farm. The corn was high for this time of year and should produce some good husks, providing a bit more income for the local farmers. Husks actually pulled in more money than the corn itself as it provided the cellulosic biomass that was fermented into ethanol. Most of the farmers in Maple Grove grew corn since the Husk Processing Plant of the Michigan Energy Corporation was located right in the heart of Maple Grove at Layton Corners. Will was thinking about the processes of turning the husks into fuel. His knowledge of the process was still in its infancy, but he knew that enzymes were used to reduce the tight grid of the cellulose to a pulp, which was then heated and converted into the raw fuel. Will made a mental note, *Might be fun to discuss this with Uncle Jax someday.*

Uncle Jax, crazy Abner, and a small group of investors had founded the Michigan Energy Corporation over twenty years ago. Uncle Jax had managed a group of scientists who developed a new process for turning corn husks, and other biomass, into ethanol. Scientists had discovered the means of doing this in the past, but Uncle Jax's team developed a revolutionary enzymatic process that was cheap and efficient, along with several additives that made it compatible with existing diesel and gasoline engines. The MEC could not build production facilities fast enough. After two years, MEC had converted five major refineries and tapped into existing pipelines. Fuel prices fell ninety percent as well as the crude oil previously used to produce it. This led to the United States finally gaining not only energy independence, but taking over the market as the world's largest energy exporter as well. Southwest Asia was sent into turmoil as most countries had failed to use oil profits to build infrastructure. It took over a decade for the region to stabilize, but when it did, western based, democratically elected, republics had sprouted and civil rights were, for the most part, restored.

Two other favorable results followed. Terrorism, which had bred violence throughout the world, lost its funding from crude oil profits and was expeditiously defeated by Western countries. What was left of the defeated groups turned inward, attempting to take control of their failing governments. But without the weapons provided by oil, the terrorists were crushed by the groups that favored freedom who were heavily funded and armed by Western countries.

The greatest aftereffect was the end of the Millennial Depression. The Millennial Depression was a period of great global economic turmoil. Unemployment had hit twenty five percent in developed countries as years of fiscal abuses and lackadaisical behavior had led to near economic collapse. Governments had few options as years of budget deficits had left them impotent in coping with the deteriorated situation. And, as when faced with similar catastrophes, the American people climbed their way out of the deep hole, and Uncle Jax had led the way.

Will turned left on Ditch Road, sped two miles to Bishop Rd. and swung north on the loose gravel. He was irritated hearing the small stones rebounding off the bottom and sides of his Trig, no doubt tarnishing the paint job. About a quarter mile later was

Will's first destination on this night's journey, the house of Dako Avery. Dako and Will had been best friends since 7th grade. An outsider, Dako and his family had moved to Maple Grove from Oakville, Ontario when Dako's father gained employment as a scientist at the MEC Research Center in Flint. Will recalled seeing the new kid in school that year: they tended to stick out in small schools such as New Lothrop. Dako was a big kid, yet too friendly to be intimidating. He and Will were in the same class, and during gym one day, the teacher had the class do a push-up contest. Will and Dako were the last two survivors: Dako due to his strength and Will due to his lack of weight, either muscle or fat. Both boys had revealed their competitiveness as they struggled and dripped sweat from their forehead. Will finally won out as Dako collapsed, hitting his chin on the gym floor in agony, hurt feelings more than anything. The two boys gained respect for each other which formed the initial bond of their friendship. The young lads were inseparable after that, always competing in academics and sports until their body types led them into different competitive arenas.

Will pulled his Trig into the empty driveway around the back of the two-story, oblong house and dismounted. He walked over to the elm tree, climbed until he could safely jump onto the roof of the expanded family room, crawled on all fours, opened the window of Dako's bedroom, and crawled inside. This was Will's typical entry into the house as it avoided all contact with Dako's family. Not because he didn't like them. He actually loved Dako's family; he just preferred to avoid the required small talk that would certainly occur if he found them at home. Will also entered the house in this manner for the sake of its uniqueness, and Will always made an effort to be unique. He was fortunate not to have the need to fit in to any type of clique or run with the herd.

"What's up, Loper?" Will was greeted by Dako whose large frame was plumped into a bean bag chair. His face was buried in an Australian travel book, from which he did not bother to remove his attention upon Will's arrival. Dako had a fantasy about moving to Australia when he graduated high school and planned on taking Will with him. His bedroom was decked out with an assortment of pictures from the land down under: Bondi Beach, Palm Beach, Ansons Bay. They all decorated the room like a travel agent's office. Dako's curly, black hair was uncombed as usual. He finally looked up at Will with his sharp blue eyes which were sunk low into a jovial square face. He was big, about 210 lbs. and tall for his age. He was the starting fullback and linebacker for the New Lothrop Hornet football team three years running.

"On my way to the Sperling's bonfire. Thought I would stop by and pick you up." Will guessed Dako's reaction and was correct.

"No way, I'm not spending my Saturday night at a Grover party," Dako growled.

"Hello!" Will stated sarcastically. "You *are* a Grover, moron!"

This comment was met with a snarl from Dako, "Thanks for reminding me that I live in the middle of nowhere."

"Saw Uncle Jax today," Will changed the subject. "Actually talked to him."

"Yeah? How'd that go?"

"I don't know. He seemed a bit different. Slower, older than I would have expected him to look. We're going to get together again. Apparently, he's going to be around the house for a while. He's going to help me a bit with history. Maybe it will get me a few more points on the Uskey. I could use the help. Hard to believe, eh?"

"He's your uncle. He's getting old. Probably wants to make up for lost time. Maybe your Aunt made him do it."

"He's Jaxon Warren: he doesn't have to do anything."

Dako offered his support, "He's no better than you."

"*He's Jaxon Warren!*" Will repeated.

"Yeah, you're right. He's much better than you," Dako stated with a bit of jest. Will conceded with a nod of the head.

"Come on, Dako, I can't go to this party alone," Will pleaded. "Her mom is going to annoy me. Her dad is going to try to bond with me, and her brother will harass the crap out of me. And if I decide to once and for all kick his ass, I may need you there to back me up. There isn't going to be a single person at the party I would want to talk to."

"Talk to Ronni. She'll listen to you all day."

"I don't date her for her conversational skills," Will noted, and they both smiled. "And no, she doesn't listen to me. She humors me."

"So do I," Dako smiled. "Tell me again, why do I have to go?" Dako asked.

"Because you're my best friend, and you have to share in my suffering. What are you going to do? Sit around here all night?"

"Practice is killing me. I'm sore, Loper. I need my rest," Dako griped.

Will knew better, as he was certain Dako was the one dishing out the punishment in practice. "Stop whining like an eight year old. Put a shirt on and let's go," Will commanded. Probably the only person in the greater New Lothrop area who could talk to Dako this way without receiving a beating. "Besides," Will continued with his argument, "Ronni is related to half the teenage girls in Maple Grove. The place will be crawling with pretty young things, so you might just have a bit of fun." Maple Grove was known for its large families. Both of Ronni's parents were Grovers, and this resulted in Ronni having about twenty cousins, on each side. Add family friends on top of that, and you easily had well over a hundred people likely to attend the bonfire.

Dako paused for a moment, letting Will's comment sink in. Will knew the thought of pretty girls would win him over. Dako put his book down and slowly started to shift his body, groaning at the initiation of each reluctant movement. He walked over to the closet, slipped his vintage Van Halen tee shirt around his thick neck and pulled it over his bulky chest. "You owe me big time for this, Loper."

"Real sorry to drag you out of your room to a party!" Will badgered his friend, despite sympathizing with Dako's reluctance.

Will went over to the small wooden desk in the room and picked up Dako's tablet. He unfolded the device, opened the contacts list, and hit the phone number of Aryn Krause. Aryn rounded out their trio of friends, and Will knew she would be home fretting about the start of school. Aryn was a complete Type 'A' personality and was continuously planning her next accomplishment and executing the required tasks to reach her goals. Will was always impressed with her focus, not to mention her intelligence.

The video feed kicked in when Aryn answered. For a split second Aryn's face showed confusion. The video caller ID had read Dako's name, and she was not expecting Will's mug to show up on the video.

"Hey, Will," she greeted with a smile. "What's up, my friend?"

"Hey, we're heading over to Ronni's for the bonfire. Meet you there?"

"Why?" she asked reluctantly and with slight sarcasm.

"Because it's the last Saturday night before school starts, you live four miles away, *and* you have nothing better to do." Aryn lived in the far northern sector of Maple Grove.

Aryn paused for a moment, as if debating her options, and for the lack of any reasonable argument, agreed. "Ok, I'll be there later though."

"See ya." Good enough for Will. Aryn was a book worm, and Will always felt like he was dragging her out of the house.

"Let's party," Dako charged as they both walked out of the room and down the stairs. Will was happy that no other Averys were around. It saved him from answering the usual questions. They went out the back and both jumped on the Trig, the carbon fiber frame easily supporting both their weights. They drove back south to Ditch Road through the darkness which had descended on the corn fields. They traveled east for about ten minutes before seeing the flames rising up in the distance from the bonfire. Cars were parked on the south side of the road near Ronni's house, at least a hundred, maybe more. But there was certainly no lack of room for parking in this part of Maple Grove as long as you didn't mind walking. Ronni's nearest neighbor was a mile in either direction from the house as her father owned and plowed all the acreage on two square miles.

Will was not concerned with parking or walking as he pulled the Trig up to the house and stopped in the yard. They both dismounted and Will lowered the kick-stand. The young men stood there for a moment in silence, out of sight from the crowd in back of the house, hesitating at the thought of what awaited them on the far side.

"You ready for this?" Will asked.

"No," came the firm reply from his friend. "No human being should be subjected to this ritual."

Will sighed. "Let's go." And they slowly walked forward in unison.

As they rounded the side of the house, they were greeted by the prodigious fire, its flames billowing toward the clear night sky. It appeared that a diminutive forest had been sacrificed judging by the pile of wood that was the source of the flame as well as the assortment of logs in reserve. Will took a moment to sympathize with the flame. This fire sought only to grow, to expand, to reach out and seek its highest ideal. Yet it was shackled with the constraints of those who held power over it.

They were first spotted by Ronni, who was standing on the opposite side of the bonfire, talking with several girls who Will thought he should know. Ronni was understatedly beautiful. She had been blessed with every attractive feature known to the male psyche. She smiled energetically and took off gracefully running toward Will, her hair jouncing with each step. She never took her dazzling green eyes off of him as she approached and swung her arms around his neck. Will slightly bent his knees in anticipation as she planted her soft, red lips to his, and he wrapped his arms around her slender body.

Time passed, probably only a few seconds, and Ronni pulled back and looked into Will's eyes.

"Hi, Honey!" she greeted. The best moment of the evening had now passed for Will. It would be sheer torture from there on out.

Ronni was perpetually giddy. Happy on the surface, driven by need and want in the depths of her mind. For as much as she was beautiful, she had grown to rely on it as her primary resource. Using it to get that which she desired, successfully, from an early age. And she wanted Will. Not just his body, but his mind and spirit as well. She wanted him all to herself, to have and to hold, forever. She was not certain as to why. That would have required a much deeper analysis than what Ronni was capable. But it was undeniably a driving force that came from deep within her.

"Eh," Will replied. He was temporarily mesmerized by the kiss but was quickly whisked back to reality upon the sound of her voice. Ronni had the unique ability to hypnotize men with her looks and cause near seizures when she spoke. It was not necessarily the tone, but rather what was behind it, which was nothing of any substance. Ronni had good grades. She could memorize the school text pretty easily and smile at the teachers just enough to maintain a 3.6 GPA.

Ronni turned to Dako. "Hi, Dako. Glad you could make it! This party is rocking, and now that you're here, everything is perfect. I'll get you guys a beer, so you can start drinking and have fun." She disappeared in the crowd with a bounce.

Dako smiled politely and nodded before Ronni ran off, failing to disguise the cringe he felt at Ronni's spiel. Dako and Will unconsciously relaxed.

Although the legal drinking age in Michigan was eighteen, Grovers tended to relax such restrictions at their parties. The unwritten rule was about age sixteen for boys, and girls were given another year to mature. A rule no doubt that lacked any type of sound judgment but was also ridiculously backwards. But in the rural New Lotrhop/Maple Grove area, it was part of the culture.

Will and Dako began to wander over to the south side of the fire when Will felt a hand on his shoulder. His reaction was mild as it did not feel menacing. He turned around to face a middle-aged man with a rough but kind face: Carl Sperling, Ronni's father. Carl Sperling was a farmer, had been his whole life, as his father was before him, and so on, and so on. He had the face of a farmer also. It was tan and coarse from so many hours under the sun, but the eyes revealed a sense of fatigue, brought on by years of hard work or regret.

"Hello there boys, glad to see you," Mr. Sperling greeted them pleasantly.

"Hi, Mr. Sperling," both replied, almost simultaneously.

Will had a lot of respect for Mr. Sperling. He was one of those generous types, always there to help his neighbors with pretty much anything. Just last spring, he spent half a day replacing his neighbor's sewer line. The neighbor was out of work and the line had become plugged from the roots of a nearby tree. Efforts like that earned him a good reputation in the community. He wasn't necessarily smart by today's standards, but he could size a person up quickly.

"Last party of the summer, sure was a dry one." Mr. Sperling always thought like a farmer. There was an uncomfortable pause, Will knew what was coming. "Will, can we have a chat for a minute?"

Here it comes, thought Will. Mr. Sperling wanted Will for a son-in-law and would pull him aside on occasion to drop hints in regards to his intentions for his daughter and Will. Will surmised he was only looking out for Ronni, but he could do without the pressure. Mr. Sperling moved away from the fire. Will looked at Dako, rolled his eyes, and began to follow. Dako responded with a mimed laugh as he stepped away, quickly finding two young girls with which to tempt, their minds more than their bodies.

When Mr. Sperling came to the edge of the corn field, he stopped, looking out over the crops with a sense of self satisfaction. "I'm not going to plow these three acres that face the road next year. I'm thinking of bringing in some landscaping dirt, leveling it out, and putting down some grass seed. I figure in about three years I could use it for something else." He turned and looked Will in the eye, grinning ever so slightly. "Maybe put a house up."

Will knew where he was going and concluded the best policy was to stay quiet. If he was lucky, Ronni would notice and save him.

"Have you thought about what you're going to do after high school, Will?" Sperling asked. "I know you're still pretty young, but we would be happy to have you as part of the family. If you wanted, you could help out here on the farm. It's not glamorous, but it pays well enough. I know it's not what you're used to, but you could pick it up pretty quickly. Hell, it's mostly all automated now. Stable job, good family, those are the important things in life, Will."

As Will stood facing Mr. Sperling, he felt a sense of unease at these words. He had to willfully suppress the contents of his stomach from erupting like a volcano. Sweat beads began to form on his forehead, and a sense of dread filled into him like lava.

Sperling paused for a moment, and turned to look back towards the fire. "A lot to think of for a young man, I was there once myself. Marrying Becky was the best thing I ever did." Will thought his eyes revealed differently. "We got married two months after I graduated high school. Thirty years and six kids later, we're now waiting on our first grandchild. Went by fast, but I loved every minute of it, Will. Even the hard times during the Millennial Depression. Worked with the community to dig ourselves out of the economic mess this country had gotten into."

With a little help from Uncle Jax, Will thought.

"Hey Daddy, you're not boring my boyfriend with farm talk, I hope—he's here to have fun," Ronni said as she walked up with a beer for each of them. Will grabbed it and drank it like he had just found an oasis after wandering in the desert for days. The cool liquid felt good. The psychological effect was better.

"Nah, honey, just talking. I best run along and chat with the others." Mr. Sperling looked at Will again. "Something to think about, Will." Mr. Sperling kissed Ronni on the forehead, and walked back to the fire.

"What was that about?" Ronni inquired.

"Oh, nothing. Just small talk," Will lied. "I better go find Dako," Will said as he tried to escape.

Ronni surely suspected that there was something more to the conversation between the two than just small talk, but Will had enough of the subject. Ronni ran after Will but got distracted when she spotted two of her friends coming from the road and changed her route. The latest local gossip was more intriguing to her.

Will found Dako talking with two attractive girls at a picnic table. Dako was a stud when it came to women. He was smart enough not to play the field, but he enjoyed the fact that he could. Will sat down and joined in, only partially participating in the conversation. He was more concerned with downing his beer as he could not get the conversation with Mr. Sperling out of his head. Will had been punishing himself all summer for not having a plan after graduation. He was torn. He loved New Lothrop—plenty of friends around and there was Ronni. *She isn't perfect, but who is?* Will thought. He was drawn in by the security and acceptance that he felt. His thought-process continued. *Not a bad place, good people. Uncle Jax came back here.*

While he was distracted by his own mind, the two girls got up and found entertainment elsewhere. Dako had not said anything as he could see Will was in deep thought, so he painfully had a conversation with Ronni when she sat down a few minutes later.

"You need to be more careful who you hang out with, Ronni," Jim Sperling snarled as he sat down at the table.

Will came out of his trance and looked at Jim, Ronni's older brother. Jim was not very bright. He combined this characteristic with a short attention span and a shorter temper. A bully in high school, he failed to grow out of those characteristics into his early twenties. One could say he peaked at about age seventeen. Jim, as well as Ronni, spent too much time with their mother while growing up, which meant they grew up in front of the television. Unlike Mr. Sperling, Ronni's mother was pretty messed up. She drank more than what was healthy and had been seen on several occasions with men other than her husband. Unfortunately, the kids would spend their days with her while her husband was busy working the long hours typical of a farmer.

As Jim grew into adolescence and expectations grew of him, he became fearful, and rather than take on the challenge of living up to those expectations, he chose to lash out at others. His insecurity grew over the years and any potential within him faded. In high school, he could barely keep his grades high enough to stay eligible for athletics. Jim's realization of his own failures drove his anger even deeper. He was a deep, dark, black hole: full of animosity that he never attempted to hide.

He now spent his days unloading husks at the MEC Husk Processing Plant. Perfect job for Jim. Physical work with minimal brain function required. The trucks come in to the dock; Jim hooks up the vacuum tube to the truck, and the machine does the work. Jim removes the tube, and the truck leaves. Eight hours a day, five or six days a week.

"Isn't it time you showed some sign of intelligence?" Dako shot back.

Will attempted to defuse Jim's hostility. "We're here because Ronni invited us, Jim, and we are going to be together for quite some time, so you better get accustomed to it."

"Just leave us alone, Jim. Stop being a jerk," Ronni retorted.

"The last thing we need around here is a spoiled rich kid. You don't fit in here," Jim shot at Will.

"Now you're really showing your ignorance, Jim," Dako shot back. "Every dime Will has ever received from his uncle was earned through work." This was true: Jaxon Warren was not prone to disperse money to relatives, although he took good care of Abby. He would do anything to help somebody succeed, with the exception of giving a handout. He believed it set a bad precedence. Money was meant to be earned through some productive means. Giving it away for free, Jaxon thought, would only encourage more requests.

"Your uncle is another story," Jim was pressing for an engagement. "Making all that money at the expense of hard working people. Farmers like my dad and hard workers like me are getting pennies while he sits back and rakes in the cash."

Will was annoyed by the flippant remark but kept his tongue; he had to keep his cool. Besides, he didn't want to put a stop to Dako's obvious enjoyment just yet.

"You're dad makes ten times as much from crops as a farmer did thirty years ago. Back then, farmers could only sell the corn, now they have a market for the husk and can sell it for more than the corn! And you have Jaxon Warren to thank for that. An idiot like yourself would have been digging ditches and getting paid a fraction of what you make at MEC." Dako wasn't afraid to lay into Jim. Exposing idiocy was one of his favorite pastimes.

"Anybody could have done what he did," Jim continued. "Hell, I could have done it if I had the money. It takes money to make money."

"It takes a bit of brains to make money, Jim. You lost out," Dako pushed.

Will kicked Dako under the table, signaling his friend to be careful. Jim was a fighter, known for drinking too much and starting a fight with anybody within arm's reach. He was full of hostility, probably due to his lack of success in life and few prospects for improving it. He had potential but also an innate indolence and a tendency to overindulge in alcohol.

"Maybe we should step to the side of the house and settle this?" Jim stood and challenged Dako.

"Let's settle it right here," Dako now stood.

As Jim started to come around the table, he was grabbed by a large hand on his shoulder.

"Back off, Jim!" Carl Sperling yelled, and he spun Jim around to face him. "Damn, you can be a dunce sometimes."

How about all the time, Will thought.

"How many times do I need to tell you, Jim? You don't start fights! How the hell did I raise a son that lacks such common sense? You have a problem with somebody, so you try to start a fight? At our own party for Pete's sake!"

"He started it, Dad," Jim retorted.

"No!" Carl shouted. "You did. I heard the whole conversation from the moment you walked over and sat down. Why do you always need to create drama, Jim? You need to straighten up! Now get out of my sight." Carl pointed with his finger off in the distance, not in any particular direction. He just wanted Jim away from him.

Jim looked dejected. His eyes were down as he turned and walked away. Will almost felt bad for him, being rebuked in public by his father had to be humiliating for him. *But he got what he deserved*, Will thought.

Ronni, visibly upset during the conversation, got up and ran toward the house.

Carl turned to Will and Dako. "Sorry about that, boys. You're always welcome at our house. Stay as long as you like." He then turned and walked away.

"I hate that guy," Dako railed.

"That makes two of us," Will agreed while standing up. "But he's Ronni's brother. I just have to put up with it."

"No, you don't, Will. Maybe it's time to dump her." Dako had been dropping hints like this throughout the last year.

Will paused. "I can't do that. I really like her, Dako." Will started to walk away to find Ronni. Dako pursued.

"It's our last year of high school, Will," Dako pleaded, and he grabbed Will by the shoulder, spinning him around. "Get rid of her, so we can have some fun. We'll be out of here in nine months, my friend." Dako was getting excited now. He pointed into the fire with his free hand, gently turning Will with the other. "What do you see when you look into the fire, Will? I see us on a beach in Australia a year from now, two hot chicks, living the dream. Eh? What do you think?"

Will smiled. "I think you're crazy." Will smacked Dako in the stomach. Ronni disappeared from his thoughts as he continued to gaze into the fire. "I can't believe we are going to be out of here in nine months."

Will sunk deep into his own thoughts. Around the fire, some danced, some talked, and many drank. All appeared to be having fun. But Will couldn't help but sense that there was fear underneath the cosmetic social layer of the psyche that people revealed at parties: fear of not being in control of one's own destiny, fear of the unknown, fear of the human condition, he could not define it. Will realized he did not fit into this world, and neither did Dako or Aryn. That was why they were friends. They were misfits, and they were good with that.

Will spotted Aryn as she emerged out of the darkness on the other side of the fire. She maneuvered through the crowd and found her way to Will and Dako. She was dressed in her usual summer apparel, jeans and a long sleeve tee shirt. Aryn had a collection of about a dozen tee shirts with cities portrayed on them. Today was Chicago.

"What's up, boys?"

Dako filled her in. "You missed all the excitement. Will here has been accosted by the Sperling family since we arrived."

"Can we please find something else to talk about?" Will pleaded.

Aryn showed Will some mercy. "You'll have to give me the details later."

Ronni ran up and greeted Aryn. She had apparently recovered from, or at least suppressed the earlier incident with Jim. Aryn did not have much use for Ronni's nonsense and gave her the minimal respect required. They had run in different circles since elementary school and had been grouped into different cliques at an early age. The animosity had persisted. Aryn perceived her as a 'non-thinker,' a general term that Aryn used for those she judged to use too little of their brain matter.

In return, Ronni despised Aryn. She did not like Will having such a close friend who was female. The relationship inflamed Ronni's insecurities and drove the wedge even deeper between the two. It suited Will as he preferred to keep his relationship with Ronni separate from his friendships.

After a brief, but polite, conversation Ronni peeled off to mingle. She was not known for her attention span either.

"I got some interesting scoop today," Aryn teased.

"Pray tell," Dako pressed.

"Mr. Ronsel is going to assign us to read 'A Brave New World' this semester." Aryn loved books and was an avid reader. Not only did she like to read but she had an amazing memory. This allowed her to minimize her studying and concentrate on reading every book in the library. Thanks to Uncle Jax, she had available to her any book worth reading.

"Ooh! What news!" Dako teased her sarcastically.

"Shove it, Dako. It might help you to read a book now and then, at least something with a subject outside of Australia," Aryn retaliated.

"What's it about?" Will cut in.

"It's an old book, part of that social science fiction genre. It's supposed to take place in some dystopian society. Should be a fun read, something different at least." Aryn was correct. Social science fiction was not something assigned in school that often.

"Hey, are we all doing the school newspaper thing again this year?" Aryn asked. "First meeting is Thursday after school." All three had pretty much ran the school newspaper their junior year, and Aryn was excited about doing it again.

"I'm in," Will said.

"Ditto, but I have practice after school, so you'll have to sign me up," Dako indicated.

They stood around the fire for the next hour having those delightful conversations that only teenagers can have: cajoling, bantering, and teasing each other, in the back of their minds knowing that in less than a year, they may be parting ways and possibly never see each other again. Their friendship had been forged over the years through many escapades, adventures, and those fleeting teenage moments in which bonds are built for a lifetime. They not only shared similar levels of intellect but also drive. They represented the best of the class and their generation, and yet were completely unaware of this gilt-edged status.

***

Will awoke to the sound of sparrows and robins contesting for the food in the feeder outside the sunroom at the back of his house. He felt his body, still heavy with sleep, sinking into the large bean bag chair. He gazed around the dark room shielded from the sun by the cellular shades across the large windows. Aryn and Dako were both still sleeping on separate couches. They had left the party and drove their bikes to the west of town to a turn off where Easton Road veered south. They sat on their bikes at the edge of the cornfield and watched the sun rise together.

He slowly rose from the chair and stepped out onto the deck. His face warmed from the sun, and he paused for a few moments to enjoy the feeling. Judging from the position of the sun, he concluded it was around eleven o'clock. *Great morning for a run*, he thought. Will loved to go for a morning run. It was his way of meditating, thinking through the many ideas and thoughts that crept into his mind. Some good, some bad; it gave him a chance to sort it all out. Nobody bothered him on his run, all that he had to listen to was his own inner voice.

After a quick change into his running gear, Will ran out the front door, hearing voices singing a hymn from the Methodist Church across the street.

"…was lost, but now am found, was blind, but now I see…"

One of those voices was likely his Aunt Abby. Fortunately, she had stopped making Will go to church two years ago. He went occasionally because he liked the people, but running was his way of praising God, it gave him a chance for a good one-on-one with the higher power. Will started running his route that would take him around the perimeter of the west side of town, 1.1 miles in total. He thought it felt like a four lap day.

As Will rounded the corner of Butternut and New Lothrop Road, he felt the cold stare of Abner Troffe. Crazy Abner, who looked at least twenty years older than the sixty some which he had lived, stared at Will through his fierce, gray eyes, which were crowned by burly eyebrows. His Roman nose erupted from his face and tugged at the deep crevices that formed in his ashen skin. His once black hair, now streaked with silver, clung to his scalp and hung about his shoulders like an old cotton mop head.

The house, which sat on the corner, was a reflection of its owner. With its gray siding hanging on a sagging frame, the house was situated in a way that led one to believe it could collapse at any moment. Abner's fragile body could be seen, daily, sitting uncomfortably in an old moth-eaten chair on his porch. His only interests in life apparently being the game of chess he could be seen playing with a phantom opponent, known only to him, and watching Will run by.

Abner was the co-founder of MEC. Jaxon was the management guru, whereas Abner was the scientific genius. During the midst of the company's initial success, Abner sold his share to Jaxon and left the company. Why he left was probably New Lothrop's best, and only, kept secret. Uncle Jax never spoke about it, and Abner just never spoke. Will found the old man spooky.

Once past Abner's, Will's thoughts wandered to his future, which pre-occupied his thoughts most of every day. He knew he was smart but was continuously frustrated by this lack of direction within himself. First, there was Ronni: he really liked her. The feelings he felt were strong. *Could it be love?* He thought to himself. *She has her faults, but nobody's perfect. How the heck am I supposed to know what love feels like?* Will wished his dad was alive to help him figure this stuff out. But then again, most of his friends avoided their fathers like the plague.

Then there was school. *What type of degree to get? Who knows,* he thought. *I like science and math. I suppose that narrows my choices down to a few hundred occupations. What school to go to? Ronni will probably want to stay local.* He picked up his pace to about five minutes per mile. *Should I let Ronni dictate where I go to school? Is that what love is about? Maybe I should go wherever I want and let her follow. That will never happen. She won't leave her family. God only knows why not.*

The thoughts were coming fast, but Will knew they would slow as his pace settled into a rhythm. He could feel his breathing deepen as his blood flow quickened. It always took a few minutes to warm up. He was about a half mile into his run now, and the thoughts slowed. Overtaken by the silence between words, the moments of presence, taking in the sights and sounds without the chatter, he rounded the corner and turned south on Northwood Street. The elms on this road were particularly amazing as they lined both sides of the street. It gave a person the feeling of running through a translucent tunnel with the sun shining down through the tops of the trees.

Will's mind was quiet now. The beating of his heart and the subtle sound of his shoes striking the pavement kept time as his system assumed control of his movements. He was now in his mental state of inner stillness and could maintain this for the rest of the run, especially on this Sunday morning in New Lothrop. About twenty minutes later, he had finished his run. Will slowed to a walk and felt the stillness of the air as his chest heaved. He closed his eyes for a moment. "Thank you" were the words that escaped his lips as they had many times before.

LOPER

3

"False image and status are sought by the weak. Truth is sought by those with the strength and intestinal fortitude to use their reason. To which group do you belong?" —Jaxon Warren

The intense summer sun struck Brianna Larkin's tanned face as she stepped out of the West Wing Lobby. She winced at the simultaneous attack of the heat and humidity which collided with her dim mood with the ferocity of a high speed locomotive. Her current temper, brought on by the meeting that had just concluded, was boiling inside but was well hidden as she smiled automatically at the Marine guard underneath her hawkish nose as she passed, dismissing his salute with a nod. Her slim body felt heavy from the layers of rhetoric that had been laid on her over the last two hours, and it required extra effort to move along the walk toward her awaiting car, which would take her back to Georgetown. *At least it was Saturday, and the traffic would not be that bad,* she thought.

It had been a hot summer in Washington, the hottest since the drought of 2012. The environmentalists were clamoring, once again, and raging that it was another sign of global warming due to fuel emissions. The savants had warned of global cooling, of a coming ice age, until the drought of '88. At which point they flipped position 180 degrees to that of global warming. She knew the truth about global warming, it was more of a political issue than emissions related. Global temperatures were certainly rising, mostly due to changes in solar luminosity, volcanic eruptions, and variations in Earth's orbit around the sun. But these causes were much less dramatic and certainly did not roil her voter base. That required something, and someone, to blame. Her base was convinced that banishment of emission-producing fuel would solve the global warming issue. Brianna sought the destruction of Jaxon Warren. Their means were the same, and their ends mutually inclusive.

In Brianna's mind, politics had more to do with power than with ideology. She had framed her dialogue over the years to manage the beliefs of her target voters, the lower third of the income spectrum: a class that she emotionally worked with fear. In truth, The Enlightenment had led to great success both economically and socially. However, there were still those susceptible to influence, and others who felt a claim to the treasures held only by the elite of the business world, e.g. Jaxon Warren. She had become the hero of the working class: the farmers, laborers, and tradespeople who felt left behind by the scientific advances of the last several decades. As The Enlightenment began to unfold, she saw the chasm forming between the newly established lower, middle, and upper classes. Like many politicians before her, she successfully manipulated the most vulnerable in society, inciting them with beliefs that they too were entitled to the riches earned by so many others.

Deep within, she knew it was a sham. Everybody had profited during The Enlightenment. Unemployment now only existed in the faulty calculations of government bureaucrats and the politicians who utilized the data as a means of keeping the population in a state of fear.

This political acumen, over which she draped a thick layer of media savvy, had thrust her upon the congressional stage to become one of the most powerful politicians in Washington. And it had just paid off although not exactly as she had planned.

What Brianna Larkin lacked in beauty, she more than made up with influence and charisma. She was gifted with that exceptional ability to create an image of a situation, be it true or false, and sell it to her constituents, even her peers on occasion. Being of less-than-average height, she often had to look up to her male colleagues in the Senate, but she made certain they knew that she was looking down the IQ scale at them. This indignation was overlooked as Brianna was preferred as an ally and dreaded as an enemy.

She could feel the soft curls of her chin-length, black hair flatten from the humidity as she approached the waiting car. The chauffeur opened the door, and Brianna climbed into the back of the stretch limousine, immediately relieved by the air conditioned interior. Daniel Vicksburg, her Chief of Staff, was inside waiting for her. Brianna thought he was particularly striking in his custom Tom James suit. She was always impressed at Daniel's ability to portray composure and professionalism and was well aware that he had the ability and political acumen to run for elected office himself. But alas, he was only a man to Brianna, which meant she would use him for his abilities and dispose of him at her will. He was a tool, nothing more. However, his service had been replete with loyalty, and despite the many other offers over the years, he had chosen to stay with Brianna.

"Damn it's hot out!" she exclaimed as the door shut behind her. "I should have gone back to Michigan for the summer recess."

"That would have been stupid," Daniel replied bluntly in his low, deep voice. He looked up from his tablet on which he had been reviewing poll numbers. His brown eyes were set deeply into his sharp face, revealing the unmistaken appearance of a strategist yet handsome enough to get elected if he chose. "Screw the weather, what happened?" Daniel asked, unable to hide his impatience.

Brianna glanced at him quickly before turning her gaze out the window. "In six months, I'll get defense." She tried to hide her disappointment but was certain Daniel would pick up on it. Two weeks ago Davis Lanzen, Secretary of Defense, had a mild heart attack while jogging. He was seventy-five years old and, as

Brianna had thought at the time, *an old geezer who was well past his prime.* Immediately, the political transmission shifted gears, and the lobbying began to search for who would lead the Defense Department of the most powerful nation in the world. "Lanzen will stay on to wrap up and make a smooth transition."

"It's a cabinet position," he said, dolefully. Brianna continued to stare out the window. "It's not Secretary of Energy, like you wanted, but it's the second most powerful cabinet position." Brianna had planned on persuading the President to force the retirement of the Secretary of Energy and appoint her to the position. Her intent had been to regulate MEC to a point of collapse and nationalize its facilities.

"We can use the massive budget to sway votes our way in congress and gain more influence," Daniel continued. "A well placed purchase to a business in a congressman's home district will be a great tool in reaching our objectives."

Daniel instinctively leaned in a bit closer and lowered his voice despite the fact the privacy glass was raised behind the driver. "This also puts us in a perfect position to pursue our other goals." Daniel left the insinuation hanging.

"I wanted to beat him on his own ground," she retorted. "This will be an end-around."

"The end justifies the means," Daniel shot back.

Brianna did not argue further. She knew he was right but could not forgo the setback that she felt. The President was well aware of her power but was suspicious of her motives as he knew that Brianna had been tossed out of the energy industry, specifically MEC. He couldn't risk such an appointment, but he required her skill. The Department of Defense was the moral, financial, and technical leader of the World Defense Organization, formed by the democratically elected governments of the world and a key unit of the League of United Republics. The latter group forming after the collapse of the ineffectual United Nations. Their mission was simple: maintain world dominance by the democratically elected governments of the world at almost all costs.

Brianna had been hired right out of college at MEC as a chemical engineer and had shown promise as she moved up the lower rungs of the corporate ladder with ease. Shortly after receiving her first mid-level management position, it became obvious to her superiors that she had been covering up her incompetence by committing MEC's cardinal sin of management: taking credit for the work of others. She was fired and vowed to herself that a failure such as this would never happen again. Brianna was angry after the firing. Angry because she knew they were right. It was her first and only complete failure in life, and it exposed her weaknesses as a human being. She believed there was nothing worse than someone who was completely inept, and she had fit the bill. She would never forgive them or, for that matter, herself.

Her father arranged a job for her as a low-level staff member of a family friend who had managed to get elected as a congressman. She learned quickly the political ropes and, after being in Washington for four years, was already a congressional Chief of Staff. A vacant Senate seat was available a short time later in her home state of Michigan for which she ran. Many politicians, including Brianna, ran on a variant of the "us against Wall Street" slogan. She utilized her skills and the anti-business rhetoric more successfully than her opponents and won the election.

Brianna lacked leadership skills, which she made up for with intelligence, and a gift of personal persuasion. She could spin a lie better than the best in Washington and could tell her lies in a manner that made people afraid to not believe her. In the business world, results mattered. In Washington, results were irrelevant. Image was everything.

She had met Daniel during her first staff position. He had been the brightest and most ambitious intern and was her only choice as chief of her staff upon being elected to the Senate. Daniel came from a humble background in rural Michigan. He was abandoned by parents not yet ready to face the reality of parenthood. He grew up in foster care, fortunately for him, landing in a family willing to groom his obvious intelligence. After graduating from law school, he moved to Washington with the honorable intention of working to improve the system. During the last two decades, he had matured and proven himself and was considered, by many, the most effective campaign and staff manager in congress.

Shortly after winning election to the Senate, Brianna had discovered she was not alone in her animosity toward Jaxon Warren. She formed a coalition with two other senators and a dozen representatives who believed that he had too much power for one person, and they intended to put an end to it. They remained in the background for now, meeting in private, working to gain influence within the bureaucracy. They called themselves SLOT, Senators Larkin, Owen, and Torrence: after the original members of the group.

"We'll make the most of it," Brianna said as she was startled by the vibration of her secure tablet. She removed it from her inside jacket pocket and, without bothering to unfold it, tapped the small indented button on the rear. This switched the frequency to match the receiver of the tiny implant in her ear, keeping the caller's voice private. Daniel turned away and looked out the window, noticeably irked that she would reward his loyalty with even the slightest distrust.

"Go ahead," she answered dryly, knowing that the voice modifying application was morphing her voice into to that of a man. The caller would be completely ignorant to the fact that she was a woman, let alone a United States Senator.

"I'm short on time, so I'll be curt. This transaction has to occur today or no deal," explained the caller.

You're getting prepared for a mobilization, she thought. *Just as expected. That should give me at least thirty to forty days. My initial preparations are paying off.*

Senator Larkin paused for a moment to quickly calculate any necessary moves on her part. There was only one thing he could be up to that made sense. Calidum. "Send me the account number, and I'll transfer the money today based on the terms we previously discussed." She terminated the call.

Senator Larkin stared intently at the seat facing her, clutching her tablet close to her chest. She knew she had to be careful. Taking the wrong side would be disastrous in this game. But she had come to Washington to run with the big dogs, and she well knew an opportunity like this could not be passed up. The timing was perfect.

The car rolled to a stop in front of her complex, and she turned to Daniel. "Meet me in the office tomorrow morning and have the rest of the staff there. No later than seven."

Daniel turned to her with clear irritation in his voice. "Tomorrow's Sunday, Senator."

Brianna ignored the slight insubordination. "I don't care. Make it happen. It's time they earned their pay, and we have a lot of preparations to make for this transition. I'll make it up to them later." She never would. She would have him work the staff hard the next six months and then hire a new team when she got to her new post.

The driver opened the door, and she exited without any further commands.

Daniel sighed. *She can really be a bitch*, he thought, not for the first time. She would never make up to the staff what they had given her. He had found it difficult keeping people on board. Senator Larkin was incredibly demanding and insensitive. *Yet I'm about to become the Chief of Staff to the Secretary of Defense*, his thoughts continued. *She must be doing something right.*

***

Will sat nervously in the library on Sunday morning, tapping his fingers on his knees to an unrecognizable drum beat. Aunt Jeanna had answered the door and directed him upstairs. She said Uncle Jax was in his study taking an important phone call and would be up shortly. *What am I doing*, Will thought. *This is crazy. I'm about to talk to one of the most successful human beings in recent*

American history, and I can't think of a thing to say. Uncle Jax is going to think I'm an idiot! He rose from the chair and paced across the floor, stopping to gaze out the glass walls, searching the landscape and his mind for what to say to Uncle Jax.

Will heard light steps coming up the stairs, and his heart shifted again, quickening its pace to the point Will felt a tinge of dizziness. Turning, he watched Uncle Jax's head come up through the floor as he climbed the last few stairs of the circular staircase. He was holding a coffee cup and dressed in cargo pants and a long sleeve hiking shirt. Will noticed Uncle Jax's mouth was turned down, and his face seemed to have a few more wrinkles in it. His mind was obviously elsewhere. His eyes paused on the floor for a moment, then, with a start, he looked up at Will.

"So you want to talk a bit about history. Eh, Will?" Jaxon asked rhetorically as he walked over and sat down on one of the oversized couches.

Will answered anyway, "Like I said, Uncle Jax, I really would like to kick butt on the history portion of the Uskey."

"Why is that?" Jaxon asked candidly.

Will was a bit stunned by the question and stammered in his reply. "Uh…Why is what?"

"Why do you want to do well on this exam, Will?" Jaxon stared deep into Will's eyes waiting for an answer. His focus and intensity were now turned on.

Will sensed that Uncle Jax already knew the answer. He walked over to the couch opposite Uncle Jax, his eyes fixed on the floor as if the answer was written in the lines of the fine wood floor. "I'm not even sure what I'm doing here," Will blurted out softly.

"Listen, Will. I know we have not spent much time together over the years, but I'm your uncle. I'm not going to sit here and ramble on about my view of history. This is going to have to be a bit more interactive in order to produce any benefits. Your goal needs to be to learn and understand, and if you're not properly motivated, it will all be a waste of time. Now I want you to sit in that chair and, most importantly, think before you answer. The world is full of people who refuse to think, or worse, open their mouth without truly listening and thinking through a response. Don't be just another sheep. Now take your time and answer the question."

Will was a bit surprised at Uncle Jax's firmness. He obviously was accustomed to letting people know who was in charge. Will cupped his hands over his eyes and rested his elbows on his knees. After a few moments, he let his hands fall and looked back at Uncle Jax, who had not removed his gaze from Will.

"I don't know what I want to do after high school is over. I know I want to go away to college, but I don't know where, and I don't know what to major in. About the only thing I do know is that I want to ace this exam and, at some point between now and next June, figure out what the heck I am going to do." Will felt slightly embarrassed in the manner he blurted this out, but it was the truth as best he knew how to say it.

"That's more like it," Uncle Jax encouraged with a smile. "For this to work you have to be honest and forthcoming with me, Will. I certainly will be. Believe it or not I was once in your shoes." Will found that hard to believe. "Pretty much every seventeen year old is going through the same process. Now we have identified your short term and long term goals: that's a good start. Too many people get stuck with focusing on instant gratification. You have to be aware of both."

Uncle Jax took the opportunity to start the lesson. "History is made up of complex experiments with real empirical results, Will. Socialism, communism, capitalism, autocracies, democracies, oligarchies, times of war and times of peace—all with the resultant successes and failures. History is a legacy handed down from one generation to another although occasionally we find some artifact that may have been omitted or overlooked by a few generations, which proves to be of value and runs perpendicular to accepted history. Some even have said that history is written by the victors, which may have been true in the distant past, but I believe has been less prevalent as we've evolved.

Many of the atrocities over the last one hundred and fifty years could have been avoided if people just took the time to study those experiments. Thus was the first quarter of the 21st century."

"When studying history, Will, you have to look at politics, economics, and culture, including religious and social institutions. These are all intertwined with each other. No one segment stands alone. You have to look at it from a high level of ideas, movements, and data to the lower level of the underlying emotions that are the real cause of human events."

Will sat up a bit more straight. He reached out for his tablet, which was on the coffee table in between them and tapped a few buttons on the screen to start recording. Uncle Jax gave no objection and continued.

"History of the 21st century can best be classified as pre-Millennial Depression, Millennial Depression, and post-Millennial Depression. In fact, you'll find, at some point, that your life will be reflected in the same manner. We all have a tripartite life, we live up to a point, a profound event occurs, and we continue our lives greatly shaped by that event."

Jaxon now spoke with ease, which put Will at ease also. He was able to relax a bit in the comfortable seat.

"That event can be different for many people. For some, it's marriage or having kids. For others, it can be a death of someone close or losing a job, perhaps. The event can be anything."

Will started to feel brave but still spoke with some hesitation. "What was yours, Uncle Jax?"

Uncle Jax turned his head to the right, looking at nothing in particular. Will wished he would have kept quiet.

"The Marine Corps," Uncle Jax stated and paused for a long moment before turning back to face Will. "It changed me in many good ways, a few bad I suppose. I was smart but naïve going in. It taught me how the world worked and the power of self-motivation. It also showed me the baneful and malevolent side of human nature, which was nothing more than a glimpse into the darker chambers of the human mind. After the Corps, I just had to work hard and things seemed to always go my way. I met and married Aunt Jeanna, and life just took off like a rocket."

Jaxon paused, as if remembering, not just historical facts, but more of the thoughts and feelings he undoubtedly shared with many in the early part of the century. He looked back at Will and continued. "The turmoil was already growing in the early part of the century. The political system in the United States was dominated by two political parties, neither of which had been effective. The terrorist attack that occurred on September 11th changed the mentality of the United States, and the world, profoundly. We became involved in two wars, financially costly but more importantly, in the cost of American lives."

"During the later years of the war, we had a global economic meltdown that was just a precursor for what was to come. People suffered while politicians played on emotions to gain that small edge that would put them in power. The wars eventually ended, but the scars were deep, and the world was not much different. We had rid ourselves of thousands of terrorists and several dictators, but there were many who filled in the remaining void. It was always us against 'them,' whoever 'them' happened to be. People didn't realize that we were just dealing with the superficialities. We were destroying evil on the top, physical level but refusing to deal with the root cause and look within the human mind, as well as spirit, and analyze motivations."

"Both political parties had structured the election process so that other groups, third parties, as they were called, had considerable, additional, hurdles to cross to get on the election ballot. In essence, it was a two party system, and both parties would go to great extents to win elections. It was all about power at this point. The concept of representing the people of the United States was no longer a concern of those elected officials."

"Socially, this political reality had become acceptable. The electorate, which is so critical to the democratic voting process in a legitimate republic, had become enamored with entertainment. People were more concerned with watching sporting events and other passive mental activities such as watching television shows, of which there were literally hundreds to choose. They had willingly removed themselves from the political process. Worst of all, reading had declined. Most studies showed that 25% of Americans had not read a book in the last year. I'd say that number was a bit low. People were losing the ability to think for themselves, and the politicians were happy to fill the vacuum with their propaganda."

Will was surprised at what he was hearing and had a hard time believing that this could be true. But Uncle Jax had lived it, not him. Either way, he was fascinated.

"People felt helpless, many turned to drugs and alcohol. Use of both were rampant throughout the world at that point. The problems were obvious; the will to overcome just wasn't there. People continued along this path, which eventually affected the work place. People didn't work hard enough and smart enough to make American business competitive. Instead of working to get a real education, many chose to pay diploma mills large sums of money for issuing a degree, educations that were impotent in the work place and useless to employers who needed real skills."

Will kept quiet as he was enthralled with the level of detail with which Uncle Jax was remembering the past. He felt slightly embarrassed that he was so ignorant of recent history and was content on just listening.

"To make matters worse, the two major political parties were taking the country in the direction of socialism. Are you familiar with socialism, Will?"

"Uh," Will stammered searching his mind for an answer. "I remember reading about it in economics class. Something about the re-distribution of wealth."

Apparently that was good enough for Uncle Jax, so he continued. "Socialism is difficult to teach. Unfortunately one has to experience it to truly understand it. Basically it is an economic system and political philosophy that advocates the control of the means of production by some kind of cooperation of the state and private enterprise. In America, we have experienced a form of socialism promoted by social politicians that focused more on regulation and re-distribution of wealth."

"Regulations were used to force private businesses to meet standards set by the government that supposedly were beneficial to society. Some turned out to be good, for example, the removal of lead from paint was passed into law to protect people from lead poisoning. On the other hand, government was forcing other businesses to alter their product in a way that would increase costs and make them less affordable. A good example of this is the government interventions into the health care system that took place several years before the depression."

Jaxon shook his head, as if in disgust. "Re-distribution of wealth was the most damaging aspect of socialism. People, through a combination of effort, intelligence, and opportunity, produce wealth. They are placed somewhere along the social stratification based on their success in doing so. In a free society that is a fair system, in my opinion, at least."

"Yet, politicians took this as an opportunity to wage class warfare and pandered to the bulk of the general public. Rather than extol the accomplishments of the most successful, laws were passed to tax those deemed as 'rich'. Behind closed doors decisions were made to spend this revenue on programs the lawmakers thought would win them the most votes come election day. This process may have led to their re-election, but it had a devastating impact on the economy. Those who were being heavily taxed lost their motivation to create wealth as it was just being stolen by the government. And those on the receiving end were content and developed a feeling of entitlement."

Jaxon paused, and glanced at the clock on the wall. "Maybe we should wrap this up for now, Will. That's a lot to absorb. I have to go to the Foundation for a few hours."

Jaxon was referring to the Warren Foundation, a charitable organization which he had founded and directed. Its founding principle was "To make the world a better place for having lived in it." This was a principle and driving force for Jaxon Warren throughout his life. The Foundation, as it was referred to, had an annual budget of three hundred billion dollars, which it used to address a wide range of issues: from hunger, to human rights, to natural disasters. There had been accusations that Jaxon ran the Foundation like a military unit and was aggressively increasing its influence around the world. Will had never thought much about the criticism, just rhetoric he supposed.

"I've been asked to speak at Oakland University this Thursday night," Jaxon noted. "It's a fundraiser for their school of business, and they want me to speak on The Enlightenment. It might play along well with our conversation. Interested?"

Will didn't have to think long about that. Any chance to spend more time with Uncle Jax would be great.

"Sure," Will enthusiastically responded. "That would be great, Uncle Jax."

"Ok. The event starts at eight o'clock. I'll pick you up at 7:00."

As Jaxon finished his sentence, a growing thunder emerged from outside. "Sounds like my ride is here. Give your uncle a hand getting out to the pad. Eh, Will?"

Will and Jaxon exited the rear of the house after stopping by Jaxon's study to retrieve his briefcase. They jumped in the electric golf cart Jaxon always kept parked out back, Will in the driver's seat. Will drove the 200 yards to the landing pad where Jaxon's custom Bell helicopter sat, rotors spinning, waiting to take him to the Foundation.

"Thanks, Will. Sorry I had to cut things short, but duty calls. Think about what we have talked about today. And never believe something just because somebody says it, not even me. The ability to question and critically think about subjects is a trait and skill you need to develop fully. See you Thursday, Will."

At that, Jaxon Warren rose out of his seat and walked to the awaiting helicopter, stooping a bit as he walked under the oscillating rotors. The co-pilot had appeared from the far side and lowered the stairs, and Will watched as he climbed into the helicopter, the door shutting behind him. Will pressed the accelerator of the cart and pulled away, back towards Riverside.

4

"Man was born free, and everywhere he is in chains."
—Jean-Jacques Rousseau

Jaxon gazed out the transparent armor of his executive helicopter, watching Will drive away in the golf cart. He had the armor installed on all the vehicles he used for transportation as there had been several attempts on his life over the years. Mostly lunatics seeking fame. He had narrowly escaped an attempt to cut him down with a shotgun shortly after he started MEC, a crazy farmer who, it was revealed at his trial, had feared the change brought on by the harvesting of corn husks. Jeanna had insisted on the armor ever since.

Jaxon was satisfied with the meeting he had just concluded with Will but was keenly aware of the work that lie ahead and the fact that he needed to manage his plan carefully, progressing slowly with great care and attention. Springing too much on Will would lead to failure but moving too leisurely would produce the same results. *Managing a group of people was much easier,* he thought. *Developing a single person was certainly a much bigger challenge. I'm up for it. I have to be. And Will's made for it.*

"Good morning, Mr. Warren," the pilot greeted Jaxon. "ETA to the Foundation is 10 minutes."

"Good morning, Colonel Payne. No hurry. They can wait for me."

Colonel Payne was an Army reservist who had worked as Jaxon's helicopter pilot for the last twelve years. He had been flying helicopters for close to twenty years, eight of which were spent on active military duty. He was widely known as one of the best pilots in the military with over eight hundred combat sorties. Jaxon had heard, through his military contacts, of his heroics which had won Colonel Payne the Bronze Star and, after making initial contact, convinced him to leave active duty and join the Foundation's team of pilots.

Jaxon opened his black leather briefcase and removed his tablet. He unfolded the device and the nano-display filled in over the seams. The home screen appeared after reading his thumb print, a red icon flashing to notify him that there was an urgent, secure message awaiting his attention. He unlocked the message, which automatically ran the decryption software.

"Larkin met with POTUS. Will be appointed to Calico."

Jaxon deleted the short message. He turned and looked out the window as the Bell was still ascending and traveling eastward over New Lothrop. Senator Larkin had been a thorn in his side for some time. It started out with some nuisances, some rejected permits for new plants, difficulties with pipeline construction approvals from the federal government, all issues that could be overcome. But the increasing level of frequency with which they occurred had caught his attention. He set his staff onto investigating what might be the underlying issue, and it turned out that the name of Brianna Larkin appeared frequently. She continued to step up her rhetoric against the energy industry and especially the Michigan Energy Corporation. She claimed that farmers and MEC workers were being exploited, which was typical political manipulation used to stir up class animosity. After getting a briefing on the senator from his staff, he knew there was something different about this one: she was out for revenge.

He had never heard of Brianna Larkin until just a few years ago, and since then, she had shown her disdain for him in public on many occasions, making false accusations of government influence peddling and other ridiculous claims regarding the environmental impact of biomass fuel. The information she distributed was completely without merit, but Jaxon was intrigued by her technical knowledge of biofuel. It was only then that he found out the cause of her scorn. She had been fired from the company and had apparently harbored some bitter feelings. Now she was about to be appointed Secretary of Defense. He knew he would have to keep a close eye on her. She had proven to be a more effective senator than an MEC manager.

The helicopter approached the roof of the Warren Foundation's headquarters building which sat at the north end of the Foundation's campus on the south end of the city of Flint. It was twenty buildings in all, half of which were hangars that stored machinery, aircraft, heavy and light duty vehicles, food and logistical supplies. There was also an armory and a small barracks that was used during training exercises. These had proven necessary as the Foundation ran missions in some of the most lawless areas of the world.

The Foundation employed twenty thousand people globally with chapters at most universities and college campuses, insuring volunteers for missions. Jaxon gave scholarships to some, others saw it as an opportunity to contribute to creating a better world. The fact that they received a few college credits for a mission didn't hurt either. In both cases, Jaxon thought it rounded out their education with some real life experiences, and employers agreed.

As they descended, he could see a group running in formation from the obstacle course of the outdoor training area. *Surely a bit bruised*, he thought, remembering how he threw his body into the course in his younger days like a goat-skinned ball leaving the basket of a Jai Alai player. Or, so he thought at least. He was not always the strongest or the fastest, but few could match his determination and drive.

The remainder of the campus was made up of administrative and training facilities, along with an airstrip with the capacity for even the largest aircraft. This campus was where each mission was planned out in great detail. Mission scope was specified, schedules and budgets laid out, teams selected, and mission completion defined. Jaxon had organized the Foundation around a project management philosophy identical to the MEC. In both cases, it had paid off quite handsomely and was now used globally as a model for business and industry.

Colonel Payne gently sat the helicopter down on the HQ building's helipad. Jaxon unlatched the door and jumped out, not waiting for assistance from the co-pilot and regretted this maneuver when his knees and ankles painfully compressed upon landing. He took several steps to stretch out his joints before noticing the strong wind blowing from the west. Jaxon turned his head to look at the cumulonimbus clouds forming. *Looks like a storm brewing*, he thought as he continued to the private rooftop entrance that would lead him straight down into his office.

Jaxon climbed down the stairs and entered his office through the hidden door on the south wall. The office was lined with zebra wood paneling, and the pneumatically controlled door closed and sealed behind him, completely hiding its existence. Only Jaxon's hand print placed on the door would break the seal, triggering the door to open. He stepped into the spacious room that contained his custom black ash desk, two mahogany framed facing chairs, and, closer to the main entrance, three beige love seats surrounding a glass coffee table: simple but elegant. The desk was immaculate, due in no thanks to Jaxon Warren. Jaxon had a tendency to be a bit disorderly; he kept everything straight in his head, just not necessarily in his work space. Angela, his longtime secretary, would come into his office after every visit and organize and file Jaxon's work, which was normally strewn across his desk and coffee table.

Three of the walls were lined with paintings by Jaxon's favorite artists. He had taken a liking to historically relevant art, struck with wonder in the artist's ability to capture a dynamic event while depicting a single scene. Over the years he had purchased the original Revere engravings of *The Bloody Massacre* and *A View of the Town of Boston,* which now hung on the west wall. His favorite, though, was hung directly behind his desk: Rugen's oil on canvas masterpiece, *Abel Warren's Enlightenment*, painted in 1817. Abel Warren was an ancestor of Jaxon's. He had been captured by the British and imprisoned in Canada during the War of 1812. The painting portrayed Abel kneeling on the dirt floor of his small prison cell and praying, his face was aglow from the light that shone through a small window, revealing a combination of despair and hope to an extent that Jaxon had ever seen in a painting. Abel had gone on to become a farmer, circuit riding preacher, and a strong leader in the community that he settled in southeast Michigan. Jaxon had always thought that the artist had intended that this painting represent the grace of God the moment it was bestowed upon Abel, leading him to an inspired life.

Directly below the painting, in a small frame, was a letter written by Abel Warren to his son. The letter had been handed down from generation to generation, and Jaxon's father had given it to him. It read:

My Dearest Samuel,

I believe my days on this earth are numbered and that I will soon face the judgment of our Lord. And, I believe, I am well prepared to do so. I have grown tired, and it is a fatigue that cannot be cured from a long night's sleep. This human body has grown heavy on my soul and it is time that it be discarded.

I know the early years in the Michigan territory were hard on the family, but I believe it also made us closer. We worked hard, suffered, and eventually, were rewarded for our efforts. Throughout, we always managed to love and laugh together.

Through the years, I have always strived to set a good example for all and, as I have often said to you, 'make the world a better place for having lived in it.' In this, I dearly hope, I have succeeded.

Your Father,
Abel

Jaxon walked over to his desk and paused in front of the painting for a moment. It heartened him every time he looked upon it, reminding him of the value of inspiration, not only from within, but offering it to others as well. He certainly understood the role of being a leader, and he also knew the necessity of gaining the trust of those one leads. Jaxon knew how to perform every process for turning husks into fuel; he had stood at every station on the processing floor and performed them at some point. His employees respected him for this, and it created a bond with them. Here at the Foundation, he had personally traveled each of the humanitarian missions, feeding those who were starving, injecting vaccines, and running security missions.

Something caught Jaxon's eye in the corner of the painting. He peered more closely and, underneath the protective glass, he found a crack in the canvas not more than a few millimeters in length. The painting was well over two hundred years old, and Jaxon had sent it out twice to be treated and restored. *I'll have to remember to send this in for a bit of restoration,* he thought. *Wish it was that easy with humans. Pity it has to deteriorate. Will it still exist in another two hundred years? Will anybody care? Or will it only be found in some academic art book that nobody reads. Ask a hundred young people today about the war and what kind of answer would you get? Probably a blank stare. How many people even know why the war was fought?* Then Jaxon allowed himself to ask the underlying question, *Will I be remembered two hundred years from now? Even mentioned in a history book?* Jaxon continued to absorb the painting for another moment.

He slowly turned toward his desk and wondered momentarily how many hours he had sat right there, making decisions that impacted the lives of the most destitute. Hundreds? Thousands? How many lives had he saved? How many had been lost? There still were troubled areas in the world and yet finite resources available to him. Every mission decision would save a community, a nation perhaps, but this always meant another region would be left to its own accord, dooming hundreds or thousands to starvation or death. Jaxon still wondered, every day, if he had done enough.

He walked over to the outward glass wall, a window that allowed him to gaze out over the compound. He called out to his secretary. The voice identification system of the intercom built into the rooms sound system immediately ran a comparison of the voice and made the authentication. The circuits opened and passed the message through the ether. Within a few seconds came the reply.

"Yes, Mr. Warren?" Angela responded with her relaxed and smooth, velvety voice.

"Are they here?"

"Yes, sir. They have been waiting for approximately thirty minutes."

And both of them are still alive? Jaxon thought with amusement. "Thank you, Angela. Have the Calidum crew assembled in Hangar Bay 6 in one hour please."

"Will do, Mr. Warren."

Angela had been Jaxon's administrative assistant at the Foundation for ten years now. She was the epitome of efficiency and professionalism as she executed her duties with militaristic precision. Jaxon knew that this organization ran well for many reasons, and Angela was a critical part of that system.

"I suppose you can send them in," Jaxon ordered, half reluctantly.

The office doors swung open and in walked the backbone of the Foundation: Kellen Wendt and Ray Bakis. Kellen was the Chief Financial Officer of the Foundation. A bit brash, he had been with the Foundation from the beginning. He was one of the original investors in MEC and, after creating substantial wealth, decided to continue to invest in the vision of Jaxon Warren, but this time it would not be with money, rather his expertise and drive. Kellen had proven to be a remarkable logistician and fundraiser. His years of experience in business combined with an excellent education and ambitious personality had secured the success of the Foundation for many years to come. He bought into Jaxon's credo of making the world a better place and knew his best opportunity for doing so was at the Warren Foundation. MEC had made him a rich man beyond his dreams, but he wanted that satisfaction of having a direct, positive impact on the most desperate parts of the world.

Kellen was born with the proverbial "silver spoon" in his mouth. His parents had died while he was in college, and he had the sense to put his inheritance into a portfolio of conservative investments. This served him well when the Millennial Depression hit. Others his age became stripped of their wealth while Kellen was able to prosper, buying large sums of what had become dirt-cheap stocks. He also decided to try his hand as a venture capitalist and invested in a startup company, MEC.

Ray Bakis had been with the Foundation for only a few short years. He was raised in rural North Dakota and excelled academically as well as athletically. Having working-class parents, he took an NROTC scholarship and earned a dual degree in mechanical engineering and mathematics, graduating Summa Cum Laude. During his junior year, he chose the Marine Corps option and, upon graduation, was assigned to the Marine Corps Special Operations Command. He served four years as a reconnaissance team leader and was being recruited by the CIA when Jaxon tagged him to be the Foundation's security officer. Ray was an intimidating spectacle to most, standing just over six feet with a large, muscular frame, the epitome of a Marine.

Ray quickly displayed an excellent combination of intelligence and instinct that was rewarded by Jaxon, who promoted him to run operations. Ray was only thirty-four but brought a sharp mind and vitality to the organization's highest ranking staff. He and Kellen butted heads often, but Jaxon knew this conflict drove the team's creativity in developing solutions to near impossible problems.

"Please sit down, gentlemen." Both sat down opposite each other, and Jaxon joined them around the glass coffee table.

"Where do we stand?" Jaxon asked.

The firestorm started. "We are fine financially, Jaxon. That is not the problem. The problem is that I'm being asked to approve dozens of purchase orders to companies with vague invoices. I don't even know what we are paying for. This is ridiculous," Kellen belted out, his face a bit red. "Half the invoices that I can understand are for weapons for God's sake. Have you seen how big the armory is, Jaxon?"

"Yes, I built it."

"We're a charitable organization, Jaxon. We help feed people! We need more food not more guns."

"The food is only temporary assistance," Ray cut in. "These people need to be defended against the corrupt cronies who still linger in the crevices of the world. Without doing so, we will jeopardize the long term success of any mission we pursue."

"Is that all we are doing, Ray?" Kellen asked. "Defending them? I can see what is going on even from back here in the states."

Jaxon was well aware that Kellen had never become accustomed to being left in the dark on many of the organization's practices when it came to executing a mission. But Jaxon distributed information strictly on a 'need to know' basis. And everything always worked out well in the end.

"I'm well aware of the Foundation's mission, Kellen. Remember whose name is on the building." Jaxon paused and continued, "I trust our field managers. I'm sure they have not submitted requests for anything they don't need. Get those purchase orders cut. We have no time to waste."

Kellen sat back in his chair obviously irritated.

"Operations?" Jaxon inquired of Ray.

"We have twenty humanitarian teams preparing—one hundred members per team. If we get all the supplies on time," Ray shot Kellen a condescending look, "they will be ready in three weeks. That leaves us with a week of contingency to stay on schedule before wheels up. We have ten units of special operations creating plans for security and support—the usual twelve man teams. Intel and admin make up another hundred. So just over twenty-two hundred in all. The planning phase will be complete in a week, which leaves three weeks of training. Green lights all around as of right now. Given the recent purchase of the additional drones, this should be a satisfactory number to complete the mission while minimizing risk."

It was these special operations units that made Kellen uncomfortable. They had grown out of the security teams that Jaxon started after a humanitarian crew in Central America had been attacked, resulting in numerous casualties. Jaxon had slowly filled their ranks with former military special operations and intelligence personnel in order to support the humanitarian effort. The media had run several reports that Jaxon was creating a private army. And he had spent considerable effort in Washington defending his operations.

The Foundation had also purchased several dozen remote-operated drones, pilotless aircraft, that could be used to drop payloads to remote areas as well as for security purposes, if necessary.

"Let's make sure we stick to that schedule, Ray. The reports coming in from the media have noted brutal fighting on the ground. One can only imagine what is going on with the civilians that are caught in the crossfire. I want to get them some relief without delay," Jaxon instructed.

"We could send in two additional special operations teams to interfere with the enemy's progress. It won't stop them, but capping a few leaders on the front lines and disrupting some of their logistics will slow them down and put some fear into the grunts," Ray suggested.

"Good idea, Ray. But hire a contract team to do it. We can't spare any of our local staff without risking a delay in the schedule."

Kellen couldn't remain silent any longer and sat forward in his seat. "We are not a military organization, Jaxon! Over the last couple of years, you've created your own private army, and it's going to come back and bite us. We need to minimize the special operations mission to protecting our own people, nothing more. Otherwise you're asking for trouble."

Ray shot back, "That's white collar crap, Kellen. Just pay the bills and keep our supplies coming. We'll do the rest."

"You've gone too far out of the box, Ray! What the hell do you need this much ammunition for?" Kellen shouted as he slapped a stack of papers on the table. "You've pulled more than a thousand grenades and ten thousand rounds of ammunition from the armory for this mission alone."

"That should be good for the first week," Ray shot back sarcastically.

"Enough, gentlemen!" Jaxon called a halt to the conversation.

"Jaxon," Kellen started again. "I've known you for over thirty years. I've been loyal to you, and I always will be. I was there to support you from the very beginning when everybody else deemed MEC too risky to do business with. But I would be remiss in my duty if I didn't warn you that this is getting out of hand."

Jaxon stood and walked slowly to the window. He gazed out at the darkening sky and could see lightning in the distance. The office slightly shook from the first bit of thunder, announcing the storm to the city.

"This is going to be my last mission, gentlemen," Jaxon announced calmly, changing the tone of the meeting. Both men sat in silence, the stunning revelation reflected in their faces. They had expected Jaxon to continue until he one day would just keel over. He was more passionate about the Foundation, and his mission in life, than either had ever seen throughout the years. This was completely unexpected to both of them.

Jaxon picked up on their astonishment and continued, "I need to step back and let the younger managers grow. I can't run the place forever." Jaxon knew this more now than ever. He was coming to grips with his own mortality. The missions were becoming harder on him both physically and mentally. The long periods away from Jeanna weighed heavily on him as well. They wouldn't live forever, and Jaxon wanted to spend more time with her to make up for those long hours he had spent at work combined with the long absences from home. Jeanna had not said anything, but he could pick up on her feelings.

"You both have your orders." Jaxon paused. "I'm addressing the team in a few minutes, and I have to prepare. Dismissed."

Both men left the office in silence, still in such a state of shock that words escaped them.

Jaxon walked over to his desk, sat down, and unfolded his tablet. He reviewed the personnel who had been assigned to the mission and made some notes. He then rose and walked swiftly toward the oak doors leading to the executive administrative pool. The scanner was triggered by the approaching motion, and the doors swung open upon Jaxon's approach.

"I'm off to the main hangar, Angela."

"Yes, sir," Angela replied in military fashion. "Your car will be outside the hangar when you are finished, Mr. Warren. Air traffic has been grounded due to the storm."

Jaxon smiled at her. "I would never survive without you, Angela."

She smiled back. "That is correct, sir. You wouldn't."

She lifted her gaze and watched him as he limped down the hall toward the elevators. She had noticed something different in his voice that she had not heard in all the years she had known him; the usual level of energy seemed to be missing. She decided to login to the telecast, so she could watch his address.

***

Jaxon took the elevator down to the sub-basement. When reviewing the original designs with the Foundation's architect, he had directed her to put a connecting tunnel system throughout the facility. Michigan winters could be harsh, and he wanted the staff to be able to focus on accomplishing their tasks rather than the weather. It also provided a means for him to move around the facility with less notice during the more amiable seasons as most preferred to walk outdoors and enjoy the beauty of the campus and the warmth. Living through Michigan winters certainly made one appreciate the warmer weather.

He stepped out of the elevator and was thankful to see the tunnel was empty. As he made his way through the white sterile walls, he reviewed the points he wanted to communicate to the team. He didn't necessarily like these addresses but had realized over the years that they were an excellent tool in motivating teams and making certain that everybody understood the mission. A few moments later, he turned north and focused on his breathing, letting his mind go blank. He had developed an expertise in portraying calmness with a strong sense of authority and knew that was how he wanted to be perceived during this speech. He was a bit concerned as the mission would be difficult, thus the extra precautions. But he would not let the magnitude of the challenge daunt him or the troupe. Jaxon had chosen this mission, knowing it would be his last, because he knew it would be the Foundation's biggest success. The world's governments would be too slow to act and, even when they did, they would simply impose additional, meaningless sanctions. Efforts he knew would not produce the needed results and would lead to an escalation of the crisis. Some world leaders had tried to discredit Jaxon over the years, casting him and the Foundation as a rogue organization, playing God with its money and influence. He didn't care. The mission mattered, and if that meant embarrassing weak leaders, so be it.

The League of United Republics had made improvements after it replaced the United Nations as a global forum for facilitating world peace. The totalitarian states that remained at the end of the depression no longer had a voice, and quickly realized that in order to stay in power, they must reform. But the League was still a bureaucracy and slow to move.

Jaxon reached the hangar and climbed the stairs. He could hear the preparations going on in earnest as he approached the deck. He emerged and after a moment one of the managers noticed him and immediately announced a command to line up over the bays speakers. The several hundred members of the Calidum team took their positions by team designation, most being special operations personnel who were on site for training. The rest of the mission's personnel were logged in remotely to view the telecast. There was also a small contingent of the most experienced foundation members, about forty people, which formed the command and control unit.

Jaxon continued up another flight of stairs that led to a small landing above the hangar offices that would allow him to be seen, and heard, by all. He walked to the edge and gazed out over the hangar deck, taking the time to look at the men and women assembled before him, making a bond with them before he even spoke.

"Thanks for taking the time out of your activities to allow me a few words as we prepare for our mission. As I look out, I see many new faces and a few old ones. For some of you, this is your first mission with the Foundation, and I welcome you aboard. I am grateful for your decision to join us. New team members always bring a new perspective and energy, and I assure you, your input is respected. I also know many of you are college students or recent graduates, and this is your first time venturing out into the world, so please make sure to listen to the more experienced team members as they have learned the ropes over the years."

"I would also like to give my thanks to those of you returning for yet another effort of the Foundation. Your experience and expertise is essential to this difficult, yet critical mission. Make certain to take care of those around you. You're all responsible for each other's safety, and only through team work will you produce the results required of this great task."

"I created this foundation for the very purpose our creed states, 'to make the world a better place for having lived in it.' Many of the ills of the world have been overcome with the Enlightenment which, in my opinion, is still emerging. My goal was to form an organization that would go into the most battered areas of the world and make lasting change. I am proud to stand up here and state that we have accomplished this task on many occasions. And my guess is that is why you are here today, to be part of this world-changing organization and make your own stamp on history."

Applause erupted from the troupe, and Jaxon artfully paused to let it pass.

Jaxon's mouth turned down and his face subtly tightened. When he began again, his voice was a bit softer. "The situation is grim in Calidum. You've seen the news reports: North Calidum has invaded South Calidum. Not in order to defend itself, but rather to serve an evil master, that which I call greed. The North has invaded in order to take control of the zinc mines which are properly located in South Calidum, for which the North has no rightful claim. Shipments of food, for which Calidum is dependent, have been halted to the western cities as the North has cut the country in half. Thousands are starving, and thousands more will follow unless action is taken. Governments around the world are talking and debating, which is what governments do best. In the meantime, we will take action."

"Our mission is simple: Provide humanitarian aid to the South Calidumese. This will at least give them a fighting chance. Because it is a war zone, we will be sending the largest special operations force the Warren Foundation has ever assembled. We've done this to assure your safe return."

"On a final note," Jaxon paused and looked again from left to right over the assembled team. "This will be my final mission with you. Field work is for the young, and I'm not a member of that club any longer. I would like to make this the greatest humanitarian achievement to date for the Foundation, go out with a bang so to speak. And that is why each one of you has been handpicked for this mission. I have complete faith in all of you. God bless you, and I'll see you on the ground in Calidum."

Another loud hail erupted from the crowd on the hangar deck. Jaxon lifted his hand and waved. He knew he had nailed it. Short and to the point, with a little emotional twist: a formula that had served him well over the years.

Jaxon turned and descended the stairs. Ray was there to meet him with a sly grin. "Great speech, Jaxon, but you left out the fun part of the mission."

Jaxon smiled. He admired Ray's drive and sense of humor. Every organization needed a Ray Bakis, especially those with a military, or quasi-military, focus. "They don't need to hear that, Ray. We'll keep that to ourselves. Get those contractors hired and airborne ASAP."

"Yes, Sir," Ray said as Jaxon walked out the door to his awaiting car. Ray, like most, had tremendous respect for Jaxon Warren. *The man certainly walks his talk,* Ray thought.

5

"Beauty itself is but the sensible image of the Infinite."
—Francis Bacon

Will sat on his porch waiting for Uncle Jax, nervously tapping his heels on the wooden steps. He was taking the opportunity to get in a few pages of the Daton book Uncle Jax had asked him to read. Will glanced at his watch, *ten to seven, still a bit early,* he thought. He looked up the road, but no sign of Uncle Jax. He turned his attention westward from which the breeze was blowing, carrying the fresh smells associated with rural Michigan, which were noticeably sharper on this day. The air was still warm as the September sun had not yet set. Will thought the temperature seemed about average for this time of year. Which, he thought, was nothing more than a reflection of everything else in his life, with the exception of his recent interaction with Uncle Jax. *Another month and the farmers will start to harvest corn,* he thought, unsure as to why he knew this as he was no farmer. Probably just one of those things you pick up while living amongst farms. Will thought how unique the life of the farmer would be. Governed by the seasons, the weather was your best friend or worst enemy. It was an attractive life, in a certain way. Certainly no nine-to-five job, often during the harvesting season, he would notice farmers in the fields well past dark. There was also no one to answer to but yourself and no daily commute.

Will closed his book when he spotted the long, black, autonomous limousine moving its way south on Orchard Street. The clear-coat paint reflected a distorted image of the trees as the car passed beneath them. Uncle Jax had heavily invested in driverless automotive technology, which had turned out to be a big seller in urban environments. But the rural population still preferred control over their own vehicles. The lengthy vehicle pulled into the half-moon drive as Will rose and descended the stairs of the porch. The limo's door slowly opened, and Will could see Uncle Jax sitting on the far side on the beige, faux leather seats, facing forward in the six-passenger, rear section. Will climbed in and took the seat facing opposite Uncle Jax.

"Hey, Uncle Jax."

The door automatically closed behind Will, and the car began to move. It would follow a programmed route to the university that would be continuously updated via satellite during the trip, accounting for traffic patterns and any accidents or construction.

Jaxon saw the book in Will's hand. "How do you like the book so far?"

"It's a lot different than the stuff I've seen in other history books."

"Yes, no doubt about that. History is created by people, Will. People create events; people react to events, and on and on it goes. We humans have an incredible level of intelligence. Yet many choose to hand that intelligence over to others and take the easy road, the road that requires little effort, or so it seems. Our intelligence can take us to levels of creativity that result in technological advances, prosperity, and a genuine degree of civility toward each other. Relinquishing reason and avoiding the labor required to think through the problems we face has led to the darkest hours of human history: the Dark Ages, the Inquisition, the Great Depression, the Millenial Depression. On the other hand, the greatest eras have been defined by aggressive engagement of our minds and applying those thoughts to our environment: the Enlightenment, the American Revolution, the Industrial Revolution, and the Information Age."

"Where are we at right now, Uncle Jax?"

"Hard to say, Will. We're better than we used to be. But not even close to where we ought to be."

"What was it like during the Millennial Depression?" Will asked. He was getting more comfortable around Uncle Jax.

"Economically, the conditions were harsh. We had gotten ourselves into a real bind. The United States finally had to admit that it would default on its over-burdensome debt, which turned out to be the first domino. Many other countries followed with similar announcements, leading to the collapse of financial markets and a global currency crisis. Many lost their life savings as funds and pensions collapsed. These events made the housing collapse of the early 2000's look like a mere speed bump."

"Financial institutions closed, and the Treasury Department was helpless as there was no possible bailout like there was in 2008. Every week there were fewer and fewer banks that carried out global transactions which practically halted international trade. Most retail stores at the time carried foreign-made products. As their shelves emptied out, many of them closed also."

"Unemployment in the U.S. shot up to about twenty percent within a few months and inflation skyrocketed, causing the U.S. dollar to be practically worthless. The dominos fell through all industries, both domestic and global. In short, it was miserable, Will. Soup kitchens started to pop up in the towns and cities to help alleviate hunger. They were quickly overwhelmed as food prices rose daily. People had no choice but to start trading in goods rather than money."

"Families were forced to move in with each other as they could no longer afford their homes. This led to a large amount of foreclosures, and those banks that survived were unable to manage the homes that were now in their possession. Communities were burdened with these abandoned homes, many of which had been ransacked for anything of value. Within a short period of time, they were also overgrown with grass and weeds which led to rodent issues."

"Bleak enough for you?" Jaxon asked.

"It sounds horrible," Will replied solemnly.

"It was. But we had to go through it. People slowly regained their senses. Suddenly, the season tickets to the sports teams and three hundred channel cable packages were not so important. People could no longer afford the entertainment they had become so addicted to and found, once again, the important things in life. They spent more time with their families and children with their homework. Seems terrible that such a monolithic event would have to occur to bring people to this realization, but that was the way of it. We slowly pulled ourselves up, and showed once again the triumph of the human spirit."

"You pulled the country out of it, Uncle Jax. Everybody knows that," Will stated.

Jaxon turned his head sharply from the window and looked Will directly in the eye, his face taut and voice firm. "I did nothing of the sort, Will. I saw an opportunity, and I took it. I may have had a bit more drive than most, but the strength of the American character is what pulled us out of the depths of the depression. People who pushed themselves to become better, parents who encouraged their children, business leaders who adapted to the new environment—those are the people responsible for bringing the end of the depression. No man is an island, Will. Don't idolize people, especially me."

Will was a bit startled at Uncle Jax's harsh reply. "I … I'm sorry. I didn't mean any…."

"No need to be sorry, Will," Uncle Jax interrupted him, more calm in his voice. "I have to remember that you're only seventeen. Sometimes I expect too much of people."

"You can always expect too much from me, Uncle Jax," Will said, not wanting to disappoint. "It's better than the alternative."

Uncle Jax thought for a moment, and then smiled. "Why, yes. I suppose you're right."

The car continued on its preset course while Uncle Jax worked on his tablet, finishing the speech he was to deliver tonight. Will pretended to read while trying to imagine living during the depression. He realized this was a futile attempt but thought it worth the effort anyway.

About sixty minutes later, the car exited the highway and drove east on University Drive. They drove through the bustling commercial area of Auburn Hills, and within a short time, the car entered the tree-lined entrance of Oakland University. As they made their way around the traffic circle, Uncle Jax put his tablet down and looked out the window. This was Will's first trip to Oakland University, and he was pleasantly fascinated with the architectural style of the academic buildings. Jaxon must have taken notice as he began to offer Will his skills as a tour guide, pointing out the Oakland Center, medical school building, and several dormitories. Jaxon quickly reprogrammed the car to take a detour around the library, School of Engineering, and School of Business in order for Will to get a comprehensive view of the campus. The buildings along with the rolling hills created an atmosphere of academia to which Will was unaccustomed. *Likely the indication of a good architect,* he thought.

The car, now back on track, took a short road through the woods and over a vintage bridge before circling to a stop. The door opened, and Will stepped out of the car in front of the largest home he had ever laid his eyes upon, even grander than Riverside. The vastness of the Tudor-Revival style of Meadow Brook Hall lay in front and to the side of Will as he stood, aghast at the elegant architectural detail to a point that words did not fit the situation. The exterior walls were of brick, sandstone, and timbers arranged into a myriad of textures. The lights from the ground illuminated this marvel, casting scores of shadows up towards an abundance of chimneys sticking up through the tile-covered roof.

"Beautiful, eh?" Uncle Jax said.

Will found this to be a rare occasion as to which Uncle Jax's words seemed almost ridiculous in their sense of understatement.

"Somebody actually lives here?" Will asked.

"Not anymore. It's one of the old auto baron estates. The wife of John Dodge lived here and donated her estate to establish Oakland University many years ago. She lived here for around forty years," Uncle Jax explained.

Jaxon nudged Will. "Enough ogling. It's show time."

At the entrance stood a young man with a suit too big for his slight build. "Hello, Mr. Warren. Welcome to Meadow Brook Hall and Oakland University. I'll be happy to show you to the ballroom where the reception will take place."

"Thanks, son. But I've been to this campus a few hundred times. I think I can find my way," Uncle Jax replied a bit gruffly. The young doorman looked quite disappointed but wisely obeyed and let Uncle Jax lead the way through the foyer and into the Great Hall. Will noticed that this less-than-humble room itself was as large as some homes. Jaxon continued down the finely cut stone steps, his gate slightly awkward despite his attempts to compensate and hide the grimace that occurred with each placement of his unsteady footing. Upon reaching the bottom of the staircase, and revealing a room crowded with tuxedo and gown clad guests, a voracious applause erupted with echo's coming from adjacent hallways and rooms as if they were members of a clapping orchestra being conducted by an unseen figure. A stately greeting for a man who would be spending the next several hours convincing them to part with large blocks of money from their bank accounts in favor of the Foundation and Oakland University. But it was known by all that their accumulated riches would be pennies if not for the brilliance of Jaxon Warren. And each guest was here to pay tribute to the savior of the Republic.

Will estimated the brightly lit room was filled to what appeared to be maximum capacity with, perhaps, two hundred or so. Uncle Jax smiled widely and gently waved, thanking the crowd for the warm welcome.

Jaxon turned to Will and put his hand on his shoulder, leaning in so Will could hear over the continuing applause.

"You're on your own, Will. I have to mingle for a while before I speak. Have some fun!" Jaxon turned and walked away.

Will looked around and noticed the bar setup for the patrons. He walked over and asked for an orange soda, then made his way to the nearest wall and attempted to blend in, which was nearly impossible as he was wearing khaki's, a navy polo, and a suede bomber jacket. He watched Uncle Jax magically working the crowd like a pro. Will reasoned that Uncle Jax had done this a thousand times and appeared to enjoy the process. Will could see the respect in his eyes for everyone with whom he spoke. Giving each person just enough attention to let them know they were a part of his life, and he was grateful for their appearance tonight yet with the realization that there were several hundred to greet.

"You're not one of us," a voice next to Will startled him from his thoughts. He turned to find himself looking at a young woman whose eyes were locked on him. Will felt a shift in time. He was not sure how long it took him to speak, a fraction of a second or a minute. When he regained his senses, he spoke.

"W-what did you say?"

The girl, smiling with her bright red lips closed, took a step closer to Will. "You're not one of us."

The girl was dressed in an elegant blue evening dress that made her narrow body appear tall when, in fact, the top of her head only came to Will's chin. Her pixie chestnut hair was blended up in swirls that seemed to perfectly frame her fair skinned face which was highlighted by high cheekbones and a soft chin. The eyes were intense and sat beneath high arched eyebrows.

Will was able to calm himself enough to utter a sentence.

"I'm not sure what you mean."

"If you were one of us, you would be dressed a bit better," the girl explained as she looked Will down then back up. She spoke in a strong, but soft tone, with a steady, natural pace. "I'm one of the nine students who is receiving a scholarship tonight. I just have to spend a few months in the desert of Calidum, and I'll have graduate school paid for. All of us are here tonight to be paraded in front of donors and for Jaxon Warren to show what a great person he is." The last she said with a hint of sarcasm. "What are you doing here?" she asked.

"I'm here with my uncle," Will said.

"Hmm. Rich kid no doubt. Well make sure your uncle makes a big donation. We don't want to run out of food in Calidum, do we?" More sarcasm.

"My name's Will." He was now intrigued and a bit calmer, unsure of what had startled him about this girl. Will found her a bit acerbic but was enchanted.

She stared at him for a moment, as if deciding to just walk away or engage in further conversation.

"I'm Suzen," she finally said.

"Graduate school? You don't look any older than me," Will said.

"I'm eighteen. I started school here when I was sixteen."

"Wow. You pretty much just skipped over high school."

"I'm smart," Suzen stated, turning to look around the room. She had said it with not even the slightest hint of arrogance and with no more emotion than if she was giving you the time of day.

"What do you study?" Will asked, awkwardly.

Suzen turned back to look Will in the eye. "I have a B.S. in nano- engineering." No hint of vanity.

"I vaguely know to what that term is related." Will knew he couldn't fake knowledge of the subject, so he chose the honest path.

"I study the methods of manipulating matter at the atomic and molecular level. I'm going to graduate school next fall and plan on researching the use of nano-processing techniques to increase the energy density in batteries."

"That sounds fascinating," Will said, *sort of.* He was actually unsure if it was interesting or not. And Suzen looked at him as though she knew it was a lie but didn't mind.

"It turns out graduate school is a bit expensive. My advisor told me about the Warren Foundation scholarship, and next thing you know, here I am, heading for South Calidum."

Another sarcastic smile as she took a drink from the glass she was holding in her hand. It appeared to be some kind of white wine.

"So, is your uncle rich?" Suzen asked.

"Ah yes, I think you could say that." Will just realized he had not said which patron was his uncle.

"I guess he would be, otherwise he would not be here. Why did he drag you here?"

"I'm not sure," Will admitted. "He's hard to say no to."

"Don't worry, eventually you'll grow some balls," she said matter-of-factly.

Will's eyebrows rose as if he just took a shot of hard whiskey. *This girl is abrasive*, he thought with a hint of excitement.

Uncle Jax had made his way around the room and now approached Will and Suzen with a brandy in his hand.

"Well, I see you've found one of our star attractions for the night, Will," Uncle Jax grinned as he gently gave Suzen a quick one arm hug around her shoulders. Suzen was startled with the familiarity in which Jaxon spoke with Will. "I picked her out myself among the applicants. This one is quite smart, Will," Uncle Jax said smugly, as if he were responsible.

"Yes, Uncle Jax, very smart." Will gave Suzen a glance as if to say 'smart, but a bit shocked right now.'

"Thank you, Mr. Warren. It's an honor to be here tonight. I'm so grateful for the opportunity." Suzen smiled.

"Oh, it's I who is grateful, my dear. It's people like you who are going to make a difference in this world. You've chosen, at a young age, to be part of the game and not just stand on the sidelines. Many of your peers are out shopping or watching the latest sitcom tonight. You're here to receive a full scholarship to graduate school." Uncle Jax smiled mischievously and leaned in closer to Suzen. "You win!" he exclaimed with a laugh and another quick squeeze with his arm around her shoulder.

Uncle Jax looked away for a moment. "Well, looks like it's time for my speech." Jaxon looked at Will, and winked. "Have fun, you two." And he walked away.

After he had gotten out of earshot, Suzen said mockingly, "You're here with your uncle, eh, Will?"

Will picked up on the intended sneer. He smiled and said, "You never asked his name."

"I suppose I didn't. But you could have mentioned it." She was smiling again now. "So you're the heir to the throne?"

"Whoa. I'm just his nephew. I actually don't know him all that well, at least not much more than anybody else. We just recently started talking to each other regularly."

"He doesn't have any children from what I understand. How many nieces and nephews?"

Will paused a moment. Knowing the answer but, for the first time, realizing the implication. He turned his head to the side and looked at the floor briefly before meeting Suzen's gaze again. "Just me."

Suzen could see the awkwardness she had just caused.

"Your uncle is scheduled to speak for about an hour. Want to go for a walk? Nothing against him," she quickly added. "I just find these types of speeches boring."

"Sure." Will's attention was now completely diverted. They walked back up the stairs and through the Grand Hall exiting onto a patio. As they walked out, they were met by a cool September breeze. Will took off his jacket and gave it to her, which she accepted with ease.

"Thanks. I didn't plan on being outside tonight," Suzen said gratefully.

They turned and strolled through a loggia terrace and small garden, following the perimeter of the mansion. She told Will, with enthusiasm, much about Matilda Dodge Wilson, the founder of Oakland University. Will was impressed with her knowledge of the university's history and the esteem she held for her school.

As they continued through an English, walled garden, lined with daisies, roses, and numerous other vegetation by which Will was impressed, but unfamiliar, Suzen told Will more about the founder, how she was widowed upon the death of John Dodge, who had founded, with his brother, the Dodge Motor Company. After a few minutes, Will looked up as they stood at the base of a gazebo sitting upon what appeared to be a sitting room with a large wooden door and lined with brick. They walked up the carved stone steps and entered the gazebo, finding a table with several chairs. Suzen sat and Will followed. They took in the view as the interior lights of Meadow Brook were shining through the meticulously decorated windows, which bathed the mansion in an aura of gold.

"Isn't it beautiful?" Suzen asked. Will agreed. It was a magnificent home. Suzen looked at Will and must have surmised that he was taken in by the charm and grace of this place. She was slightly surprised: most people did not see the allure of the house as she did. "The sun room and library are also magnificent. Maybe someday, I'll show you around the upper levels. There is also a pipe organ. The pipes are actually built into the walls. They let me play it once."

Without taking his eyes off the house, Will replied, "That would be great. I'd love to hear you play."

Suzen smiled as they sat together, engulfed from the light of Meadow Brook Hall.

"So what is it like being the nephew of Jaxon Warren?" Suzen asked, removing her gaze from the mansion and turning her head to look at Will.

Will thought for a moment. He usually didn't like it when people asked him this question. But with Suzen, he didn't seem to mind. "Well, we really don't know each other that well, which probably seems a bit strange, being that we live so close, and I'm his only nephew. He was never around much when I was growing up, busy with his company and the Foundation, I suppose. I would see him occasionally on holidays when I was younger. The last few weeks we've talked a few times. So we're just starting to get to know each other."

Suzen told Will about growing up in Flint. Her parents were both high school teachers. They taught her to read at an early age, which instilled in her a love for learning. By the time she went to school, she could read, and her high level of intelligence was evident to her parents and teachers. They accelerated her as much as they thought was socially safe, finishing the fifth grade at age nine, eighth grade at eleven, and high school at fifteen.

Her mother died suddenly when she was ten from an arterial aneurysm. It was hard on her dad and her for a while, but they pulled through together. She received a scholarship to Oakland and, as she said, "here she is!" Attending Oakland also kept her fairly close to home, so she could visit her father as often as she liked.

They decided it was best to return to the fundraiser and retraced their steps. As they stepped down to the lower level landing, they caught Uncle Jax's eye, and he finished up his conversation before excusing himself and walking over to them.

"I have a feeling you both missed my speech," he said with a wry grin.

They were both slightly embarrassed that he noticed and neither offered a reply.

"I can't imagine why anybody would not want to hear an old man ramble on for an hour or so," he said sarcastically and with a laugh.

They realized he was just teasing them, lightening the moment.

"Sorry, Uncle Jax," Will said. "We decided to go for a walk. I hope you don't mind."

"Not at all, Will. It's a beautiful estate, and I'm glad you were able to see some of it with such a beautiful and smart young lady." Jaxon was still in his flirtatious mode from raising funds. "But, I'm afraid we'll have to leave, Will. Aunt Jeanna doesn't like it when I'm too late." This made Suzen giggle a little bit, thinking that Uncle Jax was concerned about answering to anybody. She found it amusing.

Jaxon took out his key fob and pressed the valet button. Somewhere the car started and moved its way to the front of the estate.

"I'll be in the car, Will," Uncle Jax said slyly and turned to Suzen. "Good night, Ms. Arden. I'll be seeing you on our upcoming trip."

"Good night, Mr. Warren. Thanks so much for the scholarship."

"Oh, you'll earn it, my dear," he said as he walked away.

Suzen and Will stood for a moment, not making eye contact, before Will finally spoke, "Thanks for the tour."

"Sure. Thanks for taking me away from the crowd. They make me nervous. I'm a bit of an introvert," Suzen confessed. "Maybe I'll see you around sometime."

"Maybe." Will was hesitant to leave but it felt awkward to stay. "Bye."

"Goodbye, Will."

Will walked back up the stairs and out the door where Uncle Jax's car was waiting. The door was open, and Will climbed in.

Uncle Jax immediately spoke, "I don't think I've ever seen you with quite so large a smile on your face, Will. Brilliant young lady. You have a good eye, young man," Jaxon smiled heartily at Will.

Will was a bit embarrassed and just smiled.

The car began to move out the drive, up a hill, and veered right. Uncle Jax pushed a button on his arm rest, causing the car to come to a stop. He pushed another button and the window lowered. Uncle Jax pointed his long bony finger towards a barn-shaped building, maybe a horse stable, at least at one time. It was dilapidated. The windows were boarded up. *It's likely ready to be torn down,* Will thought.

"That's where it all started, Will," Uncle Jax said with excitement.

Will was looking at the building. "What is it?"

"That was what was called the Oakland University INCubator. The new building is on the other side of campus now, but that was the original and where I started the Michigan Energy Corporation. Abner Troffe had the idea, and I had the business plan. The INCubator was designed to support new business in the state of Michigan and allow certain promising businesses use of school resources. Abner was able to use the chemistry lab to perfect his conversion process, and the INCubator gave me the arena to present our business plan to a large pool of investors. We generated enough interest to finance the patent application, and once that was granted, we secured investors to build a processing plant. The rest, I guess, is history."

Uncle Jax looked back at Will. "You never know when opportunity will present itself, Will. You must always be ready." Uncle Jax made a fist and thrust it in the air. "And willing to take action."

"What happened to Abner?" Will asked curiously.

Jaxon paused before answering. "There was a lot of pressure on the scientists at MEC. Abner had some kind of mental breakdown. That is really all I know," Jaxon said this dismissively. Will suspected there was more to the story but didn't press the issue.

The window rose as the car moved forward, calculating the path back to New Lothrop. They spoke little on the ride back. Both were tired. Will suspected Uncle Jax wanted him to ponder on the events of the evening.

Will actually thought of nothing but Suzen during the ride. It was hard for him to pinpoint what it was about her that made such an impression on him. Ronni was certainly more attractive, but he seemed to delight in every word from Suzen. It felt very refreshing for him just to listen to her.

6

"The only gift is a portion of thyself."
—Ralph Waldo Emerson

W ill walked, with little care, down the hallway of New Lothrop High School. The orange and cream lockers made it look longer than it was. Intellectually, he knew this was a house of higher learning, but at times, he viewed the colored lockers like the bars of a prison, confining his mind to a cell that was damp and gray. He was in no hurry to get to the school's auditorium as he was about ten minutes early for the school board meeting, and they usually started late. He was here to cover the meeting for "The Hornet," the student run newspaper, and thought that he and Aryn should have given the assignment to one of the freshman on the staff. As he approached the entrance, he heard more commotion than he would expect for such a mundane event. Stepping into the large auditorium, he found several hundred people milling about, which was about several hundred more than one would expect. *Oh this has got to be good,* he thought, suddenly rather happy he had taken this job and feeling as if his mind had just posted bail.

Will only recognized a few in the crowd, which was unusual as New Lothrop was an "everybody knows everybody" type of town. They were all mingling, so he made his way to the front row of seats before the stage on which the board would be sitting.

Will found a seat and claimed it, dropping his jacket in the seat next to him as he expected Aryn to arrive shortly. He took out his tablet and was ready to start taking notes, a bit excited and curious as to what would warrant such a crowd. He typed Aryn a message, letting her know he saved her a seat as more people were coming in and the noise was continuing to escalate.

A few minutes later, Will spotted Aryn strolling down the aisle. *Looks like Boston was the shirt of the day*, he thought amusingly.

"Can you believe this?" Will asked as she approached.

"My dad said word spread that Mr. Ronsel was going to have the Senior English class read 'A Brave New World,'" Aryn answered, obviously thrilled at the excitement. "And apparently some in the community are none too pleased."

"Ok. This may sound stupid, but why?"

"I think we're about to find out." Aryn pointed toward the right side of the stage.

The seven members of the school board, along with the school superintendent, the principal, and Mr. Ronsel, emerged from backstage through a long, black curtain and made their way to their seats behind the elongated tables normally arranged for their monthly meetings. The apprehension clearly showed in their drawn faces as they had only heard of the small revolt that would take place tonight a few hours ago and had little time to develop a strategy.

The crowd noisily found seats and the board president, Jess Sinton, slammed a gavel to bring the meeting to order. Mr. Sinton had been the school board president for as long as Will could remember. He was known to be a bit stuffy and more than a little filled with himself. His long, narrow face, lengthy nose, and large ears made Will think he resembled a goat.

The meeting went forward with the normal boring procedure of taking roll, reading minutes, and a discussion regarding the budget. Will dutifully recorded some minor notes, awaiting what he hoped would be a tumultuous event, allowing him to once again reveal his writing skills to his fellow students.

Mr. Sinton finally addressed the primary concern of the crowd. "Now I know why you are all here tonight, and I would like to remind everyone in attendance that this is a school board meeting and to keep all of your opinions civil and to the point. You will all get a chance to speak even if we are here all night, which I certainly hope will not be the case."

A short, portly man with a red face waddled his way down the far aisle, moving with an exaggerated swing of his arms as if he had to create momentum to move his thick legs. The auditorium lighting shined off his sweating, bald head, and he abruptly came to a stop a few feet from the stage and announced himself with a roar. "I'm Nathan Haley and demand to be recognized to speak."

Nathan Haley needed no introduction. He was well known to the community for his hot temper and desire to be the vocal conscience of Shiawassee County. Nathan wasn't necessarily a bad man, just surprisingly insecure for a man of forty-eight. He had never become comfortable with himself and used public forums in a vain attempt to bolster what he desired most: the approval of what he considered to be his peers.

Nathan was the leader of a small, statewide organization that consisted of the ignorant and the unintelligent who spent their time searching for salvation in making accusations, spreading rumors, and ridiculing all that society had to offer. They cast their mindless spotlight in every corner where they expected to find sin, and if they didn't find it, they would create it out of the innocent moments of routine daily life. They attended worship services frequently but only to portray to the community their devote nature. In short, they were the modern-day Puritans of society.

"We all know who you are, Nathan. You may proceed," Mr. Sinton reluctantly commanded.

"I and my fellow citizens were infuriated yesterday when we found out that Mr. Ronsel was forcing our poor senior class to read the filth contained in this blasphemous book." At this last point, Mr. Haley dramatically raised a battered copy of 'A Brave

New World' high into the air. A soft sound of disgust made its way through the crowd at this gesture.

Will was shocked at the animosity emanating from Haley tonight. This was even dramatic for him, and a theater was the appropriate forum.

"This vile book is filled with thinly veiled sinful acts and stands against the good family values established by our Holy Father. This book ridicules the family and demeans the spirit with atrocious tales of a godless society," Haley ranted.

Is this guy truly that ignorant? Will asked himself rhetorically as he was vigorously typing the man's words into his tablet. Will had read the book over the last week and had found its story world fascinating.

"And you, Mr. Ronsel," the oration continued. "You are the devil incarnate, and we demand your dismissal from our school immediately."

Will could feel his face warm as it began to turn red. Mr. Ronsel was one of his favorite teachers and intellectually stood at the top of the New Lothrop faculty. He was an excellent teacher and coaxed his students into thinking about literature in a manner that caused the authors words to take shape, color, and texture.

"We also demand that this foul book be banned for life from our dear classrooms and the school library." A shout rose from the crowd as if Mr. Haley had scored a touchdown with this last remark. Haley continued his rant for several minutes with the crowd cheering him on as if the meeting was a sporting event and Haley was the home team hero.

Finally, Will's blood boiled over and he could no longer contain himself. He rose from his seat and moved toward the far aisle. "How can you be that ignorant?" The crowd became silent and all heads turned to the young man who dared interrupt their leader's sermon. Aryn was startled at Will's actions as it often took quite a lot to put Will in a state of bother.

"Do you realize this is a social science fiction novel?" Will inquired as he grabbed the book from Mr. Haley's swollen hands and stared into his wide eyes. "Do you even know what that is? The whole story takes place in a dystopian society, characterized by human misery and oppression. The author's not promoting it. He's simply portraying this fictional society to the reader, for heaven's sake."

Nathan Haley stood stunned, facing this young boy who so rudely was addressing him. What disturbed Nathan the most, was that he didn't understand exactly what Will was saying. Nathan turned his attention back to Mr. Ronsel. Talking was simpler than listening for him.

"See what you've done?" he shouted at Mr. Ronsel. "You've already polluted the minds of our students and revealed your powerful treachery." Haley turned to the school board president and pointed his fat finger at Mr. Ronsel. "Fire him!"

The school board sat in their seats, astonished by what was unfolding in front of them, the aisles filling with people chanting "Fire him! Fire him! Fire him!" The chorus continued for several seconds until the crowd progressively quieted, starting from the rear. Some unseen force slowly moved through the crowd and Will stretched to see from his position at the front. Out of the dense, now-silent crowd, emerged Uncle Jax.

Jaxon moved forward with a determined look on his face toward the stage. He scaled the stairwell and took his place at the front of the board without acknowledging even their existence. He paused for a moment in front of the crowd, which remained silent.

"Have the last twenty years meant nothing?" Jaxon asked softly of the crowd, and paused, knowing that none would speak. "Has history taught us nothing?" Still no one spoke. "You're certainly not the first group to call for the banning of books. The right, the left, totalitarians, communists—they've all done it. You now join all those who believe they are the political elite." Jaxon quickly turned the crowd into his audience and fully captured their attention. "Some of the darkest hours of human history occurred because of illiteracy and restrictions of intellectual freedom which, I understand, is an abstract idea. But it is an idea that people have fought and died for throughout history, and it is an integral part of the human spirit, the very spirit that God created in all of us." Jaxon looked directly at Mr. Haley when making this last statement.

Jaxon's voice grew louder now. "How can we ever expect our society to continue to flourish if we handicap future generations in such a manner? The freedom to express ideas, even when unpopular, is absolutely necessary to the creation of the minds this country, this world, requires. The Second American Enlightenment has not occurred, Mr. Haley. It is occurring, right now! As we speak! And you wish to oppress it, extinguish its fire! And why? Perhaps you're afraid, fearful that the world is passing you by as you struggle to keep pace with it. Well, I ask you all to jump on the train. There's plenty of room for all of us. If your own ideas cannot stand up to others, Mr. Haley, than maybe they just don't have the strength. We all need to challenge our own ideas as well as those held by others, and through this conflict, wisdom will emerge I tell you."

Will stood still, amazed, watching Uncle Jax move around the stage as he spoke, gesturing in a manner that pulled you in toward him with a force no weaker than gravity, knowing, deep within one's soul, that he was right!

Jaxon whirled around to face the school board. "So what will it be ladies and gentlemen of the board? Will you bow to fear or support Mr. Ronsel in his efforts to truly educate the minds of the next generation and make them the best and the brightest?"

At this, Jaxon slightly bowed his head as if to thank the board for allowing him to speak, not that they had a choice. He then descended the stairs and took the seat next to Aryn which Will had abandoned. Will moved over to the stairs, near them, to finish recording the events of the night. The crowd slowly took their seats, and the school board continued with a brief discussion of the issue which was easily resolved. Mr. Ronsel and his Senior English class were allowed to continue with their reading with no interference from the community or school administration.

At the conclusion of the meeting, the crowd rose and began to slowly depart the auditorium. The antagonists were quiet now after being defeated, but the angry glares directed at Uncle Jax did not go unnoticed. Fear, more than anything, kept them at bay, at least for now.

"What is wrong with that guy, Uncle Jax? Is he really that stupid?" Will asked.

"Not stupid, just misguided," Uncle Jax explained. "During your life, you'll come across a lot of smart people that really do some foolish things. In most cases it's fear, fear of new ideas, fear that they are not smart enough, sometimes fear that they will not be accepted in a new world with new concepts of good and bad, right and wrong." Jaxon tenderly put his hand on Will's shoulder. "People are insecure, Will, all to varying degrees of course. Ignorance and fear are ugly. Make sure you always keep your wits about you and your mind open. Some people take pride in 'telling people what they think.' I've always found it better to listen more than talk, and when I do speak, I try to express my thoughts in a manner that will compel the listener to reach their highest potential."

Jaxon smiled and broke the tension of the previous hour. "I'm glad that I ran into you two tonight. How would you like to experience my idea of a bonfire?" They both simply nodded their heads in the affirmative and followed Jaxon out to the parking lot. Jaxon turned to look at them, still smiling. Will had never seen him so jovial. "Well, who's driving? I don't have a car here. I walked." Will and Aryn looked at each other silently, still a bit confused.

"We both have two-seaters," Aryn stated.

"I think I'll go with Aryn. I've seen you drive, young man. You're a bit reckless for me," he said to Will with a teasing grin. "And she's much prettier than you!" Uncle Jax laughed, quite amused with himself.

As they walked towards the Trigs, Will asked, "Uncle Jax, where are we going?"

"Do you know the old Dvorak Homestead?" Jaxon replied.

"About three miles west of town, right?"

"That's it, nephew!"

Aryn climbed on her Trig, followed by Uncle Jax. He grabbed on the handrails beneath his seat and commanded, "Let's go. It's party time." He followed this with another deep laugh. Aryn and Will had now adapted to Uncle Jax's merry state and relaxed a little bit. Aryn looked over at Will with a big smile and a 'Why not' look on her face. Will smiled back and started his Trig. They accelerated side by side out of the parking lot and turned west on Easton Road.

Darkness was beginning to descend upon the farmlands, and Will hung back slightly, watching Uncle Jax enjoy himself on the back of Aryn's Trig. He was certainly in an unusual state as he smiled, laughed, and encouraged Aryn to go faster. Will wished he had a camera with him as he thought how amusing it would be for the world to get a glimpse of this great man having so much fun.

Within a few minutes, the road turned south, which indicated they had arrived at their destination. The grass was slightly overgrown, but it was obvious that it was occasionally tended. The house still stood but had been abandoned for quite some time. It was barely visible from the road as a vast number of black ash trees dotted the front landscape and kept the house hidden. The north side of the property was lined with tall hackberry and balsam poplar trees which stood no less than eighty feet tall and provided protection from the north winds.

They turned right into the drive and pulled the Trigs over onto the grass. Dismounting, they removed their helmets, and Will looked over at Uncle Jax, whose demeanor had changed. He still had a slight grin on his face, but his eyes were now a bit melancholy. Uncle Jax gazed at the house for a few moments. Aryn and Will remained quiet, allowing Uncle Jax to have, what appeared to be, a moment of reflection.

Once he concluded his thoughts, Uncle Jax turned to his right and began to walk over to a large fire pit lined with stones. "The man who lived here was a good friend of mine," Jaxon said with excitement back in his voice. "Many nights, when I was a young man, we would sit around this fire pit, never a large party, at the most there would be a half dozen of us. But that was the way we liked it. We talked politics, history, debated the ideas of the day. It helped shaped me into the man I was to become."

"I purchased the property when Jeanna and I moved back to New Lothrop. I have somebody come out once and a while to take care of the lawn and trim the trees. It's the least I can do," Jaxon said apologetically. He gazed into the fire pit for a few moments, studying his thoughts.

Jaxon's jovial mood returned just as quickly as it had left. "Well, we're going to have some guests showing up in a short time, so how about you help me haul some wood out here and get this fire going?"

The three carried about a dozen small logs from behind a red shed that stood a short distance from the fire pit. Uncle Jax stacked the logs like a man who knew what he was doing and, with the help of some brown paper and kindling he retrieved from the shed, started the fire. The flames slowly crawled up toward the dark blue sky, spreading their warmth. All three stood around the fire in silence as several cars pulled up the drive. Two men and a woman exited the vehicles and joined them around the fire. The only introductions were of Will and Aryn, the others were not required. Will and Aryn recognized each of them: one was the CEO of a major automotive manufacturer, another the owner of the Flint Journal, and the woman was the Mayor of Flint. A few moments later, they were joined by two more women that Will recognized as they had learned about them in school. Both were scientists who had advanced stem cell research and discovered processes for curing several major diseases. The last of the group was a man that Will recognized as an author of several science fiction books he had read. He knew they all lived in mid-Michigan, but he had no idea that they were all in the acquaintance of Uncle Jax!

And just as in Uncle Jax's younger days, all of them sat around and discussed ideas. They debated and encouraged each other, not passing judgment, but rather looking, searching for the best ideas from science, philosophy, even a short conversation on the author's new book. Will and Aryn said nothing. They just listened and absorbed, astonished at what they were being allowed to witness. These great minds were feeding off each other, and the bonfire had turned into a symposium. After several hours, the group began to disperse. Uncle Jax came over to Will and Aryn.

"I'm going to catch a ride back to the house. Feel free to stay as long as you want." And with a grin Jaxon said, "I hope you enjoyed yourselves. Not your normal bonfire, eh?"

"Enjoyed ourselves? That is a bit understated, Mr. Warren." Aryn smiled. "Thanks for letting us experience this with you."

Uncle Jax continued, "Just remember, Aryn, you can accomplish almost anything in life. Once in a while you may doubt yourself, we all do. Have the courage to lift yourself out of your comfort zone, and your mind will be unstoppable. We've still barely scratched the surface of the potential held within the human brain. Our generation took it deeper, and now your generation has the responsibility to discover the next level of human achievement."

With that, Jaxon and the small group dispersed, leaving Will and Aryn sitting by the fire.

"That was incredible, Will. Did you recognize those people?" Aryn asked.

Will nodded. "We were just part of a gathering of some of the greatest minds of our time. I felt - so small!"

"I can't wait until we graduate. I want to be like them. I want to be smart like that, doing things that change the world." Aryn paused for a moment and turned to look directly at Will. "I've decided to become a biological engineer. I want to work in the bioenergy field like your uncle. Maybe discover something new, even better."

"You've got the brains for it, Aryn. You're the smartest person in school," Will acknowledged. "Aryn, there is a reason that Dako and you are my best friends. It's because you're both so smart. You were the only two people around who I could identify with."

"I know. I feel the same. But it doesn't feel arrogant at all, it just seems natural. I feel so isolated, but at least I have you and Dako. What about you? Any idea what you'll do after graduation?"

"No," Will said with a sigh. "I still don't know what to do. I'm sure I'll go to college, but where? I don't even know what I want to go into. I wish I were as certain as you."

Aryn knew Will's feelings for Ronni were holding him back, but she knew better than to broach that subject. He had to discover that for himself.

"You'll figure it out, Will. I know you will." She smiled and said, "Let's make a promise to each other. After we graduate from college, let's come back here and have a bonfire at least once a year. We'll invite a couple of the smartest people we know and carry on this tradition that your Uncle Jax started."

"That's a deal," Will replied.

Aryn turned back to the fire. "Whatever we do in life, I know we'll be the best at it, Will."

Will had always admired Aryn's confidence and intelligence. He knew others thought her to be a bit smug, but he knew otherwise. She was curious, smart, and happy with whom she was, and it would be impossible for her to be any different.

It was late, and they both decided to head home. Fortunately, there would be no school the following day as administrators wisely began the school year with a gradual progression. They got on their Trigs and rode together to the intersection of Durand and Easton Roads. They stopped and Aryn looked over at Will. "This is going to be a great year for us, Will. GO SENIORS!" Aryn yelled as she sped away towards home. Will smiled. *Yes, it will be,* he thought.

***

Will woke to the sound of banging on his wall door that led to the deck. He glanced over at the clock which showed 7:00 am. Confused as to who would be waking him so rudely on a school-free day, he slowly rose and made his way over to the door. He pulled the blinds open to see a ghost white Dako, mouth hanging open with a look of horror on his face. Having never seen Dako in such a state, Will quickly opened the door and stepped out on the deck.

"What the heck is wrong with you, Dako? You look like you've seen a zombie for heaven's sake."

Dako stuttered, trying to get the words to move from his brain to his mouth, but the thought was so horrible to him that he had to push with all his mental strength. "Ar...Ar...Ar"

Will sensed something was very wrong. Dako was gasping for breath. "Sit down, Dako. What 's wrong?"

Dako sat down on a piece of deck furniture. He inhaled a deep breath, and the words finally escaped through his mouth. "Aryn's dead."

Will felt a tight grip in his stomach; he gently grabbed Dako's head to get him to focus. "Dako, look at me. Aryn is fine. I was just with her last night."

"She was hit by a car last night, on her Trig." Dako lowered his head into his hands and began to gently sob.

Will felt his stomach tighten to the point he thought it was literally tied in a knot. His face contracted as he felt his anger rise. "Who told you such a thing?"

As he sobbed Dako told Will how his dad had gone to work early that morning and came upon an accident scene, which the police were investigating. He had stopped to offer any assistance as accidents normally involved local residents. One of the officers on the scene related that a young girl on a small Trig had been rear ended by a car. She had died immediately while the car had fled the scene. They were still collecting evidence and interviewing residents in the neighborhood. Dako's father had asked if the girl had been identified, and that was when he immediately came back home to break the news to his son.

Will refused to believe what he was hearing. His anger was escalating. *This is insane, it can't be true,* he thought. He ran back inside his room and threw on some clothes. He then rushed back out onto the deck, jumped the rail, and mounted his Trig, which he had left parked by the deck last night. He had gotten back late and did not want to wake Aunt Abby. Dako jumped to his feet and ran to the rail only to see Will accelerating dangerously fast up the street. Dako followed suit, mounted his Trig, and took off after Will.

Will carelessly sped through the traffic circle, leaning into the turn at breakneck pace, the fear blocked by the mixture of intense emotions working their black magic through his mind. He shot out of the turn like a cannon and weaved around a car which impeded his path. He turned again a hard right at Durand Road and accelerated even faster on the open road. About two and a half miles up the road, he found the police vehicles with the road shut down. He jumped off his Trig, letting it slam to the ground, stumbled, regained his footing, and ran up to the police tape. Just before he broke through, he was tackled by a police officer and held to the ground. The officer saw immediately that Will was under duress and tried to calm him down.

"Stop, Will," the officer had recognized him and said this only loud enough so Will could hear him over his shouts of anger. "Calm down," he said again with a bit more authority. "This is an accident investigation site, son. If you cross that line, you'll hinder our investigation." A brief moment of sanity occurred in his mind, and he realized he had no choice but to submit. Will then let his muscles go limp and stopped fighting. The officer rose, keeping a hand on Will's shoulder. Will pushed himself up to one knee and could now see what appeared to be Aryn's Trig. Fragments of the composite frame lay everywhere on the road, the unrecognizable aluminum pieces twisted and mangled. He then laid his eyes on something that would be branded on his mind forever: a shirt, lying on the pavement, soaked in blood. Boston.

LOPER

7

"This power to act according to discretion for the public good, without the prescription of the law, and sometimes even against it, is that which is called prerogative." —John Locke

J axon walked deliberately along the sidewalk adjacent to Easton Road, rapping the working end of his cane on the concrete sidewalk, the rubber cleat compressing and bulging with each stroke by its master. Jeanna had been pestering him for several months to make use of such a device but he had held her at bay with his bullish objections. But she was determined and, as usual, she reasoned in a manner to overcome the headstrong Jaxon. While attending a fundraiser at the Smithsonian Castle several years ago, there had been a special display of a cane, which had caught his attention. The walking stick was one given to George Washington by Benjamin Franklin, which he had received during his time as French Ambassador. The cane was made from the finest French crabtree and was topped by a gold handle on which was formed a Phrygian cap, a common symbol of the time for freedom and liberty. In August, Jeanna had an exact replica made, which she intended to present to Jaxon on his upcoming birthday in October. But Jaxon's deteriorating gait caused her to think better. She instead presented him with the gift just a few days ago along with its terms of use. Softened by its historical significance, he assented to her wishes.

Jaxon staggered, but caught himself before continuing under the heavy, gray sky; the surrounding trees and cooler temperature indicated fall was pressing its objectives. His jacket protected him from the cold, but nothing could provide relief from the anger that weighed on him, on the community, over Aryn's death. Yet another child had been snatched from the community, from her family, by preventable actions, idiotic actions, Jaxon thought. It had been three days since the accident, and he had not yet spoken to Will. He wanted to give him the required time to grieve along with his friends. Jaxon didn't think it much of an accident, more like a murder. He found it hard to believe that with all the progress society appeared to make during The Enlightenment that foolish events, such as this, still plagued communities, and, most importantly, *his* community.

Jaxon grieved for Aryn's family. He knew her parents as they had worked at MEC for some eighteen years. They had raised her well: dressed her for Halloween, celebrated her birthdays, made merry the Christmas holiday, and all the other more mundane events that created a pleasant childhood filled with memories of love and family. And memories they would be forever, as Aryn was no more.

He silently wished there could be some way to alleviate their anguish, and Will's as well, but again knew this effort would be futile. It wasn't that he was not empathetic, but he knew that grieving was part of the human condition, and essential to maintaining the value of human life. He had witnessed too much death in his lifetime, he thought: from war to starvation, and he knew that most of it was due to human frailty and fear.

The police had just made an arrest on the previous day. Four idiots, in their early twenties, had been driving around getting drunk. Apparently nothing better to do with their lives, Jaxon had thought when he heard of the circumstances surrounding the accident. They probably never saw the poor girl. Unfortunately, only the driver was arrested as the county prosecutor did not think he could convict on a charge of conspiracy for the passengers. Jaxon thought he may be able to use his influence to change his mind.

"Oh my," Jaxon said as he stopped and looked up. He just recalled the names of the passengers in the car as they were listed in the news article the day before. One name stuck out, Jim Sperling. No one was around to hear him, but the shock of his realization caused the words to escape his mouth. *I believe that is the brother of Will's girlfriend,* Jaxon thought. He resumed his trek to see Aunt Abby, deciding to think about that later, after he accomplished the task at hand.

Jaxon turned the corner onto New Lothrop Road. It was out of his way but deliberate. As he approached the last house on the block, he could see Abner Troffe sitting on the porch of his dilapidated house. Jaxon turned to face the broken path leading to the home and paused, waiting for some reaction from Abner. They had met in graduate school. Despite the fact that they were studying different disciplines, Abner in chemistry and Jaxon in business, they found interest in each other's intellect, out of which, their friendship flourished. A union that was supposed to last a lifetime.

Abner did not move, or glance, or in any way recognize Jaxon's approach up the path to his house. Jaxon stopped just short of the three warped, broken steps that descended from Abner's porch.

"Hello, Abner. I know, and regret, that it has been many years since we last spoke. But, as you may or may not know, certain events have transpired, for which I am in great need of your counsel." Abner remained still, staring at his game of chess. The pieces, not unlike Abner, frozen in place for days, weeks, or even longer.

Jaxon proceeded up the steps, the first, groaning like a cow begging to be milked, and the second, braying like a sick goat. The third step provided a less dramatic chord upon Jaxon's ascent to the porch.

Jaxon waited. No reply. No movement from Abner.

"Abner, if you would just take your medicine-"

Abner launched his body straight up from his decomposing chair and stared directly at Jaxon with the eyes of an angry wolf preparing to pounce on an attacker. "Why?" Abner screamed, unsteadily backing away from Jaxon. "What have you put in it? What are you trying to do to me?"

"Abner, please!" Jaxon yelled as he looked around, hoping there was nobody within earshot. Then he switched to a softer tone. "Stop ranting. I'm not trying to do anything to you. I simply came here to talk to you about the young girl's death."

The crazed look remained in Abner's eyes as he raised a bony arm from which clung his loose, wool jacket; a long crooked finger extended toward Jaxon. "You're not God, Jaxon Warren. Stay away from me!"

Jaxon realized it was useless to try and talk to him, his mind was too far gone. As he moved to descend the steps, he turned and pointed his cane at the chess board. "Rook to queen four," he said, and then proceeded to the sidewalk, not turning back.

Abner waited until Jaxon turned on Butternut Street before resuming his position in front of the chess board. He then reached out and moved his rook to queen four.

Up ahead stood the house Abby had purchased years ago for her and Will. She had been a teacher in the nearby city of Flushing with Jeanna many years ago. Abby, like Jeanna, loved the profession. Neither of them had to work, not since Jaxon had made his fortune, but they both continued with the tedious and demanding work, shaping the minds of the next generation. And there was little doubt in Jaxon's mind that the kids who passed through their classrooms were the better for it. Although Jeanna did eventually retire in order to travel with Jaxon, Abby had continued the important work of educating children.

The two-story house pleasantly glowed with a light blue coat of paint on the wood siding adorned with white trim. It sat on the corner of Orchard and Butternut Streets, just several blocks from Riverside. The covered front porch was long and extended the full length of the house with a deck in the rear of the house arranged in the same manner and a sunroom added to the east end. Abby had decorated the house nicely, creating a small library and den within the house for Will and her.

Jaxon ambled up the stone walkway, which was surrounded by the well-kept lawn and unto the porch, and rapped on the burgundy door three times. After a few moments, Abby opened the door. Jaxon noticed that her normally bright face seemed dark and lackluster, and her attire was unusually disheveled. Jaxon had chosen this time of day as he knew Will would be in school, and he needed this conversation to go unnoticed.

"Hello, Jaxon," Abby said with exhaustion but a bit of unexpected relief.

"Hello, Abby. I hope I'm not interrupting anything, but I would like a few minutes of your time if I may."

Close was not a word that could be used to describe their relationship. Neither was hostility. Jaxon had always been good to Abby, but his long absences over the years had caused them to grow apart. Abby was indebted to him for arranging the adoption of Will, for which she was grateful.

"Come in, Jaxon."

Jaxon stepped into the small foyer. He glanced to his left and noted the impeccably tidy living room. There were pictures on the mantle above the fireplace of Will and Abby throughout the years. The absence of Jeanna and him amongst them did not go unnoticed. The décor was simple as were most homes whose dwellers had lived through the depression.

She led him out of the foyer and into the dining room, which was furnished with a small table and a pleasant painting on the wall of a French café whose colors merged eloquently from the light that shone in through the two double hung windows. "Please have a seat." She politely motioned to the table. "Can I get you some coffee?"

"That would be nice, Abby," Jaxon said civilly. "The place looks nice. You've always kept an orderly household."

Abby went into the kitchen. "You should stop by more often, Jaxon. I think this is the first time you've been here in years." It had actually been fifteen years. Jaxon picked up on her reproach. He was grateful she hadn't mentioned the cane, knowing she couldn't help but notice.

"There are a lot of things I should do more often," Jaxon said with guilt in his voice.

"Is that a bit of remorse coming from the great Jaxon Warren?" Abby asked from the kitchen.

"It is what it is, Abby." Jaxon held his feelings tightly to his chest.

Jaxon heard the sucking sound of the coffee machine as the near boiling water forced its way through the coffee grounds and spewed forth into the two coffee cups Abby had placed under the dual spigots. The water carried with it the rich taste of the ground Arabica bean, leaving only the depleted grounds behind to be disposed.

"Thanks, Abby," Jaxon said as she returned and placed the pewter tray on the table. He picked up the cream and added some to his coffee, stirring it slowly with a small spoon.

Jaxon let out a sigh before speaking. "How are you and Will doing? Are you getting through this?"

"He won't talk to me," she said with obvious irritation. "He has pretty much sat in his room every day since the accident. Dako's come over a few times. I hope that is helping." She paused and looked at Jaxon, her eyes welling up. "I just don't know what to do, Jaxon."

Jaxon reached out and took a hold of her hand. "There is not much you can do, Abby. Just be there for him. This is his first real experience with death, and he has to work his way through it."

"I know. It's just so hard to see him like this."

"I stopped at Abner's, thought I would try and talk to him."

"And?" Abby asked.

Jaxon shrugged. "He's too far gone."

After taking a sip of his coffee, Jaxon wasted no more time to get to the point of his visit. "Perhaps there is something we can do."

Abby's cup slightly rattled as she must have picked up on the insinuation that Jaxon had already put together a plan, causing a tremble to run through her body. She had an idea what her brother was thinking.

"Oh no, Jaxon," she pleaded. "He's too young. He's only a teenage boy."

"He's not just a teenage boy, no sense in pretending," Jaxon said with irritation in his voice.

"Yes, he is, Jaxon!" Abby shot back. "He still needs to develop, like others his age."

Jaxon's tone was firm but empathetic. "Now Abby, we both knew this day would come. And I'm not suggesting we rush into this. I checked with the school, Will easily has enough credit to graduate in December."

"And?"

"He needs to get out of town; he has a restless spirit, Abby."

"And you know this because you've spent so much time with him?" The sarcasm was obvious.

Jaxon didn't take the bait. "I want to take him to Calidum on our upcoming mission."

"Calidum! You can't be serious, Jaxon. He's too young to be exposed to that. He needs his family and friends right now. And how do you know what's best for him? You've barely spoken to him other than the last few weeks. I've been nothing short of a mother to him since—" her voice abruptly stopped, and she paused looking down at the table, "since he was young."

"I know because I was that age once, Abby. He's ready. You can't deny him his destiny."

"You're not God, Jaxon!" Abby shouted angrily at Jaxon who was more than irked to hear this twice in one day. "And he's not some robot. He's a human being."

Jaxon stood up, his eyes darting around the room as if trying to find a tool to rout his anger. "I know I'm not God, Abby! If I were God, the depression never would have occurred. If I were God, I could make the world a better place through more desirable means. If I were God, I wouldn't have so many regrets in life. People wouldn't get sick or lose their mental faculties, and if I were God, you can be damn certain that Aryn Krause would still be alive!"

Jaxon took a few deep breaths before he sat back down at the table and looked at Abby, who reached out to take his hand. They sat in silence for a moment. "We have to leave it up to Will, Abby. It's his call."

Abby succumbed to his argument, knowing she had little choice. "I'm sorry, Jaxon. You're probably right. I'm grateful for everything you've done for us, and me. He's such a strong young man, much like his parents. When will you talk to him?" she asked.

"Tomorrow after the funeral."

"And if he accepts, when will you take him?"

"Day after Christmas. I'll make sure he's back in the spring," Jaxon said.

"You better," Abby warned. She rose from her chair and left Jaxon by himself.

***

Will stood with unsteady knees above Aryn's casket with Ronni and Dako by his side. The slight breeze coming in from the west gently rustled his long, thin hair. The container, shining under the bright morning sun as if it held some potential energy, contained only the lifeless body of his friend. *Send me some kind of message, Aryn. Let me know you're ok,* he thought. And he waited. And he waited more. Nothing came but the twinkling reflection of the sun on the sarcophagus. *Is this goodbye? Is this how it ends? You're taking part of me with you, and I want it back!* Will thought angrily. He wanted to run but could not pull himself away. He wanted to stay but knew he must leave.

Dako turned and put his hand on Will's shoulder, leaning in to speak softly. "It's time to go, my friend."

Will reached out with his hand, gently laying it on the coffin. "Thank you," he said aloud. *Thank you for the passion and the inspiration.* This he thought, maybe not in those words, but rather with a sense, a feeling that would stay with him all of his life. Will would discover, more so every year, that Aryn had become a part of him, Dako as well.

He spoke some meaningless words to Aryn's parents, knowing nothing would ease the pain either of them felt, at least not for some time. *Time,* Will thought. What did it mean? Aryn had no more time. How could it exist for him and not her? The confusion and thoughts that ran through Will's mind were unlike any he had experienced. His mind seemed to leap from one thought to another like an excited frog jumping from lily pad to lily pad. The only consistency in his mind was the pain he felt deep within. Despite its intensity, he knew this could not be physical, nor did he believe that this was normal. The more he tried to control it, the deeper and wilder it became.

Will felt the soft touch of Ronni's palm against his own. The warmth was re-assurance that he was not alone, that the world still existed. Will had been cordial to Ronni. He realized it was not her fault that her brother was involved, nor had he been driving. But the anger would swell up in Will's body every time he thought of those four imbeciles smashing into Aryn. He knew the thought was unhealthy, but he could not purge the image from his mind, nor could he find a vent for the fury that raged within him. He secretly wanted revenge for Aryn— to make them pay for removing such a spark from a dim world. But at the same time, he hoped to never see any of them.

They walked in silence as they left the cemetery until Dako spoke.

"Hey Will, isn't that your uncle's car?" Dako pointed to the end of the line of vehicles along the road.

"Yeah." He looked around behind him, scanning, but did not see Uncle Jax in the crowd. "I'll get a ride home with him. I'll see you guys later."

"You sure, Will?" Dako asked. "We could hang out at my place."

"No. I'm ok," Will lied.

"I'll call you tonight. We can talk about things. It will make you feel better," Ronni said.

Please don't. It won't. "That's not necessary. I'm ok, really," Will replied. Dako and Ronni looked at each other with concern as Will walked away.

He strolled the length of the cars, coming along side of the long black sedan. The door opened, and he crawled into the car, lowering himself into the soft seat. As Will's eyes adjusted to the interior darkness, the image of Uncle Jax, sitting on the opposite side of the car, began to take shape. Jaxon was looking at Will, in his habitual style, probably searching for Will's state of mind, or so Will thought. Will could see the genuine look of melancholy on his uncle's face. Uncle Jax didn't say anything at first. He studied Will's face for another moment before speaking.

"I'm sorry for your loss, Will." Jaxon finally broke the dead air. "She was a brilliant young girl." They sat in silence for another moment. "Donne once wrote 'any man's *death* diminishes *me*, because I am involved in *Mankind*; And therefore never send to know for whom the *bell* tolls; It tolls for *thee*.' This quote has always rung true for me, especially when the departed one had such promise. The world will be a lesser place without Aryn."

"Thanks for stopping by, Uncle Jax, but why are you here?"

"I wanted to pay my respects, without distracting from the funeral," Jaxon said dolefully.

Will understood. Uncle Jax commanded attention everywhere he went. He avoided many public events due to his prominence. Will couldn't imagine living like that. He preferred to stay anonymous.

"I understand one of the criminals in the car was your girlfriend's brother. How is that working out?"

Will was slightly annoyed that Uncle Jax did not know Ronni's name.

"Her name is Ronni, Uncle Jax," Will said, more harshly than what he should have. He changed his tone. "It's not her fault. Jim's a bad seed. Everyone knows that."

"Too many bad seeds are allowed to grow," Jaxon said as he turned his head to look out the window, seeing the coffin, still above ground. "There are still a lot of bad seeds in this world, Will, and it falls to certain people in society, those with the means, determination, and opportunity, to free this world of their presence. Not unlike a police officer shooting a criminal. However, there are evil men that fall outside the realm of law enforcement, and they must be dealt with in accordance with the harm they bring upon society."

"Somebody at your company must like him. You do know he works for you?" Will asked this almost defensively, not knowing why at first. Maybe it was a hidden attempt at defending Ronni.

Jaxon turned back to look at Will, who could see the surprise reflected in Jaxon's slightly distorted face. "He works for me?"

"Maple Grove Processing Plant," Will said

Jaxon changed the subject. "I have an idea that may help the situation." Jaxon adjusted himself in his seat, a bit closer to Will, and his voice became a bit more firm, yet the tone remained gentle. "This is not the last time you'll face adversity in life, Will. It's one of many. How one responds to adversity is important, in my opinion, in leading a successful life. I'd like to help you with that. Are you aware of what is going on in South Calidum?"

"Sure, it's been in the news. Some type of war, north invading the south, or east invading the west. I can't remember for sure."

"Those details are not important right now," Jaxon said, dismissively. "The Foundation is preparing for a humanitarian mission in the region. The war is causing serious distress among the civilian population. Thousands are starving, and it is only going to get worse. We'll be deploying in several weeks. I think it might be a good opportunity for you to get away from here. I would like you to come join us shortly after Christmas. What do you think?"

Will turned his face away from Uncle Jax and looked to the floor of the car. This was a surprise, and his mind, dulled from the last few emotional days, was trying to dispose of the accumulated muck in order to process the information.

After a few moments of silence, he said, "I have school, Uncle Jax."

"You've done well in school, Will. You easily have enough credit to graduate in December. And you'll only be gone a few months. In fact, it may be a good opportunity for you to focus on your Uskey essays."

"I'll have to talk to Aunt Abby," he mumbled.

"I've already spoken with her."

Of course you have, Will thought. Uncle Jax would leave nothing to chance. Will felt the box shutting in around him.

"I can't leave now, Uncle Jax. With Aryn's death, the timing would just be—"

"It's the best thing you could do, Will," Uncle Jax said with insistence. "You need to get away and put this behind you."

"I can't leave Aunt Abby. She'll be all alone," Will pleaded, becoming irritated. "I have a girlfriend, Uncle Jax. It's my senior year of high school, and I'm just not ready for something like that."

"Abby will be fine. She is well aware of the fine young man you're turning into. We all leave home sooner or later. It's part of life."

"Well life sucks right now," Will said as he looked up from the floor of the car and directly into Uncle Jax's eyes.

Jaxon took a deep breath and released it. "I'm sympathetic, Will. And I also know the hold this community can have on a young man. I grew up here, don't forget." He then continued with enthusiasm, "But you are ready to gain the experience that a world of infinite depth can offer. There is so much out there to learn, Will. Please, take this opportunity, run with it, leave the past behind you. New Lothrop, your family, and your friends will be here when you return."

Will wanted to end the conversation; he paused a few moments to find a way. "I'll have to think about it," he said.

"Take your time, Will," Uncle Jax said as he leaned back into the seat. He pushed a button on the arm rest, and the car slowly accelerated. The ride back into New Lothrop was silent. Both were thinking of what to do next, and they knew there was nothing more that could be said in the present.

The car pulled in front of Will's house, and the door opened. Will turned to Uncle Jax. "I appreciate the offer, Uncle Jax. And I promise that I'll think about it."

"That's all I'm asking, Will. You have some time," Jaxon said with a sympathetic smile.

***

Brianna Larkin sat with her forearms pressed to her glass top desk. She was in the office of her lavish Georgetown condo and impatiently stared at her tablet, waiting for the members of SLOT to login. Next to her tablet sat her stylus and a glass of Bordeaux, the only other items on the desk. The room, unlike the remainder of the executive suite, was simple, if not plain. It contained two barren, cornsilk-colored side walls, identical to the one behind her. The wall before her was lined with three televisions, each carrying a different major news network. A distinctive smell of lavender emanated from the azure carpet she had cleaned twice a week. There were no windows as she preferred few distractions in her office, other than the news stories being carried out on the screens before her.

An icon popped up on the side of the tablet, indicating the thirteenth, and final, member had joined the teleconference. Brianna immediately began.

"All of us our logged in now, so I'll begin the meeting. Per the security protocols we have implemented, no staff are allowed to listen in on the meeting, and the use of any member names is forbidden." She paused for objections, none followed.

"My sources have confirmed that the Warren Foundation is only a few weeks away from launching a mission to South Calidum. As usual, they will claim it is humanitarian, but my personal belief is that Jaxon Warren is trying to strengthen his ties with the South Calidumese leadership and gain power over the same zinc mines that the North is after. Thus, increasing his personal wealth and power which, we have determined, is already beyond any reasonable standard. We need to find a way to stop this." She took a sip of wine.

"How certain are you of Warren's intentions? Maybe this really is just a humanitarian mission," asked a member with a deep southern drawl.

"Unlikely," Brianna shot back as she set the glass back down. She thought this member to be a coward, but he had influence. "Jaxon Warren hasn't gained all this power by being generous. He creates business alliances through these so-called humanitarian missions and grows his empire on the backs of those he claims to be helping." Brianna knew this was a lie, but she didn't care. *Keep the end in mind*, she told herself.

"We could have the State Department revoke the passports of the Foundation's team," said the southerner.

"FAA could ground their planes and reject their flight plan. Stop'm before they even get off the ground and put Warren in his place," said another with an obvious rural Pennsylvania accent.

"Hmm. Interesting ideas," Brianna said with condescension. "But I have another I would like to propose." She paused and took another drink. "Let the mission move forward. They get on the ground, begin their humanitarian efforts, and then they completely fail. This will hurt their fundraising efforts, resulting in a lack of resources that will allow Warren to fail in meeting his long-term goals. We can use our influence in the media to make certain The Warren Foundation's image will be forever tarnished."

"How exactly do you propose to make that happen?"

"You'll have to trust me on that," Brianna said. "My team has a plan in place, but divulging it would put you at risk. The details of the plan stays only with me and my team, allowing you to reap the benefits but avoid exposure."

"Where you'ns at with your plan?" the Pennsylvanian asked.

"The plan is complete. We just have to move forward with execution."

"You have to redd things up if you're going to slap one to Jaxon Warren. He's a smart bastard with a lot of experience in the game," retorted the Pennsylvanian. Life was nothing but a series of games to him.

"Success is almost certain," Brianna replied with more than a little irritation. "I've developed sources within the organization that will give me access to vital, real-time information. I'm the only one who can pull this off. We shouldn't pass up the opportunity." She paused for a moment. There was no reaction, so she continued. "I'll make it even easier for you. You can notify me of your approval by simply logging off."

They all knew how badly she wanted this. They were safe and did not have to use up any political capital in the process. Slowly they began to log out of the meeting. After the last member's icon disappeared from the screen, she sat back in her chair and smiled. *Sometimes they were too easy to manipulate*, she thought.

She got up from her desk and walked through the vast living room and out onto the balcony. Leaning against the rail with her glass of wine, she gazed out at Theodore Roosevelt Island as the sun was setting, causing its many trees to cast long shadows. She had never visited the park, but she always found some peace when gazing out over its green acres. She allowed a memory to creep into her consciousness, a memory of a girl and her father walking through a park, the father pointing out all the different kinds of birds and teaching her their names. She remembered the excitement they shared when she saw her first bald eagle. Then she remembered the depression, seeing the father break under the mountain of stress that comes from losing one's job and not having any means of providing for his family.

Maybe one day she would visit, she thought.

8

"Opportunity is the great bawd."
—Benjamin Franklin

Will stood, facing east, looking into the sun as it rose above the horizon and began to warm the cold winter day. The frost on the nearby grass glistened as it began to melt. The birds that chose to brave the Michigan winter finished their morning song in unison as if they were part of an orchestra and the sun, the conductor, had brought the concerto to an end.

It had been ninety-five days since Aryn's death. Will was still in pain and still struggling to find his way. Abby kept telling him that the grief would subside, but he saw no end in sight. He considered drugs, but quickly disposed of that idea as he would not submit to that foolish temptation that could only lead to a bottomless pit. Uncle Jax had left for Calidum and their conversations were limited to email exchanges. He had persisted in pushing Will to join the mission in Calidum, but Will stubbornly sought comfort within the confines of his friendships and home.

The day after the funeral, Uncle Jax had gone into the husk processing plant in Maple Grove. He walked in through the front door, limped straight through the plant, not speaking to anyone. His cold eyes informing all that he was not to be approached. The few who started a greeting silently repented and made for the nearest exit, out of harm's way. Jaxon Warren was on a mission, and his face revealed its ominous nature.

He violently threw open the double unlatched doors that led to the shipping dock and quickly surveyed the dozen or so employees performing their tasks until he found the face of the one person for whom he was looking. Jaxon paused just long enough to be recognized, and all work came to a stop with eyes focused on him. He lumbered slowly up to Jim Sperling, grabbed him by the shirt collar with both hands, and dragged him over to the side of the dock, the edge of Jim's boots dragging along the concrete. Hiding his pain, and with a shift of his weight and a twist of his hips, Jaxon threw the much heavier, and younger, Jim Sperling off the dock and onto the pavement several feet below.

"Get the hell out of here!" Jaxon shouted. "If you ever come back—." He stopped short, letting Jim infer what the result would be. "I don't employ murderers or those who condone it. You're a disgrace to this company and your community."

Jim rose from the fall he had just taken and stood, wobbling, still in a slight state of shock. After a moment, his dull senses came back to him. "You're crazy, old man!"

"You're fired, Sperling. And if I ever lay my eyes on you again, you'll get more than a few bruises," Jaxon fired back.

"You have no right to fire me, Warren," Jim said angrily as he pointed his finger at Jaxon. "I've done nothing wrong."

Jaxon growled, his face turning crimson. "Done nothing wrong? You're responsible for killing a young girl, you moron. A girl with intelligence and promise; two things you're too dumb to even know exist. You may not have been behind the wheel, but you're just as much at fault as the idiot who was driving."

That had been in September.

In October, Will took the Uskey exam. He did well as all had expected of him, missing only two of the three hundred questions. The high school counselor had called him into his small, cluttered office, filled with books that were once read, and soon after forgotten. After the counselor offered a few words of support, meaningless to Will, he asked Will if he had given any serious thought to what he would do after graduation. Will related that he had not decided yet. The counselor informed Will that most of his class mates had decided what majors or occupations to pursue. Will angrily stood and walked out, vowing never to enter the counselor's office again.

In November, Will told Ronni about Uncle Jax's offer. She laughed nervously. "What a ridiculous suggestion—I can't believe he would ask you to do that; he's stupid," she had said.

"I'm thinking about it," Will replied.

"How could you even consider doing something so stupid?"

"It's been two months since Aryn died, Ronni. I'm just as lost now as I was then, and if I stay here, I could be just as lost in another two months." Will's voice filled with the frustration that had been growing within him for most of the year. "Don't you understand that we're graduating in six months?"

Ronni then moved towards him, put her arms around his neck, and pressed her body against his. "All you need is right here, Will," she said, staring him directly in the eye. "Stay here with me and don't go off on this foolish trip."

"Ronni," Will pleaded. "I need you to take me seriously." He pushed her away.

"What am I supposed to do, Will?" she pleaded, feeling his rejection. "Tell you it's ok to go? Well it's not. This is our senior year. One of the best years of our life, and you want to abandon me? Who am I supposed to go to parties with?"

Ronni had pleaded her case for another hour.

Shortly after, Will sought the advice of Dako. Dako had said, "Go ahead, Loper. Get out of here. Just make sure you're back for graduation, so we can be on that plane to Australia by the end of June."

In December, three days after his eighteenth birthday, Will accepted Uncle Jax's invitation, which brought him to this tarmac on the Foundation's airfield.

A shadow enveloped Will as Uncle Jax's personal APEX jet rolled slowly in front of him, its engines whining to a low pitch. The white aircraft was a box wing design, made from a carbon fiber composite that allowed it to fly at Mach 1.1 with a range of 9000 miles. The 7000 mile flight to Calidum should only take about eight or nine hours.

The jet came to a halt, and the twin engines idled quietly. After a few moments, the hatch slowly opened and descended toward the ground. Emerging from behind the door was Uncle Jax, clad in black cargo pants, a black crew shirt, a black jacket, and brown wool felt hat that was akin to a fedora. He descended the stairs heavily, using his cane for balance, and walked straight up to Will.

"Hello, Will," Jaxon greeted with a firm handshake. Will noticed that Uncle Jax had bags under his eyes as if he had not slept in some time, at least not well anyway. Will assumed the burden of running the mission was no more difficult than any other, but Uncle Jax was not getting any younger either.

"You've made a wise decision to join us, Will." It was only a few days before Christmas that Will had declared his intentions to Uncle Jax. "We had a meeting with some supporters in D.C. yesterday, so it worked out well that we could stop and pick you up," Uncle Jax said this casually as if he was stopping to give Will a ride to school.

A porter emerged from the hangar behind Will and grabbed his luggage, two black military duffle bags. Uncle Jax had informed him that this would be the most convenient for the field. The porter opened a hatch in the belly of the luxurious jet and disappeared inside with the luggage.

"Come on board, Will." Jaxon motioned to an approaching small tanker with hoses hanging from each side. "It will take a few minutes to refuel before we head out."

Jaxon began walking back to the plane, and Will followed, carrying only his tablet in his shirt pocket. They ascended the stairs, and Will glanced back to the now empty tarmac before disappearing through the hatch. Turning to his right, Will caught his first glimpse of the splendor of the cabin. He had never been in a private jet, and Will could already sense the rich style.

Jaxon noticed the look on Will's face, which he had seen from many a guest. "Sorry, it's so small. This is my commuter car," Jaxon said in jest with no hint of arrogance, stated simply to put Will at ease.

Will moved through the wide aisle that led into the galley before emerging into the main cabin area. The bright morning light was shining through the eight elliptical windows on each side of the spacious fuselage, making the plane's beige and cream interior appear brighter than it actually was. Next to Will were a set of seats facing each other, along both sides, with a table in between. The table top was actually a large touch screen which allowed the users to access the aircraft's wireless network. Behind the seats on the right, there was a lone chair, a bit taller and wider than the others, with its own broad table. Will assumed this was Uncle Jax's private desk. Opposite was a couch and a large screen television attached to the rear bulkhead. Will continued, moving in between the sets of chairs, feeling the soft leather as he reached out with his hand. Another door was open in the rear which led to a sitting area. Will could see a bedroom beyond that. He turned around to face Uncle Jax with a wide smile on his face. "Classy, Uncle Jax. Very classy."

"Have a seat, Will. We'll be on our way shortly." Jaxon disappeared in the forward galley as Will sat down in one of the seats mid-cabin. Uncle Jax returned shortly with a bottle filled with blue liquid. "Here, start hydrating. You're going to need it where we're going. It's an energy drink, electrolytes and that kind of thing."

Will took the drink as Jaxon sat back down in the opposite seat. The cool liquid felt good as it flowed through his parched throat. He saw the fuel truck pull away and heard the hydraulic pumps being worked as the pilot went through his checklist. A few minutes later, the plane began to taxi to the runway, turned north, and with little pause, began accelerating. Will could feel the thrust of the engines as his inertia forced his body deeper into the soft seat. The plane glided smoothly into the air, and Will could see the city shrink away, rapidly, out the large oval window next to his pair of seats. He watched until it disappeared from view.

"Congratulations on your Uskey score, Will."

"It's just a test, Uncle Jax. It doesn't prove anything," Will said humbly as he took a drink.

"Don't be modest. You're a lot smarter than you realize. You just scored better than every one of your peers that took that test. That is a great achievement and should be celebrated."

Will wasn't sure if he believed that. "If I'm so smart, why don't I know what to do with my life?"

"Well, that's why we're here, right? To get you some experience in the world, figure out your options," Jaxon said, steering the conversation to a more positive path.

"What is Calidum like, Uncle Jax?"

Jaxon's face became cool. He looked out the window for a moment and then back to Will.

"You are about to go into a war zone, one of the most lawless arenas of the world, Will. Calidum has a long history of violence and treachery, especially in the north. Its people have suffered greatly over the years. People who just want to live peacefully, not be afraid, want a better life for their children, at least those who survive."

"How did it get that way?"

"Terrorism was at its peak in the late 20th and early 21st century. The September 11th attacks in New York City hit America hard, and the desire for justice was strong. America and some allies waged a series of wars with the intent of rooting out the groups performing and sponsoring such activities. But as soon as one group was defeated, another would rise up and take its place. For several years, many thought the war on terror was permanent. Surprisingly enough, it was innovation that finally defeated terrorism."

"How so?" asked Will.

"The war on terror was expensive: in dollars and lives. During this era, there was also an increase in social spending and excessive government intervention into the economy that was occurring in most of the so-called advanced economies in the world. These poor decisions led us into the depression like we spoke about several months ago. When the government was forced to cut back on so called 'investments' in order to reduce the huge deficits they had created, investors were able to move in and inject their capital based on market demand, not political cronyism. This private investment led us out of the depression and into a period of great innovation in business, industry, and education; all areas of society began to flourish to an extent not seen in American history. The great minds of several scientists and engineers I had the fortune of working with, allowed us to create a new fuel which set the world on a new path."

"With the scientific advances in efficiently removing energy from cellulosic biomass, making it cheap and energy dense, the price of oil crashed. The major crude producers were in turmoil for years as their oil was fetching about a tenth of what it had been at its peak. Most had spent their oil money building palaces, weapons, and funding terrorism while completely ignoring the basic infrastructure and educational system required for maintaining stable economic growth. They paid for it in the end. The suffering in the region was devastating for such a long time, and the rest of the world could only stand by and watch lest they be labeled as 'crusaders.'"

"We worked behind the scenes as much as possible through various means. But resources had to be spent on moving forward with those countries that had the stability and desire. The chaos subsided over the years, but not after countless wars and thousands of unnecessary deaths."

Uncle Jax's expression had turned more somber as the images flashed through his head—the suffering, the bloodshed—Will had no doubt it was all being remembered.

A moment later, Jaxon snapped out of his trance. "In the end, terrorism was effectively destroyed, for the most part, and we had a new fuel. I just wish it had not been so painful getting there."

"The terrorists who survived moved into the desert regions of North Africa. One of those countries was Calidum. Calidum had suffered through a bloody civil war during the early 21st century and peace was realized only when an agreement was signed to form two separate countries, North and South Calidum. Each country took different paths. Most of the terrorists ended up in the north and fought for political control of the country. The south sought out investment from foreign capitalists in exchange for leasing rights to its vast zinc mines. This paid off for them, and a stable republic with democratic elections, based on a free market economy, took shape. Over the years, the south grew more prosperous while the north grew deeper into poverty and political turmoil."

"That leads us to where we are today. The son of a former terrorist has ruled North Calidum for the last two decades. Mitakus, they call him, though nobody knows his true name. He has ruled by killing his enemies and rewarding his friends. It's the usual path followed by many dictators throughout history, dictators who lost their heads in the end, literally. I never understood why some people never learn that."

Uncle Jax got up and walked forward to the galley. He took out a glass and poured himself a drink of some brownish liquid. Will assumed it was alcohol. He returned to his seat with the glass in hand. Will noticed his eyes were a bit darker. He looked tired. "Brandy helps me sleep on these flights."

And maybe blocks some of the pain, Will thought.

Uncle Jax drank his brandy in silence. Will guessed he had a lot on his mind, so he remained quiet. He finished off his blue drink and opened his tablet, reclined in the comfortable seat, and began reading. Uncle Jax had recommended he read Shakespeare's Richard the Third. Will found the story fascinating. It was like peering into the mind of pure evil. Will found himself simultaneously appalled and drawn to Richard and his continuous efforts to manipulate those around him.

After a quarter of an hour, Will glanced up and saw that Uncle Jax had dozed off. He rose from his seat, walked to the rear of the plane, and sat down at the private desk. Uncle Jax had left his computer display on within the table top. He had apparently been reading an article on human genetic engineering and gene therapy. The article contained several methods for applying gene therapy to human beings which would result in higher intellectual capacities, advanced brain function, and accelerated healing.

Will had been studying the article for some time and did not see Uncle Jax rise from his seat. He was startled when Jaxon reached out and abruptly turned the display off.

"That's private, Will," Uncle Jax said coldly.

"It was up on the screen, and I found it interesting," Will said apologetically. "Why are you reading up on genetic engineering?"

"Just research. We're using it in our labs to create a better biomass." Jaxon walked back to his seat without elaborating.

"But the article was about genetic therapy for humans," Will said.

"It's related," Jaxon said curtly.

Will didn't press the subject.

"Why don't you try and get some sleep. It will be morning when we land, and you'll likely be up all day," Uncle Jax said as more of a command than a request. Will moved over to the couch and laid down. He closed his eyes and felt the rumble of the engines easily coaxing him to sleep.

Will awoke to some jostling as the plane hit turbulence. He was not sure how long he had been sleeping, but noticed light shining in from the window and his stomach felt queasy. He sat up and looked out to peruse the landscape. As he looked down, he could see nothing but a bland, beige-colored earthen floor beneath him. No green, no sign of a river or lake, and certainly no sign of people. A current of wind was moving sand across the dead, featureless landscape.

Will saw the first sign of life below in what appeared to be a herd of animals moving across the desert floor, fear and panic emanating from their pace, as if they were fleeing a perilous fate. They moved like a flock of starlings, turning and maneuvering as a single compact unit. As they fled across the desert, their shape alternated, a bell, a football, even a crescent moon at one point as they turned and changed direction. Never once did they slow before Will lost sight of them.

"Gazelle's. Probably Soemmerings or Grants," Uncle Jax said, looking out the other window. He had awoke and noticed Will's fixation. "Fascinating eh? To survive in such an environment: little food or water. Who knows how they do it. Life will always find a way to survive."

Now that the gazelles were out of sight, Will looked around at the land getting closer beneath them. "Looks pretty deserted," Will said.

"Like most of North Africa," Jaxon said. "We should be landing shortly. That brandy really put me out; best thing for flying." Uncle Jax smiled.

Will wondered how much excitement he was going to find in a place like this.

"What do you want out of this trip, Will?"

Will looked down at the floor, gathering his thoughts. "I need to figure out what to do next, Uncle Jax. I feel lost, and I'm not getting any closer to finding my way." Will shrugged. "I certainly wasn't finding my way back in New Lothrop."

Jaxon understood. He knew Will was frustrated. But he also knew that he had to find his own way. "We'll be landing at an old abandoned air field about ten kilometers outside Traku, one of the large cities, large by Calidumese standards at least. That's where we have our Tent City set up. Tent City is what we call our compound. Not sure how the name got started, but it stuck and we pretty much use it globally. The southeast of the country has been left untouched by the northern forces as the zinc mines are in the southwest. When they invaded, they dropped straight down and cut the country in half. We've built Tent City just off the airfield."

Jaxon continued, sorrowfully, "Many of those fortunate enough to have escaped the fighting roam by our compound daily on their way to the eastern cities, dragging their belongings and their families with them. It's tragic, Will. Hundreds daily have been uprooted from their homes and lost family members. We're setup twenty four/seven with food, clothing, and water. We're keeping up, but it has delayed us in venturing out to the hard hit areas where people need the most help."

"How far away is the fighting from Tent City?" asked Will.

"Far enough to be safe. About forty miles right now and moving farther west," Jaxon said.

"Is there any hope in stopping the war?"

"The South has a standing army, but they are not doing as well as one would expect. We have a few on the team with experience in intelligence, and they have been interviewing some of the refugees. From what they have gathered, the North is much better armed than most in the region had expected. It could be a long war. Any war is too long I suppose."

Uncle Jax paused, then looked back at Will. "So here are the rules. When you are on the compound, you're free to roam wherever you like, residential tents, supply, field mess; it's all yours to explore. But stay out of the command tent unless I, or Ray Bakis, accompany you."

"Who's Ray Bakis?" Will asked.

"A remarkable man and the Foundation's Director of Operations," Jaxon replied.

"The command tent is the central nervous system of this operation. There is a lot of activity going on at any given time, and you'll just be in the way if you wander in there. You'll still get to see it, but I'll take you in at an appropriate time."

"Never leave the compound unless you are with myself or Ray. Ray will be taking part in many of the patrols to villages in need of food as well as overseeing security. Ray is military, so stick to him like glue. Don't underestimate the danger of this barren place, Will. Any nook or cranny could be occupied by a platoon of Northerners. They know we're here and are certainly keeping an eye on us. We've sent out messages on their open communication frequencies to let them know we are here only for humanitarian purposes, but I doubt they will trust us. We clear on the rules?"

"Understood," Will acknowledged.

"We run this show like a military operation, so you're better off calling me sir instead of Uncle Jax. You'll fit in and be accepted better that way despite the fact that everybody will know that you're my nephew. I won't have a lot of time to spend with you, so make sure you work hard on your essays and learn everything you can, so you can get up to speed on proper protocols. Understood?"

"Yes, Unc—Yes, sir," Will replied.

"I've made arrangements to house you with one of the special ops platoons. Ray will give you your duties. You may not like them, but you'll learn from them. Like I said, stay close to Ray and do everything he says."

The plane went into a deep dive, and Will's ears popped. He could feel the blood drain from his face as his stomach fluttered.

"Don't worry, Will." Uncle Jax smiled. "We come in steep, reduces the risk that somebody is out there with a surface to air missile wanting to take a shot at us."

Will felt a bit dizzy. *Thanks for the comforting words Uncle Jax*, he thought.

Will watched the ground approach quickly; at the last minute the pilot pulled the nose up and leveled the jet for a smooth landing. Will saw the Foundation's Tent City off in the distance and counted three large cargo planes and what appeared to be four unmanned drones, at least that's what he thought they were as he had only seen them in pictures. They taxied to the hangar and came to a stop. The hum from the engines whistled down before going silent. Uncle Jax stood and looked out the window.

"Welcome to Calidum, Will."

9

"Freedom hath been hunted round the globe. Asia and Africa have long expelled her." —Thomas Paine

W ill listened to the thumping of the canvas tent as it was thrashed against its wooden frame by the strong wind. *Does the wind ever stop in this godforsaken hole?* he thought. It was 2:00 a.m. He was lying on his canvas strewn cot secured by a carbon-fiber frame, and wide awake. He had been in country for a week, and his body's rhythm was still in the grips of jet lag. The blistering wind, and the resultant clamor, only exaggerated his misery.

Shortly after landing, Uncle Jax had turned him over to the tutelage of Ray Bakis. Ray was cordial but lukewarm. Will surmised that he did not like the idea of having him around and whatever else Uncle Jax may have asked him to do, in regards to Will's duties. Unbeknownst to Will, Ray's instructions had been clear: "Mentor him Ray, make sure the boy learns; challenge him, force him to grow," Jaxon ordered over Ray's protests. And Will's instincts were true, Ray was not happy about the situation.

As Ray gave Will the standard tour of the compound, Will was able to coax him to open up a bit. Ray told Will about his military experience and how he was lured to the Foundation by the vision of Jaxon Warren. He told Will about numerous conflicts in which he had been involved that were absurd. "Wars are influenced by politicians. Politicians can be bought. I decided I wanted to work for a man who can do the buying, and Jaxon Warren is a buyer." Short and to the point, that was Ray's style.

Tent City was massive. One hundred and sixty tents in all which included living quarters, mess tents, a gym, and even two taverns. Ray pointed out the command and intelligent tents, both identified by their black tarps, unlike the others which were all dirty beige. Ray explained this was to make all personnel aware which tents were completely off limits. The intelligence tent was actually two tents strung together, making it look more circus-like than military. As they walked, Will quickly became aware of the constant whir of drones taking off and landing. He caught a glimpse of a few of them, and Ray noticed. "Get used to it. You'll hear a lot of that. Those are the quiet ones, propellers. The jet-powered drones may actually wake the dead."

During the tour, Will told Ray of Uncle Jax's offer to join the Foundation's mission in Calidum, without revealing the events that preceded it. Ray appeared to understand when Will spoke about his lack of a plan after graduation. "Being eighteen is tough, Will. All of us have been there." He slapped Will on the shoulder and said, "You're going to learn a lot here in Calidum. Maybe a little more than you'd like."

On Will's first night, there was a safety drill at 0300. Will sat up on his cot, dazed by the proceeding siren and the frantic movements of his tent mates. One of which, "Squid," picked Will up by his shirt collar and carried him, with one hand, to his assigned bunker. Squid dropped Will into the four foot square hole in the middle of the compound and took off running into the darkness. Will shared his shelter with two others with whom he did not bother to exchange names as he was making every effort to get some sleep, even in the discomfort of a dirt hole and the annoying activity going on about him. Sleep did not come as his companions were chatty and spent their time complaining about the uselessness of such drills and the food in the mess hall that evening. Ray apparently held the drills to train the inhabitants of Tent City the proper response to an attack, but the two young men, who appeared to be very sure of themselves, disagreed that such would ever take place as the fighting was too far away. The "all clear" sounded, and they wandered back to their tents.

A thin layer of canvas cut a cross section through the tent which Will now called "home." This resulted in four equal segments that housed four people each. Will shared his segment with three men who were part of the special ops team. The aforementioned "Squid" was a former Navy Seal, another was a Marine called "Wolfman," and the third was a Calidumese translator they called "Cutter." Will realized these were nicknames, which he knew was popular among military personnel from the war movies he watched growing up. Needless to say, this caused Will to feel even more segregated from their threesome as no one offered to call him anything but "Will" or, in Wolfman's case, "Rich Kid," a term that did not sit well with Will.

Squid didn't say much. He sat on his gear chest and cleaned his rifle most of the time. Will did not know his real name, nor any of his other nicknamed tent mates. He reckoned they would have to accept him before he would find out such personal information. What he did know about Squid came from Ray and was quite impressive. He had been a Navy Seal for eight years, before joining the Foundation, and had been awarded a Purple Heart, twice, and a Bronze Star. Squid was not tall, maybe five ten. He had broad shoulders. From there, his torso narrowed considerably to his waist. His triangle shaped body was topped by an identically shaped face from which jetted his prominent nose, which was exaggerated by a shaved head. His brown eyes were stretched as if his nose was pulling them from his face. It made him look like a bald eagle.

Wolfman was from Adrian, a town a little over a hundred miles from New Lothrop. Will was a little uncertain of Wolfman's sanity. He reminded Will of the Grinch from the Dr. Suess books he read as a child, except this Grinch carried an automatic rifle and a KA-BAR, a scary looking combat knife. Squid had warned Will that Wolfman was a bit different but had assured him that when things got rough, Wolfman was the kind of guy you wanted on your side. They knew each other from the third war in Afghanistan, and Squid had actually recruited Wolfman to the Foundation. He said he was worried what might happen if Wolfman was released back into civilian society, so he convinced Ray to make him an offer.

Squid related the following story to Will: "Our platoon was on a search and destroy mission in the Bamyan Province, and finding a great deal of success, when we came along a village which was loaded with the remnants of a terrorist group. We were clearing out the huts when a grenade came rolling across the floor from a draped door. Wolfman was closest and dove on it. We all hit the deck knowing what was coming next." Squid paused. "And nothing happened. It was a dud! Wolfman just rolled on the ground laughing his ass off. Funniest thing I ever saw." Squid said this last bit without even cracking a smile.

Wolfman, upon waking every morning at 0500, would stand up, arch his back, and heave his chest forward releasing the air from his lungs in what Will could only describe as an attempt to imitate the bark of a deranged dog. Turns out he was closer to the truth than he expected. Wolfman said it was his "Devil Dog" bark. Devil Dog apparently had been a term bestowed upon the Marines by the Germans during World War One. The Germans, after being soundly defeated, claimed the Marines had fought like "Teufelshunde." Something the Marines took great pride in, according to Wolfman.

Cutter was from South Calidum, and was the son of one of the political leaders. His father had sent him to a Swiss boarding school from the age of thirteen until graduation at which time he moved on to Albion College and studied Ecology where he was a member of the Foundation's student club. He had returned to South Calidum the previous spring and was working to create groundwater availability models in rural areas before the war broke out.

Most of what Will knew of Calidum at this point came from Cutter. Cutter was a devout Buddhist, which he related was the primary religion of South Calidum, and did not carry a rifle. His father had been one of the architects of the Edict of Detroit, a pact signed by the leadership of the world's five major religions: Christianity, Islam, Hinduism, Buddhism, and Judaism. The agreement stated that tolerance and respect would be afforded to a person's spiritual belief system and that violence carried out in the name of religion was criminal and would be met with each religions method of excommunication. This pact was promoted by the League of United Republics and a direct result of the acts of violence carried out in the name of religion that occurred in the early part of the century.

On Will's second day, he ran into Suzen in the mess tent. She had just recently arrived and was suffering, equally, from the jet lag. Each day after that, they shared breakfast and their very differing experiences, but common perception, of Calidum. The conversations always seemed fresh to Will despite the repeated complaints of the heat and dust.

Will's first experience with the Calidumese, other than Cutter, came shortly after leaving the mess tent that first time with Suzen. His assignment that day was to man the "trough." Will deduced that it got its name from the similar farm usage. It was the area setup on the south side of Tent City to feed those fleeing the fighting. There were eight lines in all, manned twenty-four hours, seven days a week by four shifts of aid workers. Will had stood at the end of the long line of tables that was one of the troughs, looking at the aluminum bins filled with ill-flavored food. The food was rich in vitamins, minerals, and protein, but looked like thick porridge. Apparently, as those with more experience explained to Will, this was due to the fact that most who came through had not eaten for days and their bodies required a maximum amount of nutrition with minimal intake.

Will stood for hours serving those seeking food and refuge, looking at the distraught faces as they came through the line, always pleading with words he could not understand. But their faces revealed their desperation. "More! More!" Will was certain they were saying. But his instructions were clear as to the amounts their depleted stomachs could handle. The line supervisor had said, if given the opportunity, they would eat until their colons exploded.

Their eyes were particularly astonishing; it was as if they had been scared into retreat, pulling back to depths of the mind from which they may never return. After eating, they would move on, to what kind of fate Will would never know.

Will kept the food covered as best he could, but the incessant wind carried grains of sand that had been scooped up from the surrounding earth and mixed it with the porridge. Will did not know how people could live in such conditions. It was depressing and he wondered what kept them going. Was it nature's will to survive? Was there more for them to fear from death than this level of suffering?

He had performed his duties at the trough each day since, six hours a day. At night he would work on his essays.

As he now lay on his cot, the faces that passed through the line now passed through his mind, each one just as clear as the first day they held their plates out. *Why can't I get them out of my head?* he asked himself angrily as he lurched his heavy torso off the cot and sat on the edge, his head in his hands.

Tomorrow, the Foundation was taking its first venture out into the field. There were numerous small villages and farms that lay along the main transportation route from the eastern ports of the White Nile to the zinc mines. When North Calidum invaded, they cut straight down to this highway, and then turned west. Ray had told Will there were literally hundreds of small villages along the path of battle, each with small populations. Random reports from those who had fled were Ray's main source of intelligence, and they were all consistent, revealing many SoC's, as they referred to the South Calidumese, had stayed behind in hopes the NoC's, North Calidumese, would overlook them on their way to the zinc mines. After all, most were just poor farmers.

This was a mistake. Will thought sternly. *How could I have ever thought I would learn anything here in this god forsaken land?*

Misery is not going to teach me a damn thing. The only thing I've learned about myself is that I have sand in my ears, my nose, and my eyes. He stopped there, suddenly feeling guilty for his self-absorption.

He reclined again on his cot, closing his eyes and hoping, praying, sleep would come.

It did. But it was restless.

At 0500 Ray came in the tent, kicking each cot, rousing the "ladies from their sweet slumber" as he put it.

"Convoy leaves in one hour, be in full gear and at the armory in thirty minutes for final instructions," Ray said as he left the tent. They had spent three hours the previous night loading the two special ops trucks with ammunition, smoke grenades, illuminating grenades, stun grenades, and a few RPG's. "Just in case," Ray had stated. Will was astounded with the number of crates they were loading for the field mission. Ray must have noticed. "I like to be well prepared, Will. We're here to feed and clothe people, but don't ever forget that this is a war zone."

Will's muscles strained as they completed the task, and he could feel them tighten as they walked to a small addition on the command tent to receive their mission briefing from Ray. Twenty-four special ops personnel crowded in front of Will, who stood in the back row with Cutter.

Ray turned on the large stationary display. "Listen up. These are satellite images of the first set of villages we'll be venturing into." The Foundation had about a dozen of its own satellites in orbit whose use was shared with the MEC. "We'll drive about forty five-miles and stop here." Ray pointed just outside what appeared to Will as a cluster of buildings. "My team will move forward from there while the rest of you remain with the convoy. We'll make sure the town is secure before we radio back for the 'all clear.'"

"The satellite and drone images have shown very little activity, which is no surprise. Many civilians are probably hiding and still afraid to venture out of their homes or other areas where they are dug in. There were fierce battles at several places along this highway, so be prepared for some bad scenes." Ray looked around at each set of eyes which were locked onto his, to let this last statement sink in. He paused a moment longer on Will.

"There should be no combat troops in the area. At least none left alive. But don't let your guard down for a second. There could be booby traps, roadside bombs, or unexploded ordinance left behind. We'll have two drones flying overhead during the entire mission, both loaded with surveillance and light arms if we run into trouble. The idea is to coax the civilians out in the open so we can administer the aid more efficiently and quickly. We'll be exposed out there so I expect to see a strong sense of urgency."

"Cutter, as soon as we start getting the locals fed, I need you to start gathering intelligence. I want to know as much as possible about the weapons the NoC's are utilizing. We've all been surprised by their rapid push into the south, and we need to know why. Make certain you're on top of that." Cutter nodded.

Back in the tent, after the briefing, Will approached Squid. "Can you teach me a bit about your rifle?" Earlier, Ray had shrugged off his request to learn more about the weapons that the special ops team carried. "Not yet, Will," Ray had said, curtly. But Will was curious.

Squid smiled, obviously happy to discuss his toys. "It's an STR 5, standard issue for all Foundation special ops personnel. Shoots a 9 mm round, holds thirty in the translucent mag. Utilizes a 50 watt laser guided sight for aiming, which is also connected to the on-board chip set that sends coordinates back to HQ so they can lock on and send some extra fire power on specific targets, if needed." Squid slapped the black rifle with his hand. "State of the art, high-impact carbon fiber casing makes it nice and light: 2.5 lbs. Accurate up to 500 yards and fires at a rate of 1200 rounds per minute, never jams." Squid reached down and tapped his knuckles on his wooden footlocker.

Squid reached over the side of his cot and picked up what Will could only describe as an odd looking pair of ski goggles. He continued, "It's configured with our night vision system. On the front outer cover of the goggles is an ultra-thin light intensifier. It takes invisible light and sends it into a small processor fastened to the high-definition LED screen that is on the inside of the goggles. This is what you actually see when you are wearing them. Here, try it out."

Squid placed the glasses over Will's head and turned off the lights in the tent. The screen inside the goggles automatically illuminated, and the room took shape as if it were still lit. Will was impressed.

Squid then picked up his rifle and aimed it at the canvas above them. He flipped a switch on the STR 5 and a set of crosshairs appeared in front of Will's eyes. "When I turn the rifle on night vision mode, a processor sends a signal to the goggles, and the crosshairs show you what you're aiming at."

"Technology like this allows us to take on a larger fighting force like North Calidum. You can't get a better assault rifle anywhere in the world. In fact, they're illegal to export from the U.S."

Squid then proceeded to show Will how to hold and aim the weapon, clicking off a few dry fires, so he could get a feel for the trigger. This was Will's first experience holding a rifle as the only reason to do so in Michigan was for hunting, a sport which Will did not participate. Although Dako's dad was an avid hunter and provided Abby and he with venison each fall, which delighted Will.

Now in the cool thin morning air, Will stood, reluctantly, and moved to the trunk at the end of his cot. His tent-mates were moving about a bit faster than he. Will opened the trunk and looked at the drab clothing, sand falling off as he picked his cleanest uniform.

Squid, having noticed Will's disgust, walked over to him. "Hey, just think about all the money we're getting paid for this," he said as he slapped Will on the back and laughed. Wolfman and Cutter followed suit.

"There's not enough money in the world that would compensate me for this crap," Will said. He had not gotten used to the constant feeling of being filthy.

"Apparently your uncle's money is enough," Wolfman said, sarcastically. Will had not been completely accepted by the group.

Will got along best with Cutter. They would sit for hours in the mess tent talking about Calidum and its history as well as politics and the idea of managing nations. Will found Cutter quite intelligent and knew Uncle Jax would like him as well for this quality.

After forcing himself into the uniform, he put on his flak jacket and helmet. The flak jacket wasn't too bad, but Will could tell the helmet would take some getting used to. It gave him a headache. Will finished dressing and ate some dense energy bars with the group before leaving the tent.

***

Ray Bakis walked into the command tent, which was bustling with activity. The large monitor at the front was displaying the incoming video and data from the various drones in the air above South Calidum. Jaxon was walking around, checking in with each of the crew of about twenty that manned various consoles and analyzed the data. Jaxon spotted Ray and joined him near the entrance.

"Anything new?" Ray asked.

"No noticeable activity. I'm afraid of what you may find out there, Ray. Keep a tight watch," Jaxon warned.

"You know I will. This one has us all a bit more alert."

Ray paused, and searched Jaxon's eyes for a moment. "I'd like to leave Will behind on this one. He may not be ready for this," he said gingerly. Will's presence and Ray's assignment to tutor him left Ray in an unusual situation. Will had no experience in anything connected to the mission and, although he was showing a penchant for hard work, could be a hindrance at an inopportune time. Ray had gone into combat many times with eighteen and nineteen-year-old men and knew how unpredictable they were.

"He's ready. You'll have to trust me on that, Ray," Jaxon said this as a command, leaving no room for argument. Ray's look of concern must have been noticeable, and Jaxon softened his tone slightly. "I know you're just looking out for him, Ray. But he has to learn, face some adversity. And this is a good opportunity."

"I would just rather have him working the humanitarian side on this one, that's all." Ray persisted with caution.

"He's been doing that since day one. It's time to put some pressure on him. I'll be watching and listening closely from back here via the drones and your helmet cam. Just be careful and get as many of those people fed and transported back here as possible, so we can send them into the city."

Ray saw no more benefit to pushing his argument and nodded his affirmation. He then left the tent to assume command of the mission.

***

Will and Cutter walked by the convoy on their way to the hangar. There were twelve fully armored trucks in all and one light armored command vehicle. Will thought the latter looked like a cross between a dune buggy and a large Lamborghini, with what appeared to be two automatic weapons mounted on each side of a tall spoiler. Six of the trucks would be used to bring back the most critical of the civilians. There was only enough room for about thirty in each, which would be used for women, children, and those who required medical attention.

Will and Cutter joined the ops team that was assembled in the hangar near the armory. Ray marched in looking agitated.

"We move out in fifteen minutes. Drivers are already assigned. The drones are over the site as we speak and show no unusual activity. None the less, keep your full gear on until we've cleared the town." This was followed by a grumble from those assembled, which Ray ignored. "Cutter and Will, you two are with me in the command vehicle. Any questions?" Silence. "Good. Dismissed."

Will and Cutter walked out to the command vehicle where the driver, Wolfman, had the shell raised and the interior exposed. Will and Cutter took the back seats while Wolfman waited for Ray. Within a few minutes, Ray walked up, stood, and looked at the rest of the convoy for a moment, doing a final visual check, then jumped in the front seat. Wolfman followed, and lowered the shell, leaving Will feeling claustrophobic. Ray immediately turned on the imbedded display on the commander's console and issued an order for each driver in the convoy to respond when ready to move. After the last indicator on the screen turned green, Ray ordered Wolfman to pull out. Wolfman gripped the small steering wheel firmly and accelerated, leaving the confines of Tent City in their dust.

Light was just sprinkling on the desert plain as the Warren Foundation began its first field mission in Calidum. Will stared out the window from his slightly elevated position behind Ray. He thought about New Lothrop and wondered what his classmates were doing right about now. If his calculations were correct, they would be fast asleep.

As they drove away from the airport, the barren desert showed signs of life. They passed through trees and even a stream. But even the trees seemed to be screaming for water with their dust-covered, pale green leaves. Cutter even pointed out a few giraffe as they passed a small pond, their necks craning to watch the convoy pass.

As expected, it took about an hour to cover the forty-five miles from where their team would venture in and secure the first village. The command vehicle and lone truck drove slowly as they departed the humanitarian team, cautiously approaching the outskirts of the village.

"Looks like this is where the battle started," Wolfman said as they drew closer to the village.

Will lost his breath when he saw human bodies lying lifelessly along the roadside. Each in an awkward position of some sort, as if their body parts had lost all sense of order and natural direction, which, Will realized, was the case. Will felt Cutter's hand press on his shoulder through his flak jacket.

"Just breathe," Cutter whispered to Will, who had not realized he had stopped. It calmed Will just enough, and he released his breath. Ray slightly turned his head, but said nothing, and returned to monitoring his command display, which captured a view of the village through the telescope mounted in between the aft guns.

"Listen up!" Ray said over the communication line. "Shields down on all vehicles. Stay focused and ready. This is their battle, their loss. Remember, we're here to save lives." Will could not help but feel a slight uneasiness and a bit more claustrophobic as the dark high strength carbon-fiber of the shields lowered over the glass of the vehicle, closing the portals of natural sight. The windows flickered momentarily before displaying the video feed coming from the cameras mounted on various parts of the vehicle.

They pulled off the main road onto a wide dirt path that led directly into the village, which included dwellings, a hundred or so, that formed a ring around a large water well in its center. The walls of the huts were spotted with dings and holes, a few broken windows, but not too much damage. Will took this as a good sign that the fighting had occurred mostly on the outskirts of the village.

The road was void of any sign of life, and they pulled to a stop just short of the water well. Will could see in the display, attached to the well, what appeared to be a single piece of paper, blowing gently in the wind.

Ray turned to Cutter. "Get on the horn, let them know we're here."

Cutter grabbed a microphone from the center console and started saying something in the native language, exactly what Will did not know. Cutter kept repeating his message which blasted from the external speakers but to no avail.

With no indication that the villagers would rise from their shelters, Ray ordered Wolfman to open the shell. "Stay here and don't move," Ray said as he exited. "Cover me with the aft guns, Wolfman." At this, Wolfman took hold of a joystick located on the center console. Upon doing so, a video with cross hairs appeared on a small monitor mounted in the center of the dashboard and he maneuvered the joystick, looking for any signs of hostiles.

Ray walked for a moment then stood still, turning his head suspiciously in each direction, eyeing each building, each window. His chest lifted as he took a deep inhale. Will thought it looked like he was smelling the air. For what, he did not know. But his face grew more grim.

A heavy odor descended upon Will and filled the vehicle through the open door. They sat and awaited Ray's command. "Everybody out, form a perimeter." Within seconds the team had exited their vehicle and formed a wide ring around the well, each alert and looking for any movement.

Will found the strong smell repugnant and tried not to breathe deeply.

Cutter, who had also seen the paper, approached the well. He reached up and pulled the note with a sharp jerk, pausing to read. His fist tightened around the note, then released it, reading it again. It was as if Cutter thought the words would miraculously have changed, but, judging from the expression on his face, they had not.

Ray walked up to him, gently pulling the note from his hands. Will moved his way up next to Ray and could read the English writing.

You are poison to my people, Mr. Warren.
Get the hell out of my country.
-Mitakus

"Command, are you seeing this?" Ray spoke to his microphone, tilting his head to make sure the camera attached to his helmet was capturing the writing. He paused for an answer, then stuffed the note in his pocket. "Listen up," Ray commanded. "We need to go through these buildings one by one." Ray directed the teams into three groups of four and sent them into different directions. Will noticed the strain on the face of each as if they already knew the outcome of the search.

Will followed Ray's team. Ray noticed but said nothing. Will took this as his approval. The team moved slowly, watching and with their rifles at the ready. They approached the first hut; the person on point was one of two women on the team, and she had her rifle pointing in through the uncovered entrance, quickly scanning the area. The rest of the team moved in behind her, each systematically taking a different line of fire.

Will went in last, right after Cutter. The strong odor was now almost unbearable, for him at least. The rest of the team seemed unaffected.

Rays of light were shining through the windows and onto a bed in the middle of the single room hut. From his position, Will saw what appeared to be three people, contorted into awkward positions on a mattress. He could see that their dead skin was pale, flies feasting on their pitted sores. Ray moved in for a closer examination. Will now realized the source of the stench.

"Look at their stomachs," the woman on point said. Their stomachs were bloated to the point of rupturing. "Looks like some type of poison, maybe a nerve gas dumped into the well. Poor bastards probably ran to the well after the battle passed. Dying for a drink of water," she said.

"Cutter, you and Will standby at the command vehicle. Do not follow." Ray said, emphasizing the last and shooting a hard glance to Cutter. He and Will walked out to the command vehicle as the teams made their way around the village.

Will could see Cutter's eyes were watering as if he knew what the team would find. Will also knew, he was not sure how, that the search would reveal nothing but the same. Will didn't speak.

Neither did Cutter. They stood in the same spot for ten minutes. Waiting.

Will summoned the courage to speak. "What do you think happened, Cutter?"

"A slaughter. Ray knows it. You can see it in his eyes. And you could see it on the faces of every guy on the team who's military. They knew from the smell," Cutter said with disgust.

The teams returned a short time later. Ray's was the last. The grim faces revealed what was found. No words had to be spoken.

"Let's move out to the next village. It's five kilometers west. If we find the same situation, we're heading back to Tent City," Ray said and headed for the command vehicle.

The vehicles pulled out, and, as expected, found nothing different upon arrival at the next village.

Cutter and Will remained in the command vehicle as Ray had ordered. Eventually the teams returned to the vehicles. "Pack it in. Let's get out of here," Ray commanded. The shell was lowered, and they sped into a U-turn and back to the waiting convoy. Ray called to the team that remained with the humanitarian group over the communication link. "Follow us back to Tent City. There's no one to feed here. Let's take a different route back, through the bush, just in case they decide to ambush us on the way back." He then took off his helmet and threw it at the console. The helmet fell to the floor at Ray's feet, making no effort to retrieve it.

There was nothing but silence on the drive back. Will knew better than to ask questions. Everybody's anger could be felt in the heavy air of the vehicle. Will was watching out his window as a herd of gazelles ran frantically by in the opposite direction. Their beige orange coats flickered, and their long black horns appeared to bend backward from the raging speed of their gait, almost touching their backs as they arched to extend their stride as if each inch would deliver them from that which gave chase. They were obviously frightened by something more fearsome than the convoy. A half mile farther, Will saw the cause: a lion was burying his face into the torso of one of the herd, apparently the slowest.

They pulled into Tent City through the main gate and parked along the last row of tents as the remainder of the convoy headed to the staging area to unload.

"Cutter, Will, you're with me. Jaxon's request." They followed Ray into the tent, which was dark despite the daylight outside. The tent was sealed to enhance the illumination of all the displays. People were standing around looking at table top monitors, for what, Will didn't know, but the tone was hushed.

Jaxon was sitting in the back of the room on a chair elevated by a long riser. He looked forward, glumly. The trio approached him without saying a word. He finally turned and looked Will up and down briefly, probably assuring himself Will was unharmed.

"What kind of person kills village after village of innocent civilians? That's barbaric even for an animal such as Mitakus." Jaxon spoke softly but with rage in his eyes. "What's he after? He knows we're here to feed people, civilians at that. They mean nothing to him."

Ray finally spoke, controlling, but not hiding, his anger. "You're Jaxon Warren. He's looking to prove he can beat you. He's low tech. No aircraft, old weapons. We can attack his supply line, maybe destroy enough resources and force him to retreat."

"That's no longer a humanitarian mission, Ray. That's a war," Jaxon said.

"Sometimes a war is a humanitarian mission, Jaxon. That's what makes it so absurd," Ray replied.

"What do you think, Will?" Jaxon asked.

Will was stunned. *Uncle Jax is asking my opinion?* He thought for a moment. "If I see a dog attacking a human being, I shoot the dog."

After a long moment of silence, Uncle Jax replied, "Right you are."

"He's an animal, sir," Cutter said. "He will never stop until he has complete control of this country and has slaughtered half its people."

Jaxon looked at the large display at the front of the tent. The drones were canvassing the landscape, looking for signs of life in the villages farther west. After a minute, he turned and looked at Ray. He nodded his head. "This doesn't stop until Mitakus is dead."

"That may fracture an international law or two," Ray cautioned.

"Let the politicians worry about the law. I started this foundation to save lives, and that is exactly what we're going to do."

10

"Evil is easy, and has infinite forms."
—Blaise Pascal

M itakus stood outside of his mobile command unit, watching the sunset cross the path of his army. The wind whipped the sand into a swirling eddy under the amber sunset and cut across his face like sandpaper, his eyes protected only by the black sunglasses that adorned his face. As the sand danced around him, its light, earthy smell left him serene. Calidum was his home, and his country was embedded in every pore of his body.

He had stepped outside a few moments ago to watch as twilight descended on this glorious day, this day of victory. He crossed his arms, gripping with his hands the muscles that, like his mind, had been forged in a childhood of violence and hatred, although to him, he knew no substitute. He knew not of the games children played in Western societies, nothing of Red Rover nor that of the simple enjoyment of throwing a Frisbee, or of attending summer camp. His early memories were filled with learning how to manipulate people with fear and how to spot your enemies and destroy them.

As the sun sank deeper, it began to bleed across the horizon, a phenomenon special to the African continent he thought with certainty, due to the surface heat. Truthfully, he did not know.

He had never left the borders of Calidum. "Too risky, my enemies would surely kill me. Everything I have is right here: family, those who are loyal to me," he had told his aides. He had been in power for twenty years now, and he planned on staying until he was an old man.

His young wife had borne him a son just one year ago. Looking into the deep brown eyes of his son that day, he had a vision: he would build for him a strong and united Calidum. No more north and south, no more rich and poor, and no more starvation. He would use the wealth of the South to raise his people out of poverty and show the world that he was a great man. This would be his gift to his son.

"You should be looking in the other direction, cousin," said Bakri, his Chief of Staff, walking up beside him, stealing his daydream. "That is where you have made us a new enemy, who, I fear, is the bearer of our death." Mitakus' violent mentality flared, and he thought of reaching for his machete, which hung from his cargo belt, but his discipline kept him from cutting Bakri down on this very spot, which he certainly would have done to any other person who spoke to him in this manner. But not Bakri, they had been friends since birth, and he was the only person Mitakus trusted.

"Your weakness is your lack of vision, cousin," Mitakus said with the authority of a brute, angry that his cousin had interrupted this moment for him. "You must take risk in order to be great." He turned, smiling, and put his arm on Bakri's large shoulder, squeezing hard, reminding Bakri who was the ruler and the subject. "We will be great, Bakri. It is our destiny."

Bakri did not wince under the show of power as he stood taller and much broader than Mitakus. He looked Mitakus directly in the eye and continued, "We will be great together, Mitakus. Or be dead."

Bakri had been concerned about the plan to invade South Calidum from the moment Mitakus proposed it, but they had little choice. Mass unemployment existed in the North, Bakri knew it to be even higher than what Mitakus allowed to be reported. Starvation had spread widely throughout the country; business was only domestic as they had nothing to offer the rest of the world. Their history and relations with former terrorists left them persona non grata in the political arena.

Riling the public had turned out to be quite easy as the population had been indoctrinated through Mitakus' propaganda machine since his rise to power. He had aired several speeches across the state-controlled media, calling for a war against the heathens of the south. "God has come to me in a vision," he had said. He then proceeded to relate God's plan for the salvation of South Calidum, invading and taking over the valuable zinc mines. "The true riches of the South must lie in the hands of only the most devout and true believers of the North," he had preached. His bureaucrats had written a song of unification which was distributed to all the schools and houses of worship with orders to be sung daily.

"Victory or death are our only options, Bakri," Mitakus now said.

"I will pray and fight for the former, but I fear the latter is inevitable for the great Mitakus, and our country."

Mitakus laughed. "You doubt me, cousin? I have not led us into a slaughter. Did I not get us weapons of the best technology?" Mitakus had not revealed to Bakri how he had done this. "We will be victorious. And when we control the zinc mines, our people will once again be powerful. The world thrives on cheap energy: battery, solar, biofuel, nuclear, hydropower, and wind. These zinc mines will allow us to control one of those segments." Mitakus emphasized this as if it had already happened. "It is a weakness of the western nations and South Calidum that they have foolishly left these mines weakly guarded. Within the year, our investments into our laboratory research will pay off. We will have a genetically engineered virus that will wipe out the United States corn crop in a matter of years. Then, we will again be in control of our destiny."

Mitakus had made this argument to Bakri on more than one occasion and was aware of his skepticism. The so-called labs in

North Calidum were staffed with ignorant political appointees whom Mitakus trusted but had no real scientific knowledge. They had all received their education in North Calidum, which meant they knew nothing of science and technology. The labs also suffered from a lack of equipment which was due to the sanctions imposed upon it by the nations of the world. And instead of using his resources to run the blockade of ships that enforced these sanctions with much needed items of technology, Mitakus imported weapons only.

"I will fight with you as I always have," Bakri replied. "Sure, I was doubtful of the necessity of the invasion, but I realized we had no choice. But this attack on the villagers is a mistake, cousin, and meant only as a challenge to Jaxon Warren," Bakri pleaded. "We barely have the resources to fight on one front, and you just opened another! He is the richest man in the world and is worth more than North and South Calidum combined. Warren has aircraft. We have none. He has drones that can fly twenty-four hours a day and watch our every movement."

"We have ground troops, tanks, artillery. He has none of these. We will defeat him," Mitakus said with hatred in his voice. "Trust me, cousin, our victory is assured. I have always led us to greatness, and I always will. Do you remember when we were kids, how we struggled for food every day, how we ate with the dogs?" Mitakus knew this would trigger pain in Bakri. No child could ever forget the feeling of starvation, the burning sensation as the body eats away at its own tissue and organs. "I will never let that happen again, and I will kill whoever I must to secure our future. Calidum will be united, or we will be dead!"

Mitakus calmed and continued, "We were victorious today, cousin. We must fight again tomorrow and win."

"He is planning a counter attack as we speak," Bakri said sharply. "We need to bring forces to protect our rear, or our supply lines will be cut." Bakri had analyzed their weaknesses and devised a plan.

"No, that will slow our progress toward the mines. We left enough villagers alive. They will keep him busy for weeks begging for food."

Bakri turned to watch the sunset, wondering if it would be his last.

***

Brianna walked up the ivory staircase of the Jefferson Building's Great Hall in her black sequin dress, glancing over her shoulder as she often did from habit. She knew men were watching, as most women learn within a few years of puberty. Men had been attracted to her power, her body; whatever the reason, she could care less. She used carnality as a tool like a carpenter uses a hammer or saw. To her, sex was nothing more than a means to an end, be it revenge or securing power. And according to the reports she received earlier today, she was well on her way to securing the former. The mire was thickening for Warren in Calidum. He was sinking, and he didn't even truly know how deep he was.

The air was thick on this night with forced laughter and liquor, the ingredients of a successful fundraiser. A few well placed, sober, professionals from one of the top marketing firms in DC would ensure that the night produced millions. At the top of the stairs, she turned and strolled down the north corridor, looking below at the gathering crowd. *Simpletons*, she thought. *Fools flocking to dole out millions to save something.* What, she was not sure, despite the fact that she was a major donor. She was here for the press: *Image is everything.* A few dollars for this cause, a few dollars for that cause, and before you know it, they all depend on you. Belief was not important to Brianna, to her it was more a hindrance. But she certainly made sure her supporters believed in her.

She skimmed the Great Hall with her eyes. Tourists flocked here to see the exhibits, read the inscriptions and quotations on the panels high up near the ceiling. Not her. She found the

Library of Congress quite boring, ancient, and even useless. Her problem with the Library of Congress lay not in its mission, but in the fact that she could not control the distribution of the knowledge it contained.

She turned and glanced up in front of her, leaning the small of her back against the rail. She tried to block the clinking and clattering out of her mind. She found the laughter annoying. She looked up above the archway in front of her and read the quotation on the white panel:

IGNORANCE IS THE CURSE OF GOD
KNOWLEDGE THE WING
WHEREWITH WE FLY TO HEAVEN

Another useless quote, she thought.

"Senator?"

She turned to see Daniel Vicksburg approaching her across the marble floor. He was wearing a black tuxedo and a bolo tie over a bright white shirt.

"Sorry," he said as he approached her. "I was caught up in a call and couldn't get away."

"A call?" she asked with unhidden animosity. "You kept me waiting here talking to these do-gooders just because you had to take a call?"

"A call that will secure funding for the next senatorial election in Michigan, Senator," Daniel smugly replied with an artful smile. He was an excellent fundraiser, always had been. "Besides, you need to talk to these do-gooders. They're your supporters."

She smiled back. "Well in that case, you're forgiven. I was getting so bored with the conversation down below that I wandered up here and became just as bored with these ridiculous quotes on the walls." She pointed up to the quote she had just read. "Where do you suppose they got this one from?"

Daniel read the quote, which he remembered from some college course. "Shakespeare, Henry VI Part Two, I believe. I think

Shakespeare is reflecting on the pitfalls of ignorance, similar to what Dickens was saying in A Christmas Carol 'This boy is Ignorance. This girl is Want. Beware them both, and all of their degree, but most of all beware this boy, for on his brow I see that written which is doom.'"

"They were trying to tell the world, screaming in a way, what would become of us if we did not make an effort to curtail the epidemic of ignorance. The human race could avoid a lot of pain if it would only listen to such wisdom," Daniel said as he turned back to face her.

Brianna burst out in laughter, condescendingly. "You can really be a nerd sometimes, Daniel. I had no idea you were such a philosopher." This was a lie. Brianna knew enough about Daniel. He was intelligent, but she liked to put him in his place occasionally. Brianna had very little respect for philosophy and literature. She knew how to handle people; that was the knowledge that led to true power.

Daniel just held his smile. "Did you hear the news from Calidum today, about the slaughter?"

"Yes, that certainly is a tragedy. I'm sure the State Department will eventually figure out a way to stop the violence; none of my business." She smiled coyly and grabbed two glasses of champagne from a waiter as he passed.

A slaughter is everybody's business. Daniel was not surprised at her coldness. He had witnessed it first hand on many occasions. It was as if somebody had opened a door, and her words struck him like a January Midwestern wind. *Maybe it's time I shut that door.*

She handed one glass to Daniel, and touched the top of her glass to his. "We're on our way to Defense, Daniel. Don't be so glum. It's a party," she said snidely.

"If you are up to something, I need to know, Brianna. There is always a risk that things may not go your way and we must have a contingency plan in place to deal with the fallout." Daniel was always planning.

"Don't be silly, Daniel," Brianna said curtly. "I have nothing to do with what is going on in Calidum. Yes, I hate Jaxon

Warren with a passion. You know that. But I'm going to defeat him right here on his home turf," she said as she pointed to the floor.

Daniel knew better than to push the subject too far. He raised his glass and smiled. "Like you said, it's a party."

***

Will walked into the mess tent, his mind numb from the previous day's events and the restless sleep that followed. Earlier, he had rested on his cot, exhausted, yet unable to stumble upon even a moment of preciously needed sleep. Each instance that his eyes would softly close, the images from the village would unleash a haunting in his mind. Except in his mind, there was screaming. Not from the lifeless bodies that had lain on that filthy mattress, huddled together in the solace of death. Rather the screaming came from their souls, and their bitter specter's hideous cry was laced with anger and despair. Not only at their executioner, but at a world that would permit such an atrocious act.

He spotted Suzen sitting in the corner of the dimly lit tent. He picked up a tray, feeling the gritty sand that normally was found on the top tray, and approached the morning victuals. The smell of the spiced sausage began to awaken his numb senses. Morning brought his only relief from the clogged sinus passages that grew throughout the day from the blowing sand. After placing three sausages on his plate, he loaded several pancakes and laced them with maple syrup. He remembered the breakfast that Carl Sperling had made for him and Ronni after prom last year. They had returned to the farm after the event and sat on the deck, holding each other and watching the sunrise. Carl had made pancakes and sausage, Will's favorite. He missed good food and sleep as well as the peace his hometown brought him. Here, he was a stranger, not because people did not know who he was, that they certainly did. But rather due to the fact that there was no one, short of Uncle Jax, that had known him for more than a few weeks. People would pass by and offer a greeting, not really caring, more as a common politeness. In New Lothrop, his neighbors would greet him, not only seeing him as he was now, but at the same time knowing who he had been his whole life. He missed that sense of familiarity.

Will stepped back into reality and picked up a cup of pineapple juice and made his way over to Suzen. She was holding a cup of steaming coffee tightly in front of her gray sweatshirt. The mornings were still cool. As he sat opposite her, she shot him a disquieting look.

"I'll be right back," she said as she stood and left the table. She returned after just a moment with another cup of coffee and placed it down in front of him.

"Since when do you drink coffee?" Will asked.

"Just started a few days ago. And judging from the way you look this morning, you should too. Seems to be the only way I can keep my mind alert over here," she said as she took another drink.

Will picked up the cup of dark liquid as it released its steam and aroma. The smell was delicious. He took a sip, liking the bitter, yet inviting taste.

"Thanks," he said.

"You're welcome. I heard you had a rough day yesterday, which I'm sure is an understatement," Suzen said timidly, testing the waters as she was unsure how to broach the subject. Word had spread quickly through the camp as the members of the special ops team on these missions often sought companionship in the more gentle personalities of the humanitarian group.

"You—" Will stopped as a rush of thunder from a drone taking off filled the camp, the bawl of the engine fading as it whisked away into the sky. Most of the drones were quiet, the propeller drones at least. This one had jet engines, small, but very powerful and loud. They were intended for low altitude attacks and reconnaissance. *What is Uncle Jax up to this morning?* he thought.

Will tried again. "You heard about the village?" he asked, looking quickly around to see if anybody was listening.

"The whole camp's talking about it. We heard about the note also."

Will wasn't surprised that word had gotten out but somehow felt that it should have been secretive. He stabbed a sausage with his fork and bit off a large piece, washing it down with some more of the hot coffee. "It was terrible, seeing those people, their bodies bloated and scabbed. It must have been a terrible death."

"Sorry, not breakfast talk, huh?"

"It's ok. I came here hoping to find you," Will admitted.

Suzen took a sip of her coffee in order to hide her smile.

"I could see the devastation in Cutter's eyes yesterday. Seeing his fellow countrymen slaughtered like that, I can't even imagine. It would be like walking through the streets of New Lothrop and finding everybody dead. How could another human being do such a thing?"

"I'm not sure if Mitakus is a human being," Suzen replied. "He was raised by terrorists. His whole community was probably terrorists. He's known nothing but anger and hatred, probably had it preached to him day after day."

"I suppose you're right. He stopped being human long ago, I imagine. How's morale on the humanitarian side?" Will asked while stuffing a forkful of pancake into his mouth.

"There's a sense of accomplishment from all the people we are feeding through the trough line. The sad thing is they just keep coming and coming. Seeing the sunken, starving faces can certainly wear on you." Suzen turned her head as if she was embarrassed. "Sometimes I wish they would stop coming. So I would not have to see them anymore, the starving ones. I wish we would be done, so I can go home, collect my scholarship, and go on with my life, pretending that all this never happened. A part of me wishes I had never seen this part of the world. I know it's selfish, but that's how I feel. Feeding a starving child is, at the same time, joyous and tragic. Inside I am weeping, but when I see the life come back into their little faces, I'm ecstatic."

Will could sense the struggle she was experiencing. Not unlike his own.

"Well, keep up the good work," Will encouraged. "I'm not sure what's in store for me or what Uncle Jax is planning. But this guy, Mitakus, has picked a fight with him." Will had never known or heard of anybody who picked a fight with Jaxon Warren. He could not even imagine any person would be that crazy. But then again, it's a crazy world.

"How are your Uskey essays coming?" Suzen asked, changing the conversation to a lighter subject.

"I've been spending a couple hours most nights working on them. For modern history, I'm focusing on the end of the depression and how relatively cheap energy brought the global economy back into a state of prosperity. This leads well into my global business essay which focuses on cheap energy, a strong educational system, and a free market as the foundations of business growth."

"Sounds like you have the conclusions right. I'd love to read them when you are done." Suzen indicated this with enthusiasm.

Will felt a tinge of pride at this request. "Sure," he agreed. "I'm struggling with philosophy though. I liked the philosophy classes in high school, but I can't seem to correlate my own philosophy with any particular doctrine."

"Maybe you should just write on your own philosophy, maybe it will break new ground," Suzen suggested.

"That is pretty risky for an Uskey essay. Don't you think?"

"Greatness comes from taking risks. The best scientists, inventors, and business people all do it. With risks come rewards. I say go for it. You're smart enough."

"Thanks." Will wished he had as much confidence in himself as Suzen did. Putting his own philosophical thoughts on paper for a college entrance exam, one being read by admission administrators, seemed daunting, and a bit intimidating.

They sat in silence for a few moments as Will ate and Suzen finished her coffee.

"Ray has me starting some hand to hand combat training today. Judo, stuff like that. It should be fun," Will bragged as he finished his plate.

"Doesn't sound like much fun to me. But I hope you like it," she replied. "Just protect my ass while I'm in this country, Ok?"

"Will do," he smiled. *Although this may be hard to do given the fact that I'm not allowed to carry a weapon*, Will thought, but was too proud to say aloud.

11

"Yield not to evils, but attack all the more boldly."
—Virgil

J axon was studying the map displayed on the large OLED screen at the front of the darkened command tent. He had spent the last twenty minutes mulling over the data returned by the six drones as they followed their search pattern over southwest Calidum. *You cried havoc. Now prepare to feel my dogs of war, Mitakus*, Jaxon thought, paraphrasing Shakespeare. The high-definition cameras Jaxon had installed on the drones was paying off. As he manipulated the nighttime images on the screen with his fingers, the activity on the ground came to life, and he could even make out the shapes of the leaves on the trees with the aid of the night vision mode.

Dim light briefly filled the room, and Jaxon looked up to see Ray entering the tent through the vestibule setup to minimize the outdoor illumination. Jaxon motioned excitedly for Ray to come join him at the front of the room.

"Look here, Ray," Jaxon instructed as he zoomed in on a dense patch just west of center screen. "We found their supply route. They've been coming south along the west side of this large game reserve, which runs from the northern border to within fifty miles of the southern border with convoys each of the last two nights. Looks like about a dozen fuel tankers, large ones, probably

10,000 gallons each. A couple more trucks were evident, likely security teams. They probably are thinking that if they stay close to the reserve and travel by night, they can elude the drones. It was tough, but one of the intel people picked up the heat signatures on infra-red. These HD images confirm it. The game reserve is fed from an underground spring that comes in from the east. It's protected by the government so the only villages in the area are off to the east, along the spring. But to the west, there's nothing but desert, no villages."

Ray looked closely at the high-definition screen, clearly seeing the vehicles of the convoy. "Give that intel hack a raise, Jaxon. He just found a needle in a haystack." Ray continued analyzing the image from the drone. Jaxon knew he was formulating a plan of attack; it's what Ray did best.

"Can you pull up a daylight shot of this area?" Ray asked.

Jaxon pressed an icon in the lower right corner and an image appeared on the display clearly showing the green area of the reserve and the road running down its west side.

"Right here," Ray pointed. "This is where we can hit them, just as they move past the south end of the reserve. We can stay concealed along the tree line, and when they emerge, nail 'em!" Ray's excitement was also now evident.

"Have your team lay the plan out today, use the intel teams as necessary. Do a dry run tomorrow night; there's a nature reserve about five miles east of here that would be well suited. I want to hit them the following night," Ray opened his mouth to protest, but Jaxon cut him off, "I know it's not much time for you to prepare, but we need to stop this lunatic before he slaughters more people. And you are well aware that he will not stop until we leave, or he's dead. And I'll be damned if I'm giving in to this lunatic."

"Understood." Ray couldn't argue.

"On another note, how is Will coming along?" Jaxon asked. He had been worried about the exposure Will had on the field mission. People generally reacted differently to witnessing such a scene. Some held it in, processed, and dealt with it internally.

Others might turn to alcohol, drugs. Some just lost their mind. The veterans were ok. They had seen it all before, which made it only slightly bearable.

"Real good. I put him through some hand to hand training and he performed well. The boy has natural physical talent. He was throwing Squid around pretty good. Earned his respect, I believe. I also took him out to the firing range; seems to be a natural at that also. He has a good eye and a steady hand, listens well, applies what you tell him, and he doesn't forget. Impressive young man."

Jaxon was not surprised. "I'm glad he's doing well because you're taking him on your mission."

"Whoa, Jaxon!" Ray exclaimed with surprise. "He's not a soldier. And a couple days of training will not make him one. He is not ready for a combat mission."

"I need you to make him ready, Ray. You just said yourself he's a natural. Security on the convoy should be minimal. It'll be a good chance for him to get some real experience."

"He's not ready, Jaxon," Ray argued his point, emphasizing his words with his hand.

"Do it, Ray. It's not a request," Jaxon commanded and walked away, letting Ray know there was to be no debate.

Ray pursued him. "What the hell is going on, Jaxon! You can't take this kid out of high school and put him in this type of situation. He's not mentally ready. These guys on the special ops team have been in the military, through combat. They're well trained. A few weeks ago, Will was studying calculus in a classroom."

Jaxon turned around, angrily stating, "He's got to be ready, Ray. And you're responsible for getting him there. I can't do it. I'm too old for going on these missions. I need you to teach him. It's important, more so than you can possibly imagine."

"Why?" Ray asked.

"Don't you think I would tell you if I could?"

Ray shook his head with disgust. "You're the boss." He had to respect Jaxon's orders, but he didn't have to like them.

LOPER

***

Will looked out the window of the IG-86 A/T helicopter, the "Silent Killer," watching the ground slowly retreat. His stomach slightly tightened as the helicopter swung around and accelerated the team toward its mission. Turning back inward, he resumed tapping his heel on the cargo hatch, one of four that covered the floor. Inside the bay in which he sat, the air was dense and acrid. He studied the cold, gray interior that was illuminated from the eight round windows, four on each side. Along the top of the cargo area ran electrical conduit and hydraulic pipes which led to various enclosures near the rear of the helicopter, where a ramp had lowered for the team to board.

The flak jacket strapped around Will's camouflage uniform felt stiff, accentuated by the tight cargo belt laced around it. He could feel his calves rubbing up against his rifle which was stowed beneath his seat. He recounted the previous thirty-six hours, which had vanished in a blur of sweat and schooling, military style, and had culminated in his current airborne situation.

Will was ecstatic as Ray reluctantly informed him that he was on the assault team that would strike back at Mitakus' forces. He was certain Uncle Jax made it happen. Ray certainly was unhappy about it. But Will did his best to step up to the challenge. He knew that the team would, at best, be irate if he put them in any danger. He watched Squid and Wolfman closely during the exercises and dry runs and took note of how they moved in a crouch and held their rifles. "Keep your head down!" Ray kept shouting and slapping his helmet.

He picked up on the hand signals quickly. Squid had given him a lesson on the ride to the park. He successfully avoided making mistakes in the first few practice runs. Ray tried to hide it, but Will could tell he was impressed. After only a few runs, Ray focused more on the team than on Will. He was melding in and playing his role.

Now Will sat in the "Silent Killer" with the other twenty three members of the special ops team on the way to his first assault mission. He sat closest to the cockpit, to the left of Wolfman, who was to the left of Squid. They had both grown confident in his abilities and were accepting him more as part of the team each day.

Wolfman turned to him, "What the hell are you doing over here anyway, Will? Shouldn't you be going to English class and prom, or some shit like that?" This was the first time Wolfman had requested any personal information from Will.

Will decided to take the honest route. "I'm trying to figure out what to do with my life. You know, where do I go from here?"

Wolfman laughed loudly. "Life is what happens when reality is punching you in the face every day." Then laughed at himself some more. Squid was asleep. His head bounced up and down from the constant rocking of the helicopter.

The assault team responded to Wolfman's laughter with various shouts, hoots, and hollers.

"Time for a Jingle, Wolfman, let's hear it!" someone yelled.

"Give a rap, Wolfman!"

Without delay, Wolfman stood up and shuffled down the aisle, offering up the following tune to the team's obvious delight:

"They call me the Wolfman. I'm a crazy Jarhead.
No one is a better at pumping that lead.
Mitakus thinks he's bad, and he's coming on fast,
But the Warren Boys gonna take their steel and shove it up his
ass!"

Wolfman then arched his back to the point Will was certain his spine would snap like a toothpick, and threw his chest forward releasing a devil dog bark so loud and sharp that Will looked to see if the windows had broken.

The cabin erupted in a state of cheer and laughter to a point Will thought they may disrupt the flight of the helicopter. Despite these threats to their transportation, Ray remained calm and got everybody back on track.

"Button it up, Wolfman," Ray yelled, bringing the jovial mood to an end. "We hit the ground in ten minutes. Gear check, now!" he exclaimed as he slapped Squid on the head to wake him up and walked through the center of the team, visually checking them for readiness.

Everybody turned to their right in unison as the person to their left checked their gear. Will checked that Wolfman's ammo pouches were attached securely to his cargo belt and his night vision glasses were strapped securely to his helmet. He hit Wolfman on the helmet, just like they had trained. They both turned to their left in unison and Wolfman now checked Will's devices. When Will felt the slap on his helmet, he turned back forward and checked the front of his own gear. *Front ammo pouches good, cargo belt buckled.* He reached down and tugged on his rifle, causing the retention clamps to release. He inserted a magazine and checked that the safety was on. Just like Ray had made him, at least a hundred times, last night before the team executed their final dry run.

He reached up and tapped his ear piece which was nestled in his auditory canal. His microphone was fastened into his shirt collar which he could trigger with a slap to the device. The processor in the earpiece would give priority by rank, Ray's voice overriding all communication. Ray also could filter his based on team member.

The plan was that they would land in a central location within the reserve, about a mile from the point of attack. They would trek on foot to the southwest edge along the tree line where the road emerged into the opening. They would lay in wait there. The convoy was expected just after midnight.

"On your feet!" Ray shouted. And everybody stood in unison and held onto the overhead straps. The helicopter slowed quickly and banked heavily. Will instinctively bent his knees to absorb the shock of the landing. The rear cargo door began to open before the gunship was on the ground. As soon as the door was fully open, Ray continued barking orders.

"Move out! Move out! Move out!" Ray yelled. The team filed out and took off for a sprint to the tree line. Ray had said there was little risk upon landing, but military doctrine would still be followed as he was eager to get the team within the cover of the forest as soon as they hit the ground.

As he leapt off the ramp and onto solid ground, Will scanned the area while keeping his feet moving across the lush green grass. The sun was setting but there was still plenty of light, and Will could see that they had landed in a clearing to the east of a large rocky hill interspaced with dark green vegetation. The clearing was surrounded by various trees that gently blew with the wind, the rustling of their leaves silent beneath the whirl of the helicopter blades. *This is still Calidum?* he thought. Will was surprised at the stark contrast between the quasi-barren Calidum that he had witnessed and the flourishing, wilderness through which he was now running.

Once the team was safely within the tree line, Ray called everybody to take a knee. "Single file from here on out, keep your spacing and watch out for wildlife. Don't forget this is a game reserve. Squid, you're on point since you had a nice nap." Squid nodded.

"Move out!" At Ray's command they all stood, and Squid led the way. Ray grabbed Will and Wolfman by their arms, tightly. "Listen up, you two. Will, you're a rookie. That means you watch and learn. Only use your weapon if you absolutely have to." He turned to Wolfman. "You're responsible for him, Wolfman. He gets hurt, it's your ass." Wolfman looked pissed.

"That's crap. I'm not a babysitter," Wolfman protested.

"You'll follow orders, Wolfman!" Ray lashed back. "I'll bring up the rear. You two are in front of me where I can see you."

Wolfman took off angrily, and Will followed. He thought it best to keep his mouth shut.

They moved alertly through the thick brush. Will could not identify the noises coming from the depths of the forest and hoped he would not have to. He kept a sharp eye out and was a bit twitchy for most of the hike.

After about a half hour, Squid put his fist up in the air and held his elbow at a ninety degree bend. Each person duplicated this signal, and the team came to a stop. This was the site of their ambush. They would wait here as darkness settled.

They all assumed their positions just inside the tree line as was planned in the training runs. Will and Wolfman knelt behind a large, fallen tree, about three-hundred yards north of where the ops team would launch the attack. The drones had showed the convoy security would be heavier near the front, where the main force of their team would force an engagement. Wolfman and Will were to take a position near the rear of the convoy and remove any rear guards. They would also support the main force at the front if needed. Ray had determined this was the safest location for Will, and Wolfman was none too pleased.

Will asked a question that had been bugging him. "Why do they call you 'Wolfman?'"

Wolfman looked at Will with a smirk. "I can smell trouble, always have. Some uncanny ability I suppose. Some people can run a hundred meters in less than ten seconds. I can smell misfortune as it lies around the corner."

That was the extent of their personal conversation. Wolfman made Will verbally walk through the mission, from beginning to end, several times.

They waited several hours, and darkness had now settled over the African continent. The sky was clear, but there was no moon, the only illumination coming from the thousands of stars whose light burst through the atmosphere.

Will heard some rustling and nervously turned, only to see Ray running up from the rear with the help of his night vision glasses which the team was now utilizing. "Stay alert," Ray warned. "We should hear them within the next twenty minutes if they're on schedule." He then turned and disappeared into the thick vegetation, back towards the main force.

"He could have just radioed that to us," Will said.

"Not Ray. He's looking into each person's eyes, making sure they're ready," Wolfman replied. Wolfman twitched his nose and cocked his head.

Will noticed. "What's wrong?"

"Not sure. Could just be a smell from the game reserve," Wolfman replied. Will knew better as Wolfman continued to look nervous.

It was actually thirty minutes before they heard the noise of the engines approaching. Ray was to tag the lead vehicle with his laser which would guide the first missile from the drone that was circling just to the south. Will and Wolfman watched the trucks pass their position. Several seconds later, they heard the thermobaric missile hit the lead truck and spread its constant pressure wave, turning the vehicle into clouds of violently erupting flames as the fuel mixed with the oxygen. Will and Wolfman instinctively huddled behind the log at the sound of the explosion, even though they were a safe distance from the demolished vehicle. Wolfman peeked over the top of the tree and Will followed. There was a small opening in the trees and he could see the truck in front was flipped end over front from the shock wave and lay, turned over, blocking the road. Small arms fire erupted from the rear of the convoy, firing rounds and tracers blindly in the direction that the missile was fired.

Wolfman had a concerned look on his face.

"What's the matter?"

"The rifles they're firing. They sound like ours."

"So?" Will queried.

"So, these are high-tech weapons, only available in the U.S." Will recalled Squid telling him they were illegal to export. "The NoC's purchase all their weapons from illegal arms dealers, and the crap they can afford to buy is usually older, bulkier, and prone to be junk."

Will could feel his heart pounding against his flak jacket. He looked at Wolfman, who was still nervously watching the rear of the convoy. The security truck moved from its position at the rear out away from the tankers and cut a path between the forest and the convoy with weapons fire emanating from behind its cab. With their night vision goggles, Will could clearly see a figure with head and shoulders exposed above the side armor plating.

"Fifty cal gunner," Wolfman pointed out with excitement as if he and Will were about to ride a roller coaster at an amusement part. Will wasn't surprised. "Lock and load, Will. Things are about to get hot." Will did as told and loaded a round in his chamber while Wolfman raised his weapon to fire, simultaneously switching on the laser sight. With a remarkably accurate placement of the laser and a steady squeeze of the trigger, three rounds streaked from Wolfman's weapon and, judging from what Will saw through his glasses, disembodied the better part of the fifty cal gunners skull.

The truck lurched and then braked hard to a stop. Four figures jumped out the back of the truck, the red beams of their laser sights crisscrossing wildly.

"Shit! They have laser sights. Take them out, Will. I got the driver," Wolfman ordered.

Will immediately set the crosshairs on the lead figure, squeezing the trigger as the red enemy lasers lifted in their direction. The rifle burst forth a round, and the figure fell to the ground. The other three started firing as soon as their rifles were parallel to the ground. The cover of the forest and the downed tree Will and Wolfman knelt behind provided cover, but the bullets were cutting through the vegetation that surrounded them in a hurried fashion. Will heard gunfire erupting from the far end of the convoy as well.

Immediately, Will squeezed off another round and the next figure fell to the ground. Wolfman fired and took out the driver. Will fired again. The third attacker who was now at the edge of the tree line and firing, his shots bursting bark from the top of the tree, and dangerously close, fell with the last attacker who Wolfman had shot.

"We have to move," Wolfman shouted. "They're going to need support up front." Will nodded his head in affirmation. "Ready?" Wolfman asked. Will nodded again, and Wolfman immediately took off at a full sprint from his crouched position behind the tree, followed closely by Will.

Not more than six yards into their dash, a shot rang out and Wolfman shouted sharply as he fell to the ground. Will stumbled over him, unable to stop in time. Will immediately flipped over onto his back and rolled over to a prone position, just in time to settle his crosshairs on the NoC, lying partially behind the wheel of the truck with only his head and shoulders exposed. Will fired, hitting his target head on.

"Damn it!" Wolfman yelled, grasping at his right thigh.

Will turned to Wolfman and could see the blood flow from his leg. He reached down and ripped open the pants to expose the wound, then pulled open the top pocket of his own cargo pants and removed his field dressing pack. He tore at the top and removed the white dressing, which he slapped onto the hole in Wolfman's thigh. He finished the messy task by wrapping the medical tape around Wolfman's leg as he continued to cuss from the pain.

"Leave me here and get back to the team. Now!" Wolfman commanded.

"No way." Will grabbed Wolfman in order to pick him up in a fireman's carry, but before he could get Wolfman off the ground, a figure sprinted out of the woods, grabbing Wolfman off the ground in a single sweep of his arm and pulling Will with the other. It was Ray.

"Move it, Will," he commanded.

Will sprinted alongside Ray, his legs wobbling, back through the woods in the direction of the gun fire emanating from the front of the convoy. After about two-hundred yards, Will could begin to make out laser lines flickering about in numerous directions. Ray gently placed Wolfman back down on the ground into a sunken pit behind a tree stump.

"We'll be ok here," Ray said.

"I'm good. The bullet lodged in the meaty part of my leg, I think," Wolfman noted.

As Ray checked the field dressing, Will dashed off toward the edge of the tree line in a half crouch, going to a low crawl as he neared the edge.

Ray was furious at this maneuver but could not risk being heard. So he low crawled after Will.

Will could see without his night vision goggles as they were close to the lead vehicles, both of which were now burning. Six Calidumese were seeking cover behind a fuel tanker and firing into the woods. They must have realized they were not in the best of positions and made for the tree line for cover and take a chance that they could out flank the assault team. Will raised his rifle and picked off all six.

He scanned the area but could not see any other targets within range. Ray arrived at his side.

"What the hell do you think you're doing?" Ray said as firmly as possible without being too loud.

"I was going to lay down cover fire if needed, so you could attend Wolfman. Good thing I did as a half dozen were making it for the woods," Will replied.

Ray was silent for a moment. "Good thinking. But I'm still pissed."

The firing toward the front turned from steady automatic gunfire to a more sporadic tempo and then stopped altogether. Ray retrieved Wolfman from the pit and Will followed as they made their way toward the rest of the team.

Will and Ray, carrying Wolfman, continued through the woods. They spotted the team just outside the tree line near the burning tanker. Ray announced their arrival from behind a tree just in case somebody had an itchy trigger finger.

Ray placed Wolfman on the ground near the team. Will took a knee by Ray. Keeping his eyes outward, looking for any movement.

"We have to clear each truck, see if there's any stragglers. Will, stay with Wolfman," Ray ordered the team to move out with two staying behind to guard the prisoners who had been smart enough to surrender.

Each two-man team took a truck and found no more NoC's. Ray scanned the area to the west with his night vision binoculars. He spoke into his microphone, "Report."

Will heard the team members sounding the all clear through his earpiece.

Ray responded, "Rally on the tree line. They're either dead or ran into the desert. I don't think any got past us into the woods, but keep an eye out."

The team converged on their position, and Ray ordered Squid to take a tally of prisoners and the dead. He ran off with two others to carry out Ray's instructions.

Ray momentarily turned his attention to Will. "What happened back there? You ok?"

"I'm good," Will said through heavy breaths. "We took some fire from the rear vehicle. They had a fifty cal mounted on the truck, and Wolfman took out the gunner. We hit the ones that jumped out the back. We thought it was clear, so we took off. Wolfman got hit by somebody we missed."

Ray looked at him deeply for a moment. Squid came through the earpiece reporting they had twenty prisoners, and he counted twenty-four dead.

"Command One, this is assault leader. Do you copy?" Ray said into his microphone and paused for a response. "I've got three wounded, repeat three wounded Foundation team members and twenty prisoners. Requesting extraction, over." Another pause. "Copy that." Ray turned to face his unit. "Assault team, prepare for extraction."

Within ten minutes, the helicopter was back with a partner, Will assumed for the prisoners. The wounds to the three injured were not life threatening, and Will helped Wolfman on board. The rear ramp shut, and the helicopter ascended slowly, banked, and accelerated forward.

As they left the remnants of the ambush behind them, Will could hear Ray talking over his microphone. "We are clear of the field. You may proceed with destroying the remaining vehicles on the ground."

Ray walked up the aisle and knelt on the cargo covers in front of Wolfman and Will.

"They had STR 5's, Ray," Wolfman stated. He was sweating but the pain was eased by the shot of morphine that Ray had administered to each of the wounded.

"Yeah, they sure did," Ray said, obviously troubled. "Night vision also."

"How the hell did they get the same weapons as us?" Wolfman asked. "They're American made, non-exports by law." Wolfman was referring to the Staburn Act, banning all American weapons manufacturers from exporting military grade weapons.

"Not sure, Wolfman. How's the leg?" Ray asked as he lifted Wolfman's eyelids, looking into his pupils.

"It'll leave a scar. But it'll match the one on my left leg," Wolfman said with a forced smile that dripped with sweat. "Will here deserves a medal. He nailed eight or nine of those bastards and dressed my leg like a pro."

Ray looked at Will as if he wanted to chew him out, but thought better of it. "We'll be on the ground in a few minutes and get you bandaged up, Wolfman. You'll probably be going home soon."

Ray moved to the back of the helicopter to check on the other wounded.

Will sat low in the canvas seat, his battered legs lying limp in front of him. He removed his helmet and laid his head back against the cold aluminum bulkhead, closing his heavy eyes, releasing his breath. His mind, liberated from conscious control, ran unrestrained through the night's activities in streaks and flashes as if it were some comedic horror movie. Each scene replayed with a vividness and clarity that is found in only a very few of life's events. He had killed for the first time, and he would never be the same.

12

"There lives more faith in honest doubt, believe me, than in half the creeds." —Alfred, Lord Tennyson

J axon stood hunched and pressing his palms into the utility desk that occupied the corner of his tent, his grip so strong the pain was shooting up through his forearms. He stared into the blackened pine, wishing he could close his eyes and undo the previous night's events. Rather, upon closing his eyes, he faced the mirror of his mind, staring back at him with an accusing glare, saying "you have been but a fool." The guilt weighed heavily on him like a blanket of lead wrapped around his shoulders. He had been careless in underestimating the enemy, and it had resulted in three wounded men, good men who could have been killed. During the assault on the convoy, he had watched and listened to the staccato of the enemy fire, recognizing that it was identical to that of their own weapons. This should not have been possible. But it was his job to expect the improbable and minimize the risk. He had failed, and three men lay wounded in the medical tent. They were military veterans, all previously wounded, and they would physically heal. But he well knew the psychological impact of metal tearing into the body, fired from another human being, its unnaturalness deepening the trauma.

The injury to Will was particularly worrisome to Jaxon. Killing another human being, even an enemy, or in self-defense, is a wound to the soul which never heals. He had planned for Will to get the feel for combat, carrying a weapon, feeling the heightened sense when the first shots are fired, watching the action play out. *How could I have been so careless?* he thought.

He recalled the night, over forty years ago, still vivid in his mind, when he had tasted his first kill. The circumstances were quite different. During the early Southwest Asian wars, a tribe of terrorists had taken over a group of villages in the Paktika province. They reigned terror down on its residents for several weeks, forcing the young men to join their fight or face death and even threatening to shoot any women and girls found attending school. This angered Jaxon the most; the absurd idea of denying someone an education was tantamount to slavery, and slavery was worse than death.

The leader of this tribe, Kul was his name, was especially vicious and had been hunted by the coalition forces for over a year.

When news of the village's occupation spread, Jaxon's platoon was called upon to lead the attack. Intelligence had distributed photos of the terrorist leader as he was the main target of the mission. He held intelligence of the other terrorist cells in the province which those managing the war deemed a high priority. Their orders were to capture Kul and destroy the tribe of terrorists.

During the nighttime raid, which caught the terrorists by surprise, Jaxon had advanced around to the east of the village, hunting for stragglers who might attack his platoon by the flank. As he moved around an unkempt dwelling, a man sprang from its draped door. Jaxon screamed at him to halt, kneel, and put his hands on his head. The man obeyed. After padding him down for weapons, Jaxon moved to face the man, recognizing Kul the moment he saw his eyes, one of which was crossed.

The man knew he was recognized and the devil knew what was coming as tears welled up in his eyes, revealing his fear. Jaxon always wondered why. Did it suddenly hit him what may await him after death? Was he afraid of judgment day? Or just afraid of the unknown? Maybe he was afraid he would face the souls of those he had massacred. Jaxon didn't care.

Jaxon held the monarch of hell in the iron sights of his rifle. The man had valuable intelligence. Would Kul use this to his advantage and make a bargain for his life? If Jaxon killed him now, the world would be a better place, but Kul was unarmed. As Jaxon waged the battle within his own mind a bullet rifled into the man's skull. Jaxon had pulled the trigger of his M-16. Had it been intentional? Could it have been the adrenaline pumping through his veins? Jaxon didn't know. But the man had been freed from his evil mind. The world was now a better place.

Now Will had walked this path at the age of eighteen. Had he pushed too hard? Jaxon was about to find out. This evening he had invited Will, Suzen, and Ray over to his tent for a private dinner. The chef was preparing the food on an open grille, and the waffling scent of juicy steak and asparagus was being carried through the pores of Jaxon's tent.

Ray arrived a few minutes early. Jaxon entered the common room that was part of his two-room tent. He had dressed in nylon Sahara cargo pants and a blue polo shirt. He preferred this type of dress for these dinners in the field as it gave the illusion, for a short time, that the guests were in a more normal environment. Ray had done the same, dressed in black trousers and a burgundy polo shirt.

"How are the wounded men doing?" Jaxon asked and motioned for Ray to sit with him in two green fold-up camp chairs against the side of the tent. He knew the extent of their injuries; they had received excellent treatment in the camps medical tent. But, infections were always a concern in the field.

"They'll be fine," Ray replied while lowering himself into the squeaky chair. "We're flying them back stateside in a few days where they'll rehab. That and the chunk of cash you promised them will surely expedite the healing process."

"They earned it," Jaxon grunted. "How's Will doing?" He had not spoken to Will since before the mission, but Ray had briefed him on Will's performance.

Ray let out a sigh. "He appears to be doing well, on the outside at least. I just don't understand how a kid that young can go through this and not even show any kind of outward effects. He's one tough teenager. I mean, I remember my first time in a combat situation, and I was screwed up for a while. I suppose I kept my head, though. I just hope he's not bottling it up."

Will was proving tougher than even Jaxon's high expectations. "That's good to hear, Ray. I know you think I've pushed him too hard, but there are circumstances of which you are not aware." *And maybe some that even I am unaware,* Jaxon thought.

Ray nodded. "What did you do with the serial numbers from the rifles we confiscated?" The assault team had captured, along with the North Calidumese, about one hundred STR 5's. Weapons not allowed to leave the United States, yet here they were, in the hands of the enemy. The NoC's security vehicles had been well stocked.

"They're being analyzed by a source I have in Washington. He's tracing them as we speak," Jaxon answered. "How's the interrogation of the NoC's going?"

"Nothing of importance yet, but they'll break soon. The contractors are on it. You know their success rate."

Jaxon knew the contractors were good; that's why he paid them so handsomely. They used a combination of psychological tactics and drugs to pull the information from the minds of the interrogee. Jaxon had forbidden any strong physical interrogation. Like most Americans, Jaxon had always struggled with the use of torture to gain information. He realized that in some rare situations an argument could be made that it was necessary to save lives. But he found it repulsive. Non-invasive techniques had proven effective in his experience.

"I want Mitakus's location no later than tomorrow morning," Jaxon ordered. "You know as well as I that he is planning to strike back and strike back hard. We can't give him that chance."

"I understand, Boss. We'll get him," Ray said with confidence. "Just make sure you're prepared for the fallout. If we take him out, the media will go nuts, paint you as some type of cowboy assassin."

"I'll manage it. In fact, I don't really give a damn what the media does. I've been doing this a long time now, Ray. News stories come and go, as well as media personalities. They may beat up on me for a few days but then some other event will occur, and they'll shift their attention." Jaxon looked Ray directly in the eye. "I'm going to get him, Ray. It's the only way to stop this massacre. Are you still with me?"

Ray sighed. "Yes, I suppose. I'll call over to the interrogation room and tell'm to turn up the heat a bit." Ray removed his tablet from his pants pocket and stepped to the back of the room to make the call.

There was a knock on the wooden tent door. "Door's open," Jaxon shouted.

Will entered with Suzen, both looking like two nervous teenagers.

"Well hello, Suzen," Jaxon said, standing and taking her hand. "Thanks so much for accepting my invitation to dinner tonight." Jaxon was attempting to cover up his mood and put Suzen at ease. "I've received good reports about you during your stay here, and I wanted to give you a reward for those efforts." The former was the truth, but the latter was a bit less. He had actually invited Suzen because she was Will's age, and he had seen them together on several occasions. He was quite happy they had continued their friendship after that first meeting at Meadow Brook Hall and he realized she may be a source of confidence for Will, and possibly, a key factor in assuring his success here in Calidum.

Suzen smiled. "Thank you for the invitation, Mr. Warren."

"Please, Suzen, call me Jaxon, during dinner at least," Jaxon asked, smiling in return. Suzen nodded in affirmation.

Jaxon turned his attention to Will. "From what I hear, you had some heroic moments in a situation that was certainly less than usual for our humanitarian missions. I'm proud of you, Will."

Will just smiled and nodded, appreciating the recognition.

"Please, have a seat." Jaxon motioned for them to sit at the table arranged for the evenings activities. This room in Jaxon's tent served multiple purposes: dining room, as Jaxon took most of his meals alone; conference room; or even a social meeting room for his senior staff on occasion. The table was a simple wood foldout with aluminum legs, which were invisible under the long blue table cloth topped with blue earthenware, wine goblets, and sterling silver utensils.

There was an open decanter of red wine in the middle of the table and a place setting for each of them. Jaxon poured a full glass for himself and Ray, and slightly less for Will and Suzen. Ray rejoined them, picked up his glass, and took a long drink before recognizing Will and Suzen.

They shared pleasant small talk for a few minutes before they were interrupted by the chef who entered, pushing, with the help of an assistant, a large cart which held several plates, each adorned with a magnificent-looking Kansas City Strip steak and a small mound of asparagus crowns. He moved around the table as if in a dance, setting each plate delicately with a proud smile to each of the diners. Jaxon cut into his steak first, cooked perfectly to medium well, and placed the morsel in his mouth. His glands erupted with joy. "Perfect, Petre. You are a genius!" Jaxon complimented.

"Thank you, Mr. Warren. It is my pleasure," Petre replied and exited the tent with his assistant.

They ate and chatted, nothing of any consequence, trying hard to have a normal dinner and forget about the war, the sand, and the tragedies occurring outside the walls of the tent.

"Will has come up with some excellent ideas for his philosophy essay on the Uskey," Suzen said as they finished their meal.

"Is that so, Will?" Jaxon asked. "Please, share some of your insights with us. I would love to hear your thoughts."

Will was a bit embarrassed and shot Suzen a glare. "It's sort of scrambled right now, sir. I'm trying to put it into something cohesive."

"Now don't be modest, Will," Uncle Jax said. The table was silent, forcing Will to take the stage.

"One thing I've learned from the reading I've been doing and from our conversations, Uncle Jax, is that no single system of contemporary political thought has ever truly succeeded. The idea that the outcome of any act, as long as it brings a sense of happiness to the largest number of people, fails as the outcome could violate basic human rights. For instance, would taking your wealth and spreading it among the poorest Americans be wise? No, you earned it, and you deserve to dispose of it as you wish. Taking it away from you would discourage your ability to produce, which has proven profitable, for many, to say the least."

"Here, Here!" Uncle Jax exclaimed with jest and a raise of his glass. Taking a long sip before setting it back down on the table. "I like your philosophy already." This was met with laughter from the group.

Will continued, "And the idea of complete libertarianism, although my personal preference, also fails in the long term."

"How so?" Uncle Jaxon challenged. Jaxon had written his doctoral thesis on the Libertarian philosophy forty some years ago and leaned in that direction himself.

"History has shown, that no matter what type of government is in control, that the greater disparity in income between the upper and lower classes, the higher the probability that bad things will happen. In a totalitarian state, the government would likely be overthrown through some violent revolution, whereas in a republic such as the United States, the elected officials will choose sides, wage class warfare, or enter a state of complete stalemate, letting society deteriorate as they fight for power."

"The fact is, intelligence has never, and never will be, doled out equally by nature. The more intelligent will always control more of the resources, and some in society will tend to be jealous and believe that they have been 'wronged' by the system."

"So what is the answer, Will?" Ray asked.

"I don't know. Maybe we are meant to go through an enlightenment every so often that resets society. Each iteration creating a new and better way of thinking until we find something that works, some type of equilibrium," Will concluded.

"Very impressive, Will," Jaxon complimented. "You've obviously done your reading but also thought about it independently. You're a good critical thinker. An important, yet rare trait."

"There is a rumor going around that the NoC's who were captured are being interrogated within the compound. Is that true?" Suzen blurted out, looking directly at Jaxon. The table fell quiet. She had obviously been holding this in.

Jaxon met her gaze, pausing briefly in his response. *Don't forget she's a teenage girl,* he said to himself before answering. Jaxon had learned many years ago that most people did not understand how the world operated on a practical level. He did not think this in an arrogant manner but had learned it through experience.

"Most of the NoC's we captured were cooperative and happy to have a good meal. But they were lower ranking and didn't have the information we needed. The few officers that commanded the platoon are presently under interrogation." Jaxon knew where Suzen was going with this and also recognized it as an opportunity to reverse the rumor mill.

"What methods are you using to interrogate them?" Suzen asked.

"Remember your place, Suzen," Ray warned sharply. "And don't forget to whom you are speaking."

"It's ok, Ray," Jaxon said. "Interrogation is a difficult task, Suzen. How it is carried out in practice is directly related to the information being sought, the immediate need of the information, and the probability that the person being interrogated has the information you need. We are quite certain that the officers we captured have the information we need, primarily the location of Mitakus and the means by which he was transporting himself around the battlefield. We also believe they have the secure frequencies by which they were communicating with their command. This information is vital to our mission as Mitakus has shown his intent to kill civilians as you well know. The quicker we obtain this information, the sooner we can save lives. So, I'm using a team of professionals in order to get the information efficiently."

"Are they using torture?" Suzen asked.

"They use no physical force to obtain the information," Jaxon explained, trying not to sound annoyed. "And during the interrogation no physical harm will come to the subjects whatsoever. I was very clear on that. But they will be subjected to mental stress. It is the only leverage we have."

"Why do you do it?" Suzen asked as she continued her inquiry, doubtful if she would ever have this opportunity again. "I don't intend to be disrespectful, but you are arguably one of the most accomplished people throughout human history. You could be relaxing by your pool back in Michigan enjoying this glass of wine sitting next to your wife, or even on a cruise through the Caribbean. But instead you have chosen to live, for a time, in this desolate arena of Calidum, spending large amounts of money to stop a bloody war that was probably inevitable."

An awkward silence fell across the room again as Suzen kept her gaze locked on Jaxon, waiting for an answer.

Jaxon knew she was asking a question that many others wished to ask. He picked up his wine cup and drained the contents slowly, continuing to hold the earthenware in his hand. "My wife and I purchased this dining set in Charlevoix, Michigan while we were staying at the Horton Creek Inn, a beautiful bed and breakfast which has been our hideaway on many occasions. Simple, yet elegant. We thought it would be durable for various settings. I use it on my trips with the Foundation as it holds up well to pretty much any environment. It's made of earthenware, a ceramic material used in pottery, whose contents are kaolinite, mica, quartz, and feldspar: substances that have existed in the universe for billions of years and will continue to exist until the end of time. Yet I, as a human, will only be around for a few decades, a minuscule amount of time relative to the age of these elements. And because of this, we must be more prejudiced in our choosing of what we do with those precious few years."

"I have a letter hanging on my wall in the office at the Foundation," Jaxon continued. "The letter contains the origin of the Foundation's, and my own, motto: 'To make the world a better place for having lived in it.' Sure, I could be sitting at home with Jeanna right now, or off on a cruise somewhere in a tropical paradise, but I've chosen to fill this particular few months of my short life with work, work that will make Calidum a better place for years to come, and thus, fulfilling the Foundation's motto."

"Are you going to kill Mitakus?" Suzen pressed.

Jaxon leaned in slightly closer, resting his elbows on the table and looking deeply into Suzen's eyes. "Listen closely Suzen, and let there be no mistake in your understanding. I will not leave Calidum until Mitakus is dead. Be it at my hands or those of someone else."

At this last statement, Jaxon stood and limped out of his tent.

Suzen blushed. "I'm terribly sorry," she said to both Ray and Will. "I did not mean to offend or upset him."

"Don't worry, you didn't," Ray consoled her. "But, I think, you just caused him to solidify his commitment."

***

Mitakus unsheathed his machete and in one single motion, twirled his body around and violently sliced off the head of the messenger who had been standing behind him, the same messenger who had just reported to him that the fuel supply trucks had not arrived. The man's head rotated slowly before hitting the ground with a thud. The body fell limply forward as the knees buckled with no communication from the brain. Blood quickly colored the pale sand around the limp body.

Bakri stood with mouth agape, in a state of shock at such a useless act of violence. It was Mitakus' own decision to ignore his advice. Increasing the security of their supply lines should have been a priority. *Mitakus has lost it,* he thought.

Mitakus took a step toward the fallen soldier's body and thrust his machete into the back of the body's torso.

Bakri turned to walk away, disgusted at the waste of human life.

"Get back here!" Mitakus ordered.

Bakri stopped, turning his head slightly but refusing to look at Mitakus. "Or what? You'll kill me also? Maybe kill every soldier until you have defeated your own army?"

"Do not talk to me with disrespect. I'm your commander!" Mitakus screamed.

"And I'm your advisor. You just killed one of your own soldiers. Not because he did something wrong, but because he reported important information. He was doing his job, Mitakus!"

Mitakus looked down at the body still pumping blood onto the desert floor. His psychotic anger appeared to subside. Several moments later, while still looking at the body, he spoke, "You are right, cousin." He turned and walked over to Bakri. "Please forgive me. I let my anger get the best of me. It was not his fault. But, you know what this does to our cause. We are dead in our tracks. We do not have enough fuel for even a retreat. If I had not killed this poor messenger, he would have died tomorrow on the field of battle. We are sitting ducks!" He touched Bakri on the shoulder who still refused to face him. "Please, cousin, I need your counsel."

Bakri lifted his face to the sky and took a deep breath. He knew they faced horrible odds. "Warren knows our supply route. In order to keep advancing, we have to create multiple supply lines, have them run simultaneously. He can't hit all of them. The road running along the reserve was the most concealable. We will now be forced to run our supplies out in the open." He turned now to face Mitakus. "We can continue the offensive when another shipment of fuel arrives. But if he hits another convoy, we have to stop the offensive and retreat. Do you understand that, Mitakus?"

"Yes, cousin, I do," Mitakus said. Bakri knew he was not being truthful. "Have this poor man's body removed and given a proper burial. And then, see that your plan is put into place. I am forever grateful for your counsel, cousin. I have a plan for dealing with Jaxon Warren, one that will rid him and his foundation from our country. Please, Bakri, let us go in, and I will lay out the details for you." Mitakus then turned and stepped back into his command vehicle. Bakri followed.

***

Daniel ended the call on his tablet. He pressed his elbows on his desk and ran his hands through his black, moussed hair. Sitting back in his chair, he released a sigh that slowly died. *This is big.* He thought. He gazed at the books that lined the walls, mentally ripping the knowledge from their pages in the hope of discovering a morsel of insight. But none was found. The decision that lay before him could not be based on book knowledge; it required precise calculation and valiance. He was at a precipice, and it was his last chance to turn back.

His hand dangled over the flat screen of the tablet for a long moment and then slowly entered another phone number. He turned around in his custom, posture-fit, leather chair, and looked out the broad window of his Russel Senate Building office. He could see out across C Street into the Senate Park, and thought he should take a walk on the diag during lunch to clear his mind. The cool February air would do him some good. It would also do his waistline some good as too many hours in the office had left it soft.

He had succeeded in the game of politics by knowing which way the wind was blowing, knowing what friends to make, and which friends to leave behind. It was a challenging game but one he loved. Brianna was about to become the Secretary of Defense, yet he knew her desire for revenge on her perceived enemies, which was a driving force in her life, could lead to her ruin. She listened to him less these days, and he knew she would replace him in a heartbeat if she thought it would give her an advantage. He was a fundraiser to her, nothing more.

"Department of Justice, Ms. Branson's office," the voice on the line answered. Melanie Branson was the Department of Justice Senate Liaison. Daniel and she had been a little more than friendly on several occasions.

"Hello, this is Daniel Vicksburg, Senator Larkin's Chief of Staff. Could I speak with Ms. Branson please?"

"Please hold one minute, Mr. Vicksburg."

He knew she would take his call. People had been bending over backwards to offer their assistance now that it was widely known that Senator Larkin was to be the next Defense Secretary. He continued to gaze out the window as he waited. The sky was clear for February. He saw two men sitting on a park bench. *Two friends having a conversation?* He thought. *Or perhaps an aide passing on information to a reporter, information that could kill someone's career.* This town lived and died on secret information, be it true or not.

"Daniel," Melanie said after a few minutes. He had always found her voice very seductive, and he could see her sitting at her desk, sharply dressed. Red always looked great on her. "To what do I owe this pleasure?"

"I have a list of serial numbers from some assault rifles that ended up in the wrong hands. They were exported somehow from the U.S., and I need to know the route they took, who bought what and when, that kind of thing. Could you do me a favor and have them traced?"

"Perhaps. After you tell me what I'll get in return?" she asked seductively.

"DOJ gets to prosecute, with my ok, though."

"Do you think the rifles were stolen?" she queried.

"I doubt it. These are very high-tech and would have been under tight security. I think these rifles were intended for the end user."

"Since when do you get to tell Justice who to prosecute, Daniel?"

"Since I have the rifle serial numbers. Without them, you get nothing. With them, you likely will get a high profile, slam-dunk prosecution."

Melanie was quiet for a moment, probably calculating her options. "How big is it?"

"Let me just say that these rifles ended up in a country with known connections to terrorism."

"Terrorists?" This peaked Melanie's interest. Terrorist prosecutions were rare.

"I thought you'd be interested. Deal?"

"Ok. Forward them to me. These things are easy to trace through the national arms database. I should have an answer for you by the end of the day," Melanie promised.

Daniel tapped his tablet a few times. "They should be in your inbox right now."

"Got it. Thanks for the scoop."

"Welcome," Daniel replied and disconnected the call.

Daniel then dialed Ben Adams, a reporter from the Post.

Ben answered quickly. "Hey bud. Getting ready for the move to the Pentagon?"

"One headache after another, my friend," Daniel complained.

"I bet. I'm assuming you are calling for a reason. You never call me just to chat."

"How would you like to have dinner tonight? Capital Grille? Eight o'clock?"

"Why? What's up?" Ben asked.

"I have something I think you'll be interested in. If not, you'll just get a free dinner and a chance to catch up with your old pal."

"I'm in. See you then." Ben hung up.

Daniel took his walk, picking up a hot dog from a vendor on C Street. He walked along the diag, eating the steaming frankfurter and reassessing his plans. He could not rely solely on instinct to resolve his current situation. He had taken a college course in game theory, and this had served him well. He had drawn up a chart laying out the path that would give him the most capital. Not financial capital, but political capital. One could easily lead to the other. By the end of the day, his choice would be clear.

He returned to his office after buying another hot dog, which was delicious, and busied himself with the everyday work required to run a senatorial office: giving direction to staff members, watching the headlines for any breaking news, analyzing polling data from Michigan, etc.

It was only about three hours into his afternoon when his tablet rang with an incoming call from Melanie.

"That was fast," he said as he answered the call.

"This is big, Daniel! Did you have any idea what I was going to find?" Melanie said with excitement clearly ringing in her voice.

"Not really. But I suspected it could be big. Why? What did you turn up?"

"These rifles were originally purchased by the Warren Foundation directly from the manufacturer."

Daniel's heart skipped a beat. *That's impossible. No*, he corrected himself, *just highly unlikely*. "Are you sure, Melanie? That doesn't make sense."

"Absolutely, Daniel. The database doesn't lie. Where did you get these serial numbers from?"

"Your line is secure, right?" Daniel asked.

"Yes, of course."

"This information is just between us, right? If you run with this too early, you will get burnt. Do you understand?" Daniel warned.

"I'm no dummy, Daniel. We both know who runs the Foundation, and I'm not looking to make enemies with the richest man in the world, not to mention a cultural icon. What's going on?"

"I got the serial numbers directly from my contact at the Foundation. The rifles were taken from a platoon of North Calidumese soldiers they had captured." Daniel knew he could not reveal his source's name. That would be too dangerous.

"The Foundation is getting in gun fights with the North Calidumese? And capturing soldiers?" Melanie asked. "Wait, don't answer that. Assuming that is true, the fact that the Foundation is fighting against soldiers armed with rifles that the Foundation had originally purchased is much bigger," she pointed out.

"This is crazy. It makes no sense," Daniel said as he was quickly playing the scenarios through his head.

"There's more," Melanie said. "The rifles were sold by the Foundation to an American company, BSC (Buffalo Security Consulting), Ltd."

"That name sounds familiar." *Where have I seen that name?* Daniel thought.

"I could not find much out about it. It is some type of partnership licensed to do business globally. They're registered in New York. I brought up a satellite image of the address they have listed on the export application. It looks like a warehouse on the docks south of Buffalo."

"Wait a second," Daniel said as he flipped through the folders on his tablet. He clicked on the folder marked "Current Donors." He tapped his screen a few more times, bringing up a list of names, people, corporations – "Here it is: Buffalo Security Consulting, Ltd." Daniel immediately regretted saying this out loud.

"What? Where are you looking, Daniel?" Melanie asked.

"Uh, I have to get back with you."

"Don't you dare bring me into this and just hang up on me. You just found something. I can hear it in your voice."

"Listen, Melanie. I'm not going back on my word, but you'll have to trust me. Give me some time, and I'll call you back."

"You better," she threatened.

Daniel ended the call. He was still looking at the list of donors to Senator Larkin's re-election campaign. He sorted the list by company. There were two donors who worked for BSC, Ltd., and each had donated $1 Million. Not insignificant, but not among the Senators largest contributors either.

13

"The advancement and diffusion of knowledge is the only guardian of true liberty." —James Madison

Daniel entered a small bar about five miles south of Arlington. The only reason he knew this place existed was that he had a senator followed who was having an affair, an affair that he later used as leverage in negotiating support for a bill that Brianna sponsored. The senator had met his mistress here and would go across the street to some sleazy hotel to affirm their relationship. At the time, Daniel thought it was a reasonable place for a hole-and-corner meeting.

After scanning the bar, he spotted Ben at a far corner table looking impatient—as he should. Daniel was thirty minutes late. Ben was dressed in dirty jeans with a brown leather jacket over a black t-shirt, fitting in more than Daniel in his black suit and tie. He approached the table and sat down.

"About time," Ben said irascibly as he took a drink from his beer, the condensation from the bottle dripping down the inside of his hand. "You sounded scared shitless when you called to change the meeting. I'm assuming from the anxiety in your voice that there was a good reason for it."

"I don't want to stay very long, Ben, so I'm going to give this to you quickly. Do you know what SLOT is?"

"I've heard of it, but nobody has any real evidence it exists," Ben replied. "Some kind of loose organization of government officials trying to crimp the power of Jaxon Warren."

"Well, they do exist, are active, and the most influential member is Brianna Larkin."

"Whoa. I'm assuming we're off the record?"

"Of course." Daniel instinctively looked over the nearby patrons to make certain none were giving their conversation too much attention. "I cannot be associated with anything I'm about to tell you. But I'll give you the sources to corroborate the story." Daniel hated dropping names, but would give the minimal in order to get the story in print.

Ben reached inside his leather flight jacket pocket and retrieved his tablet. He unfolded it and began typing notes. "Don't let me stop you, my friend."

"Brianna started the group shortly after coming to Washington," Ben explained. "She hates the man. Blamed him for her firing years ago despite the fact that she was a small player in a large organization. She was out to get him from the start."

"She kept her activities with the group secret from me although I knew it existed. I stuck to the legitimate tasks of running the office, raising money, and getting her re-elected. Over time, I realized she was obsessed with getting Warren, to a point that I felt it would bring down her career one way or another. So I decided to hedge my bet. And this next part does not show up in the story. Got it?"

"Got it," Ben said and stopped taking notes.

"I contact Jaxon Warren and tell him what's going on. He asks me to keep him informed and that he'll take care of me if anything happens. So now I've got my bases covered, and I'm protected."

"You're playing a dangerous game, Daniel. Can you imagine what she'll do if she finds out?" Ben asked.

"This is how Washington works, and you know it, Ben. Anyway, early today Jaxon Warren sends me a list of serial numbers, from some high-tech rifle that is produced here in the

U.S. He says Mitakus is using them. He asks me to trace them, so I do."

"And?" Ben asks.

"It turns out they were originally purchased by the Warren Foundation and sold to a company called Buffalo Security Consulting. Somehow, I don't know how, they made it from BSC to North Calidum. BSC is a donor to Brianna's PAC and re-election campaign. So, I dig a little deeper: BSC has a single unoccupied office in an empty warehouse. That is it. No sign of any personnel. It looks like a dummy corporation."

Ben put two and two together. "So SLOT is running the guns through this dummy corporation, selling them to a known terrorist, and the profits are ending up in Senator Larkin's re-election campaign?" Ben started to laugh. "Oh, this is precious. This is huge."

"Yeah, it's great, Ben," Daniel said sarcastically. "Except for the thousands of people dying in South Calidum from facing the working end of those rifles."

"Yeah, didn't think about that," Ben said apologetically.

"I'll send you the list of donations from BSC. You confirm that it's a true dummy. I'll also send you the report from DOJ with the transactions on the rifles. I have a good idea who is in SLOT." At this, Daniel grabbed Ben's tablet and typed the names in. "You can scare the crap out of them with this story, Ben. Somebody's going to start thinking about their own ass and give you the players in exchange for their anonymity."

"What are you going to tell Jaxon Warren?" Ben asked.

"I'm going to tell him he has a traitor in his organization," replied Daniel.

***

Jaxon Warren slammed his fist against the table, which shook beneath his frustration. He stormed out of his tent looking for Ray and found him in the command tent. He asked him to step outside so they could talk in private.

"The rifles are ours!" he told Ray.

"What the hell are you talking about?"

"I had the serial numbers traced. Some corporation purchased them from us, Ray, the Foundation. And then sold them to that animal!"

Ray was shocked. He stood, making the calculations in his mind. "There are only four people, at the most, in the organization who could have arranged that; two of whom are standing right here. That narrows it down to Wendt or maybe one of his assistants."

"Kellen would never do that. I've known him for thirty-five years, Ray. It must be somebody in his office. Let's get him on a video conference."

They went back inside the command tent, and Ray moved to the communication panel. He spent several minutes on the phone before moving back to Jaxon's chair.

"I woke him up. He's going to login to the secure network from home. The call will come right to the main screen," Ray said.

Jaxon walked to the front and stood directly before the main screen. He was working to calm his breathing. He was angry but knew that he had to resolve the issue with a clear head, not with his emotions. He waited four minutes, which seemed like twenty. Finally, Kellen's face appeared on the screen looking a bit disheveled. His hair was matted down and his eyelids were heavy.

"Kellen," Jaxon said in an even and calm tone. "I need you to explain to me how rifles purchased by the Foundation were sold to a company called Buffalo Security Consulting."

"Very simply, Jaxon. I authorized it," Kellen said.

"Why would you do something like that, Kellen?"

"It was a simple cash flow issue, Jaxon. The Foundation runs on donations from millions of people throughout the world. Those donations fund us, but during mission preparations, we occasionally require a large amount of cash to fund a purchase, such as equipment, food, fuel, etc. I don't need to explain this to you, Jaxon. It's the same thing you've done for many years with

MEC. To answer your question, we needed some cash for food, so I sold the rifles to a company that supplies domestic law enforcement, BSC."

Jaxon scanned Kellen's face and could find no indication of malice. Kellen had just done something incredibly careless. He walked to the back of the tent and sat in his chair. He leaned forward and put his hands over his face. He looked up at Kellen who appeared a bit dismayed. "BSC is a dummy company, Kellen. They sold the rifles to an arms dealer who in turn sold them to Mitakus, who used them against the South Calidumese and the Foundation. We have three wounded people who were shot by rifles you sold to BSC."

Kellen let out a short, nervous laugh. "That's impossible, Jaxon. They're illegal to export!"

"You screwed up, Kellen. You didn't research the company well enough," Jaxon said, ending the call.

LOPER

14

"But when the blast of war blows in our ears,
Then imitate the action of the tiger,
Stiffen the sinews, summon up the blood,
Disguise fair nature with hard-favored rage;
Then lend the eye a terrible aspect."

William Shakespeare
Henry V

J axon awoke to banging on his tent door. He slowly raised his body from his cot, threw his stiff legs off the side, and planted his feet on the floor. The sun was shining through his screened window; he had overslept. He liked to be up before dawn to plan the day's activities with the department heads. But, that would not happen today. He pulled his nylon khakis over his legs and threw on his chambray desert cargo shirt. After slipping into his utility boots he walked through the conference room and opened the door to find a very excited Ray Bakis.

"A couple of them broke at about 0300," Ray said. Jaxon assumed he meant the NoC's. He motioned for Ray to come in and sit down at the table.

Jaxon sat down and Ray followed. "The contractors were able to get a description of Mitakus's command vehicle and his convoy as well as the approximate location. The convoy we hit was to meet Mitakus's party at a specific location and receive its deployment orders from there. As soon as I was notified, I sent three reconnaissance drones up to start searching. I'm sure they moved locations when they realized the convoy was hit, but we can easily estimate their rate of speed and narrow the search path."

"Good work, Ray. Give my compliments to the contractors," Jaxon said.

"Will do."

"I'll come over to the command tent in a few minutes." Jaxon reached over and slapped Ray on the shoulder. "This could be our day, eh?"

"I also ordered an attack drone to be heavily armed. Once we find him, we'll get it airborne." Ray stood up. "I'll be in the command tent." He walked out with the gleam of victory in his eye.

***

Mitakus and Bakri had finished finalizing their plan with the team that was sent out the previous evening. They had since driven all night as they knew the drones would be looking for them. Bakri had reminded the team that their mission may be their only hope of victory. They would know by the end of the day.

"Today we will assure our victory, cousin," Mitakus bragged as he turned away from the video screen that had just carried the image of the team leader.

"If our mission succeeds," Bakri said.

"Always the pessimist," Mitakus laughed.

"The mission is not certain. There is always risk. I give it a fifty percent chance of success."

"God will insure our success, Bakri!" Mitakus shouted.

Bakri knew better. If there was a god, he would certainly not support an activity such as this.

***

Jaxon walked into the command tent, which was a beehive of activity. Two additional screens had been erected at the front of the room, a total of three now showed the video and radar images from the drones. Jaxon took his seat near the rear of the tent. Ray was engrossed with the images as he stood close to the screens, not even turning when Jaxon walked in. He wanted this just as badly as Jaxon.

Ray turned around after a few minutes and approached Jaxon. "The contractors also got the communication frequencies from one of the NoC's. We should be able to hack in and get two-way audio/visual established."

"Excellent. I would very much like to have a chat with Mitakus," Jaxon stated.

Ray returned to work while Jaxon sat and watched the drone images on the large screens. He desperately wanted to put an end to this war. A private, charitable organization defeating an army was unheard of, and Jaxon was calculating the fallout. He had been battling the government for years, defending himself, the MEC, and the Foundation from attacks launched by those claiming he had too much power, too much money. He had been accused of many things including creating an organization to control all global business. Nothing could have been farther from the truth. Jaxon had worked hard to build strong relationships with suppliers, customers, foreign governments, all in the name of economic prosperity for all. He worked with suppliers to make certain workers were paid good wages and distributors to insure energy remained cheap, spurring growth in areas of the world that struggled before the Enlightenment. It was good for the country, the world, and for him.

"We're ready to hack in at your command, Jaxon," Ray stated.

"Put it on screen, please." Jaxon stood, ready to address his enemy. The large display would receive audio and visual from Mitakus's command vehicle as well as transmit Jaxon's image and voice. The screen jumped and flashed as the hacking proceeded. The image from inside the command vehicle took shape; there were several soldiers sitting at screens that faced outward, perpendicular to the main display through which Jaxon was looking. To the rear of the vehicle sat Mitakus, who was leaning over a table consulting with a large, bald man, perhaps one of his aides.

"Mitakus!" Jaxon shouted out.

All eyes in the command vehicle shot to the display with a look of surprise. Mitakus stood, as well as his aid, and walked forward to the screen. Mitakus's stance stiffened, and he crossed his arms upon his recognition of Jaxon Warren. The bald man looked worried. Jaxon had achieved the initial response he was seeking.

"I've destroyed your supply lines, and I have no intention of stopping until you leave South Calidum. I've hacked into your communications and have drones honing in on your vehicle. Any movement by your forces other than that of retreat will lead to its, and your, destruction," Jaxon stated. "Your move, Mitakus. Make it a smart one."

"You think you're quite smart, don't you, Mr. Warren? My forces will never retreat. We will continue our offensive to take back what is rightfully ours, and you will leave Calidum in defeat or a body bag. Either way, I do not care."

"I'm giving you a chance to save your men, I have no interest in killing them. You can retreat with your army intact," Jaxon said.

"Our intentions have not changed, Mr. Warren. And it is I who advise you to retreat and leave my country before it is too late for you and your invaders," Mitakus said.

"I'll give you some time to reconsider your position." *That should give us enough time to find you.* "I strongly suggest that you think deeply regarding your situation. You'll hear from me again." Jaxon motioned to end the call, and the screen went dead.

***

Suzen exited the security fence that surrounded the compound and assumed her position on the trough line. Despite the early hour, there were SoC's lined up for food already. She had seen Jaxon storming to the command tent as she exited the mess tent earlier that morning with Will. Will was curious to know what was happening and followed him, telling Suzen he would meet her later and help in the trough.

She could not see the command tent from the trough and could only imagine the activity going on inside as there was no outward indication. She turned back to her serving station as the lines opened after the shift change, doling out the tasteless mash of food to the SoC's who so desperately needed it.

The temperature rose sharply over the next several hours, Suzen's brow was in full sweat, and she focused on breathing threw her nose as she was instructed during her training; somehow it was supposed to keep you cooler by humidifying the air. As she gently wiped her brow with a towel, she noticed another small group approaching the trough.

She reached for her water bottle, which was heavy with condensation, and took a long drink. Setting the bottle down, she wiped her hand on her shirt and turned back to her duties. This group was unusual; they were all men, and did not look as battered as the others. All ten came to her station, bypassing the other two lines that were in operation.

***

Will stood to the side of the command tent, going unnoticed amidst the thick layer of tension that encompassed the room. He had watched, for quite some time now, the activities of the crew who were scurrying around nervously. The recon drones were all airborne as well as an armed drone. Jaxon was intently watching the video feedback from the drones.

"Ray, transfer control of the drone to me," Jaxon commanded. He removed a wireless module from the arm of his chair, a simple device, a touch pad for controlling the direction and speed of the aircraft on top, underneath a small ball for controlling altitude. The face of the controller also contained a blue and red button, each with a plastic flip cover. The blue button armed the drone, the red button fired the missiles, one at a time, from beneath the drones wings.

"Get that S.O.B. back on the air," Jaxon commanded again.

The flaps of the entry door parted and in walked Squid.

"Squid, get the hell out of here. We're hot," ordered Ray.

"It's important, Ray. I'll be outside," Squid replied with equal determination. He then turned and exited the way he came in.

"It damn well better be. Jaxon?" Ray asked.

"Go ahead. We're good in here," Jaxon responded. Ray exited in pursuit of Squid.

Outside Squid was waiting for Ray. Squid must have known it was risky going in the command tent. They had been placed on high alert since dawn. But apparently this couldn't wait.

"What the hell is it, Squid?" Ray asked.

"It's Wolfman. He's smelling something, and you know how he is," Squid said tensely. His experience had taught him that Wolfman's nose was true, but he had been trained to rely on facts and observations.

"That's it? That's all you got?" Ray shot back.

"When was the last time he smelled something and he was wrong, Ray?"

Ray continued to look Squid in the eye for a moment. "Come with me." Ray took off at a slow trot in the direction of the medical tent.

Ray spotted Wolfman upon entering the med tent. The room only contained three men recovering from the other night's activities and Wolfman was the only one sitting up on his cot looking like he was about to vomit his last meal. Ray walked over with Squid right behind him.

"What is it, Wolfman?" Ray asked.

"I don't know for sure, Ray, but something is up," he warned nervously. "It started about fifteen minutes ago, woke me out of my slumber. I had to grab me a bed pan else I would have vomited all over the floor."

Ray had some experience with Wolfman's senses, and they were good.

"I've never seen a reaction this strong from him, Ray," Squid said.

"Keep in mind he's been shot, Squid. Do you think that could be affecting you, Wolfman?"

"Could be. But I'm certain that something real bad is nearby."

Ray put his hand on Wolfman's shoulder and gently pushed him down onto the cot. "You lay back down and rest. Let us take care of any threats."

Ray turned to the exit and motioned for Squid to follow. Once out in the sunlight, Ray turned to Squid. "We're already on high alert. All the drones are out right now, so we can't do any aerial surveillance. Go to the watch tent and alert the security staff to be extra vigilant. Is there anybody in the trough line?"

"Yeah, when I left the tent this morning, I saw a large crowd in line. They must have been there since before light."

"I'm heading there now. That's where we are most vulnerable. When you're done in the watch tent, come join me," Ray commanded.

"Yes, sir," Squid responded and quickly trotted off to carry out his orders. Ray headed for the trough line. When he arrived, the situation was worse than he had expected. There were some two hundred or so in line, maybe another two hundred scattered about eating. He radioed in to the Sargent of the Guard to send four reinforcements to the trough line as Squid returned.

"I'll stay here. Get over to the other end." Ray pointed to the opposite end of the trough line. "Be mindful." Squid nodded and was off.

***

Suzen doled out food to the dust-covered woman in front of her who she had mistaken for a man due to her size. She didn't look all that famished, and her eyes were intense, not the dazed look she regularly would see from the SoC's who had gone without food for days. She scooped up another ladle for the next hungry SoC when the woman suddenly threw her plate into Suzen's face and jumped across the table. Suzen instinctively closed her eyes and blocked the plate with her hands. She bent down to hit the emergency alarm button which was attached to the post immediately beneath, and to the right, of her station. But as she reached out, an arm wrapped around and then squeezed in on her neck, her throat resting in the crook of the woman's arm. She tried to pull away, even scratching at the woman's forearm, but to no avail as the woman dragged her along the ground. Suzen didn't realize it, but she was being used as a human shield. Around her, a half dozen other Foundation volunteers were receiving the same treatment.

Suzen watched helplessly as chaos erupted around her. Fighting had broken out among the SoC's, or was it NoC's? At this point, she wasn't sure. She could see Ray about fifty meters away raising his rifle in her direction. She quickly concluded that she was in a particularly nasty spot.

As the NoC's dragged their shields to the security fence that separated the trough line from Tent City, four of the group huddled in their midst, two of which pulled wire cutters from underneath their ragged clothing. They began cutting and within less than thirty seconds had cut a large hole in the fence and the two NoC's who had done no work so far, jumped through at a full sprint.

Suzen heard a sharp crack as the arm loosened around her neck, and she was pulled to the ground by the woman's weight. She frantically scurried out from under the limp arm and turned to see a crater where the woman's face had been. She looked up to see several people with rifles, including some holding hostages as she had been a few moments ago. The head of a man nearby, holding a large set of wire cutters, exploded, a mixture of gray matter and blood spraying across her face. She screamed. The sound erupted from her throat with a savagery whose origins were unknown to her. She didn't think to scream. She wasn't thinking at all. Everything was happening so fast around her she was just reacting. The man's body fell directly in front of her with its arms and legs flopping, stopping only after the nerves lost the battle to stay alive. Another man holding wire cutters dove for the ground but was dead by the time he hit as another crack sounded and a crimson stain appeared on the clothing covering his back.

Suzen could see men running inside the camp, hunched over as shots continued to ring out.

***

Ray was in a kneeling position, holding his laser steadily on each target, and firing judiciously. Squid was doing the same. They were both being careful as the targets were holding human shields. Ray recognized Will's friend Suzen but pushed it out of his mind immediately to focus on his targets. As the bodies fell, he clearly saw two NoC's pass through the security fence at a full sprint. They disappeared behind a tent before he could get a shot off. He'd have to catch them on foot, so Ray took off running.

Ray ran inside the security fence and by two tents before turning left into the alley that separated the rows just in time to see the two men. He raised his rifle and fired, hitting one of the NoC's square in the back of the head. The other NoC turned right. Ray increased his effort, but upon turning up, he saw the man cut left. Ray pursued. The man's head was bobbing around as if he was looking for something.

"Son of a—" Ray blurted out. He reached up and tapped his microphone in his shirt collar. "Evacuate the command tent! Now!" he screamed with what little air was left in his lungs.

***

The screen took shape and revealed Mitakus sitting at his own command chair, listening to a communication.

"Mitakus!" Jaxon called out. "Have you come to your senses? Or have you chosen the path of self-destruction?"

Will heard several shots fired from outside the tent. He assumed it was the firing range but realized his mistake as the camp was on high alert and all firearm bearing special ops personnel would be on patrol or in fighting holes.

"It is you who will be destroyed. I have defeated the great Jaxon Warren," Mitakus replied.

"Look at the bottom corner of your screen, Mitakus. That is the video feed from a fully armed drone flying just outside your command vehicle," Jaxon warned. The image, which Will could see on one of the monitors, clearly showed the command vehicle with a red box around it, indicating the drone's radar was locked on, and a missile fired would be certain to hit the target.

We got him, Will thought. He looked back at Uncle Jax who raised the control device in his hand and lifted the cover from the blue button.

Something crackled from the speaker in the command tent, someone was yelling something.

"Evac- the -mand tent! -ow!"

It sounded like Ray but Will could not make out what he was saying. There was too much interference. He looked over to Uncle Jax whose gaze had not wandered from the display.

With fury motion, the back of the tent flew inward with a roar that all but crushed Will's eardrums.

***

Mitakus broke out into a loud, evil laugh as the image of Jaxon Warren on his screen turned into flying debris and swirling dust. His men had accomplished their mission: Jaxon Warren was dead. Mitakus thought of the glory this would bring him.

"This is an example of my great military expertise," Mitakus sung as Bakri continued to watch the screen. Mitakus continued his celebration until he was interrupted. Bakri cried out. "Mitakus!"

Mitakus turned around to see the source of Bakri's concern and followed his eyes to the display. As the dust was settling, an image began to appear. Mitakus moved closer in an effort to bring clarity to the image he was seeing. Slowly, a dust-covered young man took shape. In his right hand, he held the drone control. His left hand was thrust forward with his middle finger extended in a last salute to the ruler of North Calidum.

Mitakus watched Will press the "arm" button on the controller, knowing in his mind what was happening. Will pressed the "fire" button next. Mitakus watched in disbelief.

A sharp stab of fear shot through Mitakus body in that last moment of his life on earth. Each of his atrocities that had accumulated over a lifetime of violence and hate were realized in this very moment. And the fear was the realization that he may be about to answer for them.

***

Will watched as the Noc's command vehicle erupted into flames, metal and equipment flying into the air. Will fired another missile, just to make sure. He then dropped the remote and began to look around him. It had all happened so quickly, the explosion, the confusion, and then suddenly his instincts took hold, he searched through the dust, found the remote, and completed the mission.

"Uncle Jax," he whispered. And he immediately began to look for his uncle. The front of the tent was unharmed, it must have been a small explosive device, he guessed. He looked through the dust that was settling, and began to find bodies. The first one he flipped over he recognized as the woman who sat at the communication console; she was dead. He moved back farther, frantically trying to picture the location of the command chair, surely in splinters now. He found another body, it was Uncle Jax. Will's exaltation at finding him immediately was replaced by horror as he saw the thick piece of wood sticking up through Uncle Jax's stomach.

"Wi – Will," Uncle Jaxon said, releasing Will's name with short, gasping breaths. His eyes were wide open and stuck out like moons from his face which was covered in dust.

"We did it, Uncle Jax! I found the remote and killed him, he's dead!" Will exclaimed, wanting Uncle Jax to know they had won.

Uncle Jax's face grimaced into what Will thought was a smile, which he could see more in his eyes than on his face.

"Ray!" Will screamed out, over his shoulder. He turned his face back to Uncle Jax. "You're going to be ok, Uncle Jax. The medic's will be here any second."

"No, thi..this is it, Will." Jaxon was struggling to speak.

Will didn't understand. The medics would be here any moment, he was sure of it. "Tell Jeanna I love her, and I will see her again someday."

"Don't do this," Will lamented. "Please, Uncle Jax."

Jaxon was forcing his words with the last few breaths he had in his body. "Listen to me, Will. It's all yours now. I love you, always have." And taking in a breath, deeply, knowing it was his last, and wanting the message to be clear, Jaxon Warren said, "Make the world a better place."

Will watched the life drain from Jaxon's eyes, blurred by the tears he was shedding uncontrollably. He laid his head down on Jaxon's chest and wept.

Will felt two strong arms grab him by the shoulders. It was Ray pulling him away as the medical staff swarmed the tent to attend to those who were injured. Will stumbled, and his legs began to give out. Suzen rushed up as Will lost consciousness and went limp. She grabbed his arm.

"Is he ok, Ray?" She pleaded through tears muddied by the dirt and blood on her face.

"We'll find out. Let's get him to the medical tent," Ray said. "Medic!" he yelled. "I want a medic here now." A doctor emerged and followed them to the medical tent. The doctor took over for Ray as they laid Will on a table to begin his examination.

Ray pulled Suzen out of the tent. "Let's give the doc some room. Wait out here. I have to get the drones back here and re-establish security. Come find me when you know something. Anything!" he ordered, and walked out of the tent.

15

"Nothing except a battle lost can be half so melancholy as a battle won." —Duke of Wellington

W ill grimaced as a pain shot through his side. He had three bruised ribs which stung with each breath. Sneezing or coughing, which occurred daily from all the sand blowing around and making its way up his nostrils, would cause him to double over. Yet another reason to not get a good night's sleep.

It had been two days since the attack on the compound. A group of NoC's had disguised themselves as refugees and stormed Tent City. Two of them were suicide bombers who wore vests packed with old C-4. One of them was killed before he reached the target, but the other got through and detonated his vest just short of the command tent. "If I could have ran just a little faster," Ray had muttered, shaking his head.

The following day Ray had ordered the recon drones back up in the air to patrol the battle field. The NoC's were already withdrawing. Leaderless, the unit commanders had taken control of the beleaguered army and retreated in defeat, encountering violent harassment by the SoC's as they made their way back north. In an effort to prevent any future attacks, Ray ordered the attack drones and gunships to fire on all military equipment, tanks, artillery, etc.

Will was waiting with Ray on the tarmac of the air strip under the intense sun. A U.S. military jet was landing and onboard was General Janis Natts, USA, and commander of North Africa Regional Forces. Just hours after the news broke that Jaxon Warren had been killed in Calidum, the U.S. military had radioed the communications tent with word that General Natts would be arriving with her staff; no additional information was given and Ray did not appear surprised.

The jet, not too different than Uncle Jax's in appearance other than that it was painted green, landed and circled around in front of Ray and Will. The french-fry smell of jet biofuel drifting over them as it came to a halt. The hatch descended and the General, followed by three staff members, emerged into the hot desert air. Ray led the way to the aircraft and Will followed closely.

"Hello, General," Ray greeted, with a sense of recognition. "Welcome to Calidum. Better late than never," he added sarcastically.

"Hello, Ray," The General said in what Will thought was a rather deep voice for a woman. "Sarcasm accepted. I fully realize this was our mission, not yours. But you know I can't move without orders. And the politicians were too busy fighting over who was going to pay for it rather than consider the lives that were being decimated," the General replied, bluntly.

"I know," Ray replied sympathetically. "So what are you doing here now, General?"

The General looked at Will. "Who's the kid?"

"The *kid*," Ray warned, "is Will Warren, Jaxon's nephew. And he's done more in the last few weeks to bring peace to Calidum than the world has done in the last decade. So make sure you treat him with respect, General."

"No offense. I didn't know," the General said apologetically to Will. "I had a lot of respect for your uncle, young man. He was one of the great ones." Will suspected the General was trying to somehow console him. It didn't work but, he appreciated the effort. Ray took a moment to summarize the last several weeks for the General. Will attempted to tune it out, not wanting to relive it.

"Listen, Ray. I respect you and what your team has accomplished here in Calidum, but we're moving in. Your humanitarian people can stay, there's plenty of bellies to feed, but your special ops team has to go. We'll take that over. I've received orders to setup a base for long term support. It looks like the politicians have come to their senses and realized these mines need protection."

"Good. Our ops team could use a break."

"We'll be landing planes and helicopters within the next few hours," the General stated.

"Sure. I'll call in the drones and move them into the hangars. It's all yours."

"Thanks, Ray" the General said, and turned to Will, reaching out to shake his hand. Will obliged. "And thank you, young man. I'm sure I'll hear your story. If you earned Ray's respect, it must be a good one."

**

Will and Suzen gazed into the late morning light which was brightly shining on the flag-draped coffin of Jaxon Warren. Four men from the special ops team moved it into the shadow and then raised the pine box into the belly of the APEX. Will would escort his uncle's body back to Michigan for burial. Suzen reached over and grabbed Will's hand. It felt comfortable and his pain eased slightly.

"You can come back with me, if you like?" Will asked.

"No, I want to stay here and finish the mission. I owe it to your uncle." She turned as the casket disappeared into the cargo hold. "He was a great man."

"When will I see you again?" Will asked.

Suzen smiled. "Oh, someday, I'm sure." She leaned over and kissed him. "That will have to hold you until then. Goodbye for now, Will Warren." And she walked away.

Will grinned. Then looked back to the plane and slowly made his way to the open hatch.

16

"Nature arms each man with some faculty which enables him to do easily some feat impossible to any other, and thus makes him necessary to society. ... Society can never prosper, but must always be bankrupt, until every man does that which he was created to do."

—Ralph Waldo Emerson
The Conduct of Life (Wealth)

Will stood motionless in front of the large burgundy door. He was fully aware of what lay on the other side and he wished to elude or somehow bypass that which rested dormant in the den of Riverside. The depth of his own grief was plundering his strength, and his sleep. The jet lag added to his misery. It was all he could bear; the additional pain certainly carried by Aunt Abby and Aunt Jeanna would nudge him off the edge of the cliff that he so delicately balanced.

It was eight months prior, that he stood on this porch, having been called into the house from his leisurely swim by Uncle Jax. That day had launched the adventure that brought him full circle and to this moment. Just as Uncle Jax had foretold, that meeting was the epicenter of Will's tripartite life, it was his event for which he would measure life before and after that point.

As he was driven to town from the Foundation, he spotted the large granite sign that proudly stood firm and welcomed all to New Lothrop; he asked the driver to pull over.

"I'll walk from here" he had said.

He walked through town, down Easton Road, across the creek, and back up to the old section of town. As he walked, he started thinking about what to say to Aunt Abby and Aunt Jeanna, but he quickly gave up on that train of thought as it produced only ineffective results. He was distracted by a sense of alienation, as if something had separated his link to these streets that he had walked a thousand times. He stopped on the corner of Orchard, and looked around the half-empty streets; only a few cars were scattered about. The depths of the breach he felt as he stood in his hometown did not rattle Will, too much had happened. He had been shaken to a point in which he had developed a mental callous. Not a disassociation, he had not withdrawn from reality; in fact, his senses were as sharp as ever. As he turned and walked on Orchard Street, he could hear the wind blowing through the branches of the American elms and bur oaks that were sprouting buds.

There were no reporters or vigils being held in front of Riverside. Uncle Jax was not a rock star or television personality. He was simply a great man who had accomplished much in his lifetime, including saving the country. Uncle Jax's death was all over the news, including speculations of what would become of his empire given the fact that he had no direct heirs. But Will had avoided the media coverage as best he could, which is to say, completely and intentionally.

A cool spring breeze was now blowing against his back, as if the hand of Uncle Jaxon was gently nudging him. He reached up and rapped three times on the door, as the chimes had not sounded upon his approach. Aunt Abby answered. Her face was jaded and life-weary, the loss of Uncle Jax weighing heavily on her features. She took a step forward and gave Will a strong hug, after which she gently took his hand and led him into the grand house, shutting the door behind them.

"I'm glad you're home, Will," Abby said, with obvious concern in her face.

"I'm ok, Aunt Abby," he said, guessing her real question. "I still feel a bit numb, I guess. How are you?" *That was a stupid question*, he thought, feeling completely dumb and awkward.

"The same," she lied. "It's so hard to believe he's gone. Come with me, we're in the parlor." Abigail took his hand and led him forward to the center of the house on the main floor.

Will followed, his palms sweating more than he would like, Aunt Abby surely sensing his anxiety. He was unsure how he could offer comfort to anybody right now, but he knew the right thing to do was to be here, no matter how inept he would be at consoling Aunt Jeanna or Aunt Abby. As he emerged into the normally well lit room, which was dimmed, he saw Aunt Jeanna standing on the far side of the large, round room below a grand painting of Washington crossing the Delaware. She was speaking to an older man who Will did not recognize. But as he approached them, the face of the man became more recognizable, it had been cleaned up a bit, the hair combed. *It's Abner Troffe,* Will thought with astonishment. She motioned with both her hands to Will.

Aunt Jeanna looked worn, a dozen years older than he saw her just this last December. Her face seemed to hang around her eyes like the leaves of a willow. Will walked up to her and gently enfolded her, expressing his sympathy.

"I'm sorry, Aunt Jeanna. I'm sorry that I couldn't save him," Will choked, holding his gaze deep into her eyes. He wanted her to see his pain, his remorse.

Aunt Jeanna took hold of his shoulders. "It was his time, Will. I'll miss him dearly. The bareness of a world without my Jaxon feels overwhelming. But he was doing what he loved and what he had committed his life to: 'Making the world a better place for having lived in it.'" She held Will's gaze for a moment, a look of uncertainty, grief, and distress. She continued, "He was sick, Will. I suppose you figured that out for yourself. He didn't want anyone to know. That was why we were here in August, getting the diagnosis, and dealing with it. His days on this earth were numbered, one way or the other."

"He never said anything. His body may have been deteriorating, but certainly not his mind, nor his commitment," Will said.

"I think it would take a greater instrument than what nature has in her toolbox to tear down the mind of Jaxon Warren," Aunt Abby added, stoically.

"Will, look at me." Jeanna raised Will's chin as his gaze had drifted downward. He looked up into her light blue eyes, the sparkle gone, they looked more like a cloudy fall day. "These last few months have been hard on you, Aryn's death, the terrible things you saw in Calidum, and now Uncle Jaxon's death. You've handled it well, and for good reason. You're special, Will."

Will had heard this many times, from Aunt Abby mostly, and he was a bit tired of it.

"I'm not all that special, Aunt Jeanna."

"Yes, Will, you are. We have some things to tell you that are going to be hard to hear, for they will affect the path that you need to choose, the decisions you make in your life, and most importantly, how you think about yourself."

"I don't know how much more I can handle right now, Aunt Jeanna," Will uneasily stated.

"More than you can imagine, Will," Aunt Jeanna assured him.

"Will, this is Abner Troffe. I suppose you know of him," Aunt Jeanna said. Will nodded.

In a shaky voice, the unsettled Abner spoke. "Will, there's some things I need to tell you about your parents."

Will turned to Aunt Abby and Aunt Jeanna in turn, each assuring him with their eyes. He returned his attention to Abner.

Abner spoke slowly, as he was not accustomed to breathing, let alone speaking, in the presence of others. "As I'm sure you are aware, your Uncle Jaxon and I were friends. That to which you are likely unaware, is that I recruited, and worked closely with your parents, Edison and Marie. Your parents were brilliant,

Will. Both were top notch biochemical engineers, the best in their field. A bit intolerable at times, but only because the rest of us, even your uncle, felt intellectually insufficient in their presence." Abner walked to the bar at the edge of the room, poured a drink of something, and drained the glass before continuing. "We built the lab together at MEC, practically made it our home. We were a great team, played off each other's intellect, and produced, well, you are well aware of the results. One evening, the four of us, your parents, myself, and your Uncle Jaxon, stood around a small fire where we would occasionally congregate at the old Dvorak Homestead. We had achieved a level of success that was almost frightening, and we could all easily see the implications of our efforts. We were bursting with confidence, as comes with such a great deal of success, a little too much in hindsight."

Abner sat down, as if the burden of his tale was too much for his unsteady legs.

"None of us had children, and we mused on the fact that it was a shame. The conversation took an odd turn; it erupted into a discourse on genetically engineering a child, from the DNA of the four of us. I'm not even sure how it started, a jest, a serious proposal; but the idea took hold of us."

Will's body felt as shaky as Abner's. He had barely noticed Aunt Abby guide him down on the thick couch.

Abner continued, "The next day we started on our design. Most of the technology existed, and we arrogantly thought we could make it work." Abner dropped his head, and then raised it to look at Will. "We first created an artificial womb, just a clear plastic tank, filled it with amniotic fluid, and kept it at body temperature. We enriched our germ cells and an ovum from Marie, creating an embryo that attached to the walls of our artificial womb. I had developed the machines that simulated the placenta. We set up two systems in case one failed. To our surprise, both succeeded. After watching them both grow in our test environment for several months, and gaining confidence that we had succeeded, we named them. The girl, after the legendary female with the body of a goddess and a mind of a genius, Aryn we called her. The boy, we named after William Shakespeare."

Oh no, this could not be possible, Will thought, the level of shock rising in his system like an ignited fire. This tale tore through his mind, stretching it, the seams desperately holding. But they held, as much as he hoped they would break and give him some relief.

"We provided the fetuses with gene therapy during this same period," Abner continued. "The idea was that it would lead to improved cognitive function. In fact, you probably never recall being forgetful of something. And that is because we included an 'ingredient', if you will, for eidetic memory function."

"What are you saying? I'm some kind of robot or something?" Will asked, angrily.

"Oh no, Will," Aunty Abby answered. "You are quite human. One thing that you cannot instill through the genetic process is that of maturity and emotional intelligence. We couldn't tell you before now, you were not mature enough. And as you know, you are not perfect, Will. You'll make mistakes, poor decisions, but you'll likely make fewer of these than most others. You're not superhuman, either. Just think of yourself as having improved characteristics over others. But never forget that with experience comes wisdom. That you have to earn on your own."

"Edison and Marie were not your only parents, Will." Abner continued. "Jaxon and I are in the mix just as much, physically. Near the end of the process, I couldn't handle the pressure. Something popped in my mind like a muscle pressed too harshly in duty. I left the company, and soon after Edison and Marie were killed in the lab explosion. Jaxon gave you into the care of Abby, and Aryn to her parents, upon signing an oath of absolute secrecy. After Aryn died, and then Jaxon, I realized that I had to pull myself together as I knew it was important for you to hear this. I started taking my medication."

"Will," Aunt Jeanna broke in. "You are the sole heir to not only Uncle Jaxon, but of all the founders of MEC as well. Everything has been left to you, other than Riverside and more money than I'll ever need, that is. You now own the whole of the Warren Empire, the corporations and the Foundation. This was a decision Jaxon, I, and Abby, made several years ago. After Jaxon's diagnosis last summer, we realized we had to accelerate the plan. And that is why he spent the last seven months evaluating you. He knew it was a long shot in such a short time, but Jaxon was very happy with your progress."

Will was aghast, stunned. He had not thought about this since Suzen's offhand remark several months back. "But Aunt Jeanna," Will protested. "I'm not qualified in any way whatsoever to take over for Uncle Jax. That's insane. I can't do it."

Aunt Jeanna moved to sit next to him. "You are qualified, Will, more than any other human being on earth."

Will's jaw tightened. Something cracked within him, like a plate of glass in his mind. He began to feel a dull pain emanating from the center of his chest. He stood, his sadness now overshadowed with anger and confusion. He tried hard to remember something he had forgotten, looking for some flaw that would disprove what they had just revealed to him. But he found nothing. Without saying a word, he bolted down the hallway and out the front door. He leapt down the porch stairs and past the awaiting car. He was now at a full sprint running down Orchard Street. As he passed through the traffic circle, his heart was pounding through his chest and he was feeling dizzy. But he did not slow down. Not until he came abreast of the church, he heard the singing voices emanating from the morning worship service, its windows open to the cool spring morning.

Thou art giving and forgiving,
ever blessing, ever blest,
well-spring of the joy of living,
ocean depth of happy rest!
Thou our Father, Christ our brother,
all who live in love are thine;
teach us how to love each other,
lift us to the joy divine.

He stopped and, bending over and placing his hands on his knees, tried to catch his breath. His emotions began to subside, feeling the words of the carol as they calmed his mind.

> *Mortals, join the mighty chorus*
> *which the morning stars began;*
> *love divine is reigning o'er us,*
> *binding all within its span.*
> *Ever singing, march we onward,*
> *victors in the midst of strife;*
> *joyful music leads us sunward,*
> *in the triumph song of life.*

He couldn't hate Uncle Jax, not even in the least, nor Aunt Abby and Aunt Jeanna. And he was glad to finally know the truth, however unsettling. He walked slowly the short distance to his home, went into bed, and slept for twelve hours. He had matters to take care of tomorrow.

***

Will awoke to a light knock on his wall door, but did not open his eyes. He was groggy, and in his haze was contained a glimmer of hope that he had dreamt the mornings events. The knock came again but louder. Will surrendered and opened his eyes. The fog lifted and hope faded, no dream. Through the glass of the wall door he saw Ronni silhouetted against the night sky. How long had he slept? Ten, twelve hours? *It wasn't enough,* he thought. He labored to raise his body from the bed, walked over, and opened the door.

"Hi! I heard you were back." She stepped in and kissed him. Will was dispassionate. "Come on, let's get out of here and have some fun. I'll fill you in on everything that's happened at school why you were gone. You missed so much!"

That was it. That was all she said. No mention of Calidum. Will knew that the death of Mitakus and the withdrawal of his army was airing on every news station. Not to mention his uncle's death! Will needed an escape, so he gathered some clothes, put them on, and followed Ronni out to her car, still hazy from his sleep. He slipped into the passenger seat of the old sedan and Ronni peeled off down the street, going west out of town. The urgency of her flight from town removed what was left of Will's grogginess, and he was now fully alert. She turned south on Durand Road and babbled about meaningless gossip and topics, the words bypassing Will's mind, which was elsewhere in his new world. Ronni was part of a world that was now foreign to him. She looked as strange and altered as New Lothrop had that morning as he made the walk to Riverside.

Ronni turned west on 6 Mile Creek Road. The dirt and gravel stones flew up from the skidding of her tires. She was laughing and driving more erratically, having much more fun than Will. He turned to look at her and noticed, for the first time, that her eyes were glassed over, as if something other than Ronni was driving that car.

"Ronni, you better pull over and let me drive," Will said cautiously.

Ronni laughed. "Oh, come on. We've raced down this road a hundred times." She accelerated.

"Ronni, I'm serious. Slow down!" Will was commanding now, no more requests.

This only seemed to encourage her. "You are obviously in serious need of some fun." The tires slid across the loose gravel as she took the next two curves in the road and blew through the stop sign at Reed Road.

"Damn it, Ronni. Stop!"

Ronni lost control of the car and it spun around, stopping perpendicular to the road, its headlights illuminating a large oak tree. Ronni continued laughing as Will got out of the car. Will stood in front of the head lights, his shadow cast to comical proportions against the tree.

"That was fun!" Ronni exclaimed as she rolled out, the door groaning on its hinges. She stumbled up to Will.

"What the hell is wrong with you?" Will screamed.

"What is wrong with you?" Ronni screamed back, abruptly changing her mood.

"You could have killed us!"

"Lighten up. I was just having fun."

"I've got a reason to live, Ronni!"

As soon as the words left his lips, he wished that he could have retrieved them. He meant what he said, but he hated to hear himself say it. The statement hung in the air like a dense fog. They both stood in silence, staring at each other, each knowing the truth of what Will had just uttered.

Will broke the silence. "Ronni," he sighed, looking for the right words, or rather, the right sequence of words that would make amends. "I've changed. I'm not the guy you were dating last year."

"I don't want you to change," Ronni whimpered.

"Please, I need you to leave me alone," Will pleaded. "I wish you all the happiness in the world. But our lives have diverged, and it's time to go our separate ways."

"You bastard!" Ronni screamed and then sat down, cross legged in the road. She was now sobbing heavily. "All I wanted was to enjoy our senior year. Then you went and left me to go on some meaningless trip with your uncle. That was stupid, and you're an idiot. We had everything we needed right here."

"You had everything you needed, Ronni. Not me," Will explained as he sat down next to her. "I needed more. Something inside me knew there was a world out there that I fit into."

"But what about me?" Ronni cried. "What am I supposed to do?"

"You need to find your way, Ronni. Just like I did."

Ronni continued to sob, probably hoping for some offer of reconciliation from Will. But none came. After several minutes she stood, and Will followed. She looked at Will but made no movement. Will knew it would take her some time, but she would be ok.

"Goodbye, Ronni."

Will turned and walked into the darkness. He needed to think, and he had an important decision to make that was long overdue. He knew where to finally find the answer. Continuing his walk to Jacobs Road, he turned north. The night air was cool and seemed to sharpen his senses as he walked under the clear sky filled with an infinite number of stars. He heard a cow moan in the distance and the occasional rustle caused by a scurrying rodent. When he came to Easton Road, he cut across the field to the old Dvorak Homestead. He went into the shed, pocketed the matches, grabbed some paper, and an armful of wood. Then placing the contents into the fire pit, just like Uncle Jax, he made a fire and sat on a thick log.

The fire started a flow of memories: sitting on this very log with Aryn, talking about their dreams; the poisoned bodies in the village; of the screams coming from the men he had shot; the memory of Uncle Jax lying on the ground, the slab of wood sticking out of his abdomen; and of Mitakus and the look on his face when Will fired the missile. With each memory his chest tightened, the knot causing him to convulse. His mind was searching for a way out, a place to run and hide from the vivid images, but no haven could be found. The pain that had arisen in him now banged its head against the door of insanity, seeking escape from the burning memories. With a crash, the door gave way and Will's emotions erupted into a cry of despair. Yet the door revealed no derangement, only soft snowflakes that slowly floated, cooling his soul.

A few moments later, he had calmed and his mind cleared. A breeze whirled around the fire rustling the leaves. Will deeply inhaled, feeling free, from what he did not know. But his mind was seeing more clearly than just a moment ago.

Will sat for hours. The knowledge of this magical area was carried on the breeze that was rustling the trees, and Will continued to breathe it in deeply, reaching for each bit of its elixir. Realizing that Uncle Jax was what the world needed, but now it needed something more. Mankind has not created such beauty in this world by remaining on the path but rather by forging new ones, leaving the trail and seeking out new territories, either of the physical nature or of the mind. He visualized the paths that lay before him and made his decision.

The headlights of a car that was approaching the curve in the road flickered as the driver made his way across the uneven rural road and then turned into the long driveway. As the car drew closer, Will could make out the red coating of Dako's repainted sedan, which pulled to a stop. Dako emerged from the driver's side without saying a word and joined Will on the log next to the fire.

"How'd you know I was here?" Will asked.

"Ronni called, told me what happened. Remembering what you told me about the night Aryn died, I figured I would find you here," Dako said.

"It's not her fault. She is who she is. We were never in the same world. It just took me a while to figure it out."

"That's the way life happens sometimes, I guess."

"Uncle Jax left everything to me." Will was not going to reveal all he knew. Neither he nor Dako were ready for that. But he needed someone to talk to.

"I guess that makes you a very rich man, buddy. What are you going to do?"

"I think I feel the magic of this place now," Will said as he craned his neck, looking at his surroundings. "I don't know how to define it, but over the last few hours, I've felt a sense of wisdom in this place. And I believe it has been here for a very long time. For the first time in my life, Dako, I know exactly what I'm going to do. Take me home, will you?"

"Sure thing, buddy."

17

"The only guide to a man is his conscience; the only shield to his memory is the rectitude and sincerity of his actions. It is very imprudent to walk through life without this shield because we are so often mocked by the failure of our hopes and the upsetting of our calculations; but with this shield, however the fates may play, we march always in the ranks of honor."
—Sir Winston Churchill

Will stood on the landing that protruded into the Huron River, tightly grasping the ashen remains of Jaxon Warren. He wondered at the irony that such a great man, a man bigger than life, was reduced to the contents of an urn no bigger than a football. But only his body. For Uncle Jaxon's spirit could never be reduced nor could his imprint on this world. Behind him were Aunt Jeanna, Ray, Aunt Abby, Abner, and about two dozen others, several whom he recognized from the fire on Aryn's last night. It was a small group. Politicians had requested an invitation, but Aunt Jeanna had politely turned them away. There were a couple university presidents in the crowd, paying tribute to their most generous donor.

It was on this very spot that Uncle Jax had proposed to Aunt Jeanna, right here in Riverside Park. Aunt Jeanna had told the story of how Uncle Jax had held her hands in his, declaring that their friendship had turned into something deeper, love. He then asked for her hand in marriage.

Will had been given the duty of releasing the ashes from the urn. He could hear the voice of Uncle Jax. *Step forward, Will. It's time to let me go.* But it was probably just his imagination. He moved forward with hesitation, approaching the rail, shaking ever so slightly from the emotions he was feeling. This man had changed his life, taught him how the world worked, turned him into the man he was. He owed everything to Uncle Jax.

Will stood for a moment, reluctant to part with even the smallest physical remains of this great man. But he succumbed to the mission, stepped up to the railing, opened the urn, and hurled the remains of his cherished uncle into the slithering current of the river. The urn slipped from his fingers as if Uncle Jax were pulling away, telling Will that it was time for him to leave and that he was strong enough on his own. Will leaned against the rail, breathing shallowly and unable to suppress the pain of loss that he felt. The loss that can only be felt from those special people in your life, those who touch your heart and mind through some unique manner that leaves the deepest pit in your stomach. As he stood there in his anguish, two words slipped from his lips, "Thank You".

***

Will marched across the walkway adjacent to the Jefferson Memorial, his black, wool peacoat keeping him warm from the brisk, dawn temperature. A thin layer of fog had formed over the Tidal Basin, which rolled to the north and encompassed the grand obelisk, Washington's monument. The cherry blossoms had emerged from their winter hibernation and were near full bloom, lighting the area with a sense of midday. Up ahead, he could see Senator Brianna Larkin sitting on a park bench, her red full-length down coat contrasted against the morning backdrop. She was looking in the direction of the White House, which was just out of site at this level. Her four-man security team milled about in the immediate area. Their eyes were alert, always searching for the slightest deviation from the norm. One was watching Will closely as he approached.

After he had reunited with Ray at the Foundation, Will contacted the Senator's office. Daniel Vicksburg had arranged for the private meeting after an abundance of effort. Will motioned for Ray to stop short of the Senator as he continued toward the bench. Ray had been Will's constant companion the last several days, supplying Will with the mentoring and advice he needed in Uncle Jax's absence. But they had differed on their ideas for Senator Larkin.

Brianna was making no attempt to hide her feelings of satisfaction as she looked smugly over the basin, not altering her gaze as Will approached.

"You have ten minutes, young man," she told Will without taking her eyes off the basin. "What is so damn important that you had to call me away from my official duties?"

"I wouldn't worry about your official duties, Senator," Will warned as he remained standing. "I'm here to save you."

Brianna laughed. "Save me from what?"

"Yourself. I came here to tell you that you will call a press conference for tomorrow morning. At that time, you will announce your resignation from government service."

Brianna turned her head and looked at Will for the first time, smiling with astonishment. "You're as arrogant as your uncle. Resign? I'm about to be sworn in as Secretary of Defense." She turned away again. "But I'll play your little game. For what reason would I possibly resign?"

Will raised his hand in which he held a thick, large, manila envelope. "The day after tomorrow, this package will arrive at the FBI headquarters and the Post will run a corresponding story, front page. This package contains a detailed list of transactions and corroborated sworn testimony that ties you to the sale of weapons to a known terrorist, the animal formerly known as Mitakus."

Brianna's smile dimmed. Daggers sprung from her eyes as they narrowed on Will. "You're insane. I was not part of any such transactions."

"This same package will find its way into the hands of a certain arms dealer in Greece. A man whose link to this illegal arms deal, can only be traced through you, Senator. Now I'm only an eighteen year old kid, who hasn't even graduated high school yet, but my guess is he is going to want to sever that link."

"You're bluffing!" Brianna exclaimed, unable to hide the panic and anger that had crept into her voice. She had the look of a wild animal caught in a trap.

"And after you resign," Will continued, "Daniel Vicksburg will be appointed by the Governor of Michigan to fulfill your remaining term. He's been quite helpful to the Foundation."

The dread spread to Brianna's face as the realization of her situation took shape. "I've been playing this game longer than you have been alive. I...I have a lot of friends in this town, young man. You do not want to do battle with me. I will snap you like a twig!"

"Yes, your friends, SLOT I believe they're called? They'll be scattered to the winds after the first newsbreak. Your career, and likely, your life, as you know it, is over, Ms. Larkin. Your hatred ran so deep that you broke the law in order to insure my uncle was killed. Was it worth it, Ms. Larkin? Do you feel like you have satisfied your revenge?" Brianna did not answer. Will walked closer and sat on the bench next to her. She waved off the security team that had begun to react.

"I seek no revenge on you, Ms. Larkin."

Brianna's voice was now desperate. "What do you want? What can make that package in your hand disappear?"

"I am obligated under the law to report this crime, Ms. Larkin, and I will not falter in my duty. But I am here to offer you an alternative, salvation if you will. When the company let you go, you could have learned from it, transformed who you were, and used your energies for a good cause. Instead, you chose a living death. You chose revenge. Right now I'm sure you would like to do the same to me."

Will continued, "Here is your life preserver, that which I will use to pull you out of the icy water into safety. After your news conference tomorrow, you will be flown by private jet to Calidum. Our relief efforts there must continue due to the destruction that was caused by Mitakus. You will work there as a volunteer, under an assumed name."

"You must be joking. One word from me, and these goons will shoot you dead," Brianna said, pointing to her security.

"If I die, your path to salvation is erased. You'll go to jail and likely be killed by the Greek," Will warned her. "If you accept my offer, you will remain in the employ of the Foundation, serving at various active overseas missions. You will never be able to set foot in the United States again as you will be a wanted criminal. But you'll be safe, as long as I am alive." Will looked in her eyes, making certain she understood.

"Why are you doing this?" Brianna asked.

"The world requires a new way of thinking, Ms. Larkin. And I plan on being the change that I wish to see in the world. I must be on my way now. A jet will be waiting at the MEC private terminal, Dulles. Directly after your press conference. I recommend you be on board."

Brianna turned back, stoically facing the basin. For a moment, Will thought he saw the look of shame. He stood, turned, and walked away.

***

Will gazed in awe at the painting in Uncle Jax's office, his office now. The painting he was looking at was of a man, apparently in prison, and appearing to be receiving the blessing of God from a beam of sunlight shining down on him. That was his guess anyway. There was a framed letter that hung below the painting, to someone named Samuel and from his father, Abel. Will was unaware of the relation Uncle Jax had to either of these items, but he surmised they were of importance to him based on their location.

Will had made his decision. It had been a long nine months, but his purpose was now clear. He had focused the anger and pain into an energy that coursed not only through his body but his mind as well. He had been given a gift, a legacy. Certainly a responsibility like no other. But Will also realized he was too young to take this on alone. He had more growing to do. Fortunately, Uncle Jax had the foresight to place excellent people in just the right positions, and they would remain there until Will was ready.

He had asked Ray to arrange for a video broadcast today, his first speech to the Foundation as its leader. The crew was set up in his office, just a few feet in front of the large desk. And in fifteen minutes, his speech would be carried live to all offices and branches of the Foundation, from Flint to all continents, all university chapters, to all field operations. The Foundation members were now eagerly waiting to learn their future. One of those members was the former senator from Michigan.

"We're on in five minutes," stated the sandy-blonde haired video producer. She had a crew of five, one who applied his make-up, which had caused him some discomfort. But the crew assured him it was normal and that he would look pale as a ghost without it. So he obliged.

Will nodded and took a seat in the long backed chair. He ran his hands along the smooth armrests. He missed Uncle Jax, and could not help but think that the world would now be looking at him. He had become the world's richest man overnight, and he was only eighteen. He was certain he could forego the responsibility and sell off all the companies and properties, patents, and equipment. He could probably give the Foundation to Ray. Yet, he knew this was not an option. Uncle Jax had given him everything for a reason and, despite his death, Will knew he could not disappoint him.

"One minute, Mr. Warren." Will could not get used to being addressed in this way. He missed being called Will, as only a few did so. He had gone the last three days with nothing but

'Mr. Warren this' and 'Mr. Warren that.' He straightened himself in the chair and looked directly into the camera lens facing him. A crewmember quickly approached and attached a wireless microphone to the lapel of the fitted dress jacket he now wore. Again, something he was told that was now expected of him.

The producer held up five fingers and counted down. "Five, four, three, two, one," and then pointed to him as the light on the camera illuminated.

"Hello. I am Will Warren. As you all know, the founder of this organization, Jaxon Warren, passed away several weeks ago and handed the reins of this organization, as well as all of his corporate assets, to me. I do not accept this load lightly. After spending a small amount of time on the Calidum mission, I have seen firsthand the powerful effects of this organization and its people. You have given thousands around the world a better place to live, a better education, and the ability to sustain a new way of life, one of peace and prosperity. For this, I am grateful as was Jaxon Warren. With his dying words, he informed me that I was to carry on his mission, and 'make the world a better place for having lived in it.' And I am here to inform you that I have every intention of doing so."

"I realize that I am younger and less experienced than all, or most of, you, and that I still have to attend to my education. But I assure you that Jaxon Warren has left this organization strong, and with the right people in the right positions to assist me in continuing our work. Despite my disadvantages, I assure you that nobody is as committed to the future of this organization as I."

"Jaxon Warren was a great man, but a man none the less. He certainly had his faults, but his dedication to this country and using his personal resources to improve life on this planet was boundless. He loved America and what it stood for, freedom and liberty. Jaxon Warren held these principles with him as he moved America out of the Millennial Depression, not as a politician, but as a business man, and the country, as well as the world, is better off."

"As to the immediate future, I have accepted an appointment to the United States Naval Academy. I believe this commitment to the United States military will allow me to learn the leadership and technical skills necessary to successfully run this foundation and the Michigan Energy Corporation. During this time Ray Bakis will lead this foundation and the Board of Directors will continue to operate the MEC."

"I leave you all in fully capable hands to successfully complete the missions you have been assigned. Thank you all for being part of this family, Jaxon Warren's family, and now my family. You have achieved great things in the past, and I have no doubt the future will hold the same success. Good night."

***

Will and Dako sat on a bench against the wall in the Foundation's executive hangar. The crew was preparing the APEX to take Will to Baltimore, where he would board a bus to begin his career as a cadet.

"You have a lot of guts, my friend," Dako said. "It's not too late to change your mind and come to Australia with me." He turned to see Will's reaction.

Will smiled, slightly. "Yes, it is, Dako. I've made my decision, and the world knows it."

Dako laughed. "Yeah, I guess you would look pretty silly now if you changed your mind."

The pilot came over and informed Will that they were ready.

Will and Dako stood. "Well, this is it, Grover. You're a good friend, Dako. The best. Good luck in Australia."

Dako embraced Will strongly. "I'll miss you, Loper. I know you can do this. You're the strongest person I know."

"Uncle Jax once told me that you're not just raised by your parents and family, but also by the community in which you grow up," Will said. "I think he was right. I am who I am because of Uncle Jax, Aunt Abby, Aunt Jeanna, and the people of New Lothrop: my teachers, my neighbors, and all the others who line its streets. I am and always will be grateful. Goodbye for now, Dako."

"Goodbye, Will."

Will turned and walked away, disappearing into the jet.

T .L. Blankenburg was born and raised in the great state of Michigan. After graduating from New Lothrop High School he joined the United States Marine Corps, serving in Operations Desert Shield and Desert Storm. Since receiving an honorable discharge from the military, T.L. has worked in the private business sector. His Military and business activities have allowed him to regularly travel around the world, which has guided him to weave global issues and the modern human condition within his stories. T.L. is a graduate of Baker College, Indiana University, and Oakland University. He resides in Michigan with his wife of twelve years.

www.ingramcontent.com/pod-product-compliance
Lightning Source LLC
Chambersburg PA
CBHW070558130626
46556CB00001B/210